F D

Dieter, William, 1929-

The cactus garden

DATE DUE

MY 25 '90			
JE 11 '90			
JY 7 '90			

Books by WILLIAM DIETER

THE CACTUS GARDEN

BEYOND THE MOUNTAIN

HUNTER'S ORANGE

THE WHITE LAND

THE
Cactus Garden

THE
Cactus Garden

WILLIAM DIETER

ATHENEUM   NEW YORK

(1986)

F
D

Library of Congress Cataloging-in-Publication Data
Dieter, William, ——
   The cactus garden.
   I. Title.
PS3554.I36C33 1986   813'.54   85-48131
ISBN 0-689-11802-3

Published simultaneously in Canada by Collier Macmillan Canada, Inc.
Composition by Maryland Linotype Composition Company,
Baltimore, Maryland
Manufactured by Fairfield Graphics, Fairfield, Pennsylvania
Designed by Harry Ford
First Edition

for my sisters . . . J U N E , J O Y C E , J E A N

Between the dark and the daylight,
When the night is beginning to lower,
Comes a pause in the day's occupations,
That is known as the Children's Hour.

LONGFELLOW

THE
Cactus Garden

ONE

Looking down from the window of the hospital cafeteria, which was on the third floor, Dr. Larimer could see that the river had been trapped in the trees and turned to silver. Not the silver of ice but of the sun, a trick, an alchemy of late afternoon. It was November and the god of November was a jealous god who resented any attempt by anyone or anything to flee his kingdom. The river had tried and he had caught it, had cast it when the angle of the sun was just right into an inlay of glossy metal.

That hadn't been true in the morning. The river, the Mississippi, had been surging and black-bodied then, a serpent twisting innocuously yet deceptively through the trees, planning its escape. "If I can make a quick break and gain the bluffs," it seemed to say. "If I can reach the Minnesota side I'm sure I can get away, I can be free before the winter—"

(3)

It failed. The god of November caught the serpent river in the afternoon, late, and coated it with silver, making it an example that the doctor could see easily through the naked oaks and hickories of the river bottom.

He knew that more than just the river was trying to escape the upper Midwest these days. He'd seen hordes of geese veeing silently overhead all that week, heading south. Even the clouds seemed to be trying to get away, fleeing across the sky during the day only to pile up on the southern horizon towards nightfall like wind-driven schooners on an uncharted reef. On the bluffs across the river a few sumac still blazed but the doctor could see that the other trees were bare, their leaves long since swept away to empty stubble fields and hidden fence corners farther down the state. The winter would follow quickly now, soughing raw and sullen out of the north. Perhaps tomorrow the river would try again to dash across the bottoms and gain the bluffs before the treacherous afternoon sun. . . .

"Dr. Larimer, please," blared the intercom abruptly, breaking the stubborn stillness that pervades hospitals, even their cafeterias. His name sounded again, followed by the code 252, and Larimer drank the last of his coffee and placed the Styrofoam cup on the dirty dish track and left the cafeteria.

Code 252 was Cardiac Intensive Care and Larimer was quite sure he knew why he had been paged. It had to do with Irvin Donner, the seventy-five-year-old man from the little hill town of Viroqua who had been brought to Emergency that morning in bad shape and had grown steadily worse through the day. CVA. Progressive paralysis. Vitals labile. Pneumonia a virtual certainty. His age was against him, his body failing him at the worst time, or perhaps merely the appointed time, who could tell? Perhaps life had its own god of November. How much could Donner's body, big as it was, endure? Seventy-five years of living had

(*4*)

assailed it, three-quarters of a century's worth of falls, fevers, breaks, inflammations, grief, loss. Time eventually ran out for the old ones like Donner, sometimes quietly, sometimes with a jolt. For Donner the jolt was an aneurysm in his head. It didn't ask if the moment was propitious or if the host was prepared, the pounding blood found the flaw in the ancient artery wall and simply blew out, dropping the big strong body into helplessness, forcing it first into an ambulance and then onto assorted hospital surfaces, the lungs damaged from emesis aspiration and the suddenly blocked nerves screaming for new instructions. How do I swallow now, how do I breathe? *Help me, help me*, in the stricken eyes, and the wife waiting in a numb perplexed exclusion just around the corner in the cold white corridor, inarticulate with fright.

Dammit, why did hospitals insist on white? Corpses were white. White was the color of death, not life. Why not paint the halls red and the rooms competition orange, blue trim everywhere, or maybe hunter green, but for Christ's sake not white! Thinking it, nearly speaking the words aloud, Larimer realized he was angry, angry not at color but at age, age and the betrayal it brought.

His anger dissipated quickly when he arrived at Intensive Care. The charge nurse rose up out of the monitor-choked enclave of the nurse's station and approached him. She reminded him for a moment of a nurse from some late-night hospital movie. Joan Fontaine in a white cape gliding prophetically toward Cary Grant.

But no, not true, this was La Crosse City Hospital, Cardiac Intensive Care, and the nurse was Kirstin Olsen, a woman so professional, so coldly proficient that she seemed to be one of the monitors. "Dr. Larimer?" She held a clipboard in her hands as if it were a weapon and she the duty guard. You will stop here for proper identification. You will not pass.

(5)

"Yes, nurse?"

"I asked that you be paged, Dr. Larimer." Her voice was nearly uncivil with efficiency. "I need to talk to you about the seventy-five-year-old white Caucasian male admitted this morning."

"Yes."

"The patient has developed some respiratory problems you should be aware of." She lowered the clipboard. They had been properly identified, doctor and nurse both, they had spoken in their own voices the words that were their names. But the patient would remain *the patient* henceforth and always, he could no longer be Mr. Irvin Donner from wooded Vernon County in west-central Wisconsin, he must become the core and center of that unit's, that shift's, that hospital's aseptic universe. "About thirty minutes ago the patient became dyspneic and cyanotic." Her words were no more and no less animated than the metronomic blips of one of the machines behind her. "I started oxygen at four liters per cannula."

"Yes, that's good. What's his respiratory?"

"Forty-eight per minute. Also, doctor, he appears to have developed rales to the bases."

"We'd better get a chest film. Make it portable." He continued down the hall and the nurse fell in beside him. At the door to the patient's room he turned to her and said, "Is the patient febrile?"

"Yes. 101.8 rectally."

At bedside, the nurse stood back obediently while Larimer bent over the white-haired, large-headed, 250-pound body with its hairy arms and huge hands and desperately heaving chest, now tubed and wired and plugged like the central unit of a lab experiment. He listened to the lungs and the heart and scanned the bedside monitors and then returned to the nurse's station, where he sat at one of the tiny desks and entered notes on the patient's chart. The nurse dialed X-Ray and in a voice like an extended dial tone ordered a stat portable chest. When she hung up, Larimer asked her if she wouldn't please draw some blood for gases and then picked up the telephone and dialed Stan Howell, the staff respiratory specialist. "Stan, can you come up, please? I've got a problem situation here I want you to look at."

When Dr. Howell arrived the two men conversed briefly and then disappeared into the patient's room, and when they emerged approximately ten minutes later, Dr. Larimer went directly to Kirstin Olsen. "The patient's wife is still here, is she not?"

The nurse answered that yes, to the best of her knowledge Mrs. Donner was still in the hospital.

"Any other family?"

The nurse answered no, none were present that she knew of. She understood, however, that there were grown children living elsewhere . . . Seattle . . . California. . . .

"Seattle is not in California, Kirstin." He smiled when he said it, wanting to make it light, feeling an almost desperate need for levity at that moment.

Nurse Olsen did not. "Seattle is in Washington, doctor."

Larimer sat at the desk again and wrote new orders in the same combination of symbols and shorthand and cramped script he had employed for twenty-five years. East from the oak tree eighty paces, north eighty-five, on a straight line west from the twin rock outcrops, pi times the diameter squared, and there beneath your feet you will find the treasure. He was taking his time with the orders, deliberately, there was nothing more to do. The same Time that had betrayed Irvin Donner in the small hours of the morning would now have to come to his defense. Twenty-four hours, forty-eight, seventy-two would give them the answer. Attack the developing pneumonia, watch the fever, stand back and wait. Larimer knew that some small part of his delay at the desk stemmed from pure dread, dread of having to seek out the patient's wife and report to her. She wouldn't be prepared, wives never were. Oh, for the miracle news—there is complete recovery, you may take your husband home with you today—yes, for that they were always prepared. But he didn't have those glad tidings to give her. All he had was that failed sanctity of institutions about the most advanced scientific and medical technology being brought to bear. He wished the ubiquitous, endlessly beeping monitors could be programmed to tell a wife that the man she loved was very probably dying.

Because he *was* programmed, Dr. Larimer would have to tell her. He was pledged to do it, it was an addendum to the oath he had taken long ago and still believed in. Peter at the dike, Horatius at the bridge.

He stood up from the desk and shot the ridiculous cuffs of his overly starched smock and patted the pens in his breast pocket and sought out Mrs. Irvin Donner where she sat in the little cubicle at the far end of the hall, the one that smelled of lemon furniture polish.

The woman he found there was exactly what he expected, a startled face lifting from an unread magazine, neat dress, small stout body. My God, why did big men always pick little women?

"Mrs. Donner?"

The woman stood up, and all the days of her living with the patient flew into her eyes. Soft gentle eyes, somewhat imbedded. He also saw steel-gray hair, unstyled, and one of those Slavic faces that are broad and stolid and always faintly masculine. And frightened, so terribly quietly frightened that Larimer would have given anything not to have to look at her. But he did, he was pledged.

"Mrs. Irvin Donner?"

"Yes?"

"I just left your husband, Mrs. Donner."

No spoken question from her. The riveting stare voiced most of the words she would speak.

"Mrs. Donner," and the long-held breath let out, "I wanted to tell you that we're in a holding pattern with your husband now. There's really no . . . no progress I can report to you. We're attempting to contain the damage. Too early to tell for sure, but very possibly severe. It was a CVA, a stroke, massive, which is in a critical phase just now. The next few hours, twenty-four, forty-eight . . . pneumonia is the main concern at the moment. We're initiating certain procedures . . . oxygen mist, that sort of thing, to assist his breathing . . ."

The doctor stopped talking, but the woman did not stop searching his face. She had pinned his eyes with hers, daring him to look away, to reveal by aversion the truth of what his words both expressed and didn't express. "Is there . . . will he . . ."

"Do you have children, Mrs. Donner?"

"They're my husband's, they're not . . . ours. Four of them. They're grown, of course . . . scattered."

"I suggest you notify them . . . if they want to see their father. Mr. Donner seems to have kept in good physical condition for one his age, but it's that same age that is the enemy here, don't you see? In a younger person . . ." He let it drift away. He wanted to finish this session; he could no longer abide the impaling eyes.

"Are you saying that the children . . ."

"It's a critical time, Mrs. Donner. Forty-eight . . . seventy-two hours . . ."

"Won't the children being here frighten him?"

He coughed softly. "Your husband won't recognize them, Mrs. Donner. He won't know they're here. At best,

(9)

they'll be just forms to him. Movement, possibly. It's for the children themselves that I—"

"They're not close to their father."

"It's a precaution, you understand. There are no guarantees that even if they came . . ."

"I know how to reach them."

"Yes."

"I carry the phone numbers with me. I've always carried the numbers, I don't know why."

"There's a room off the lobby downstairs that's reserved for family use. It has telephones. You had better avail yourself, Mrs. Donner, I should think as quickly—"

"Yes, I see. Thank you, doctor," she said, stronger now, remembering her manners, falling back as they all did on the diversion of formality. "Thank you, Dr. Larimer," and she looked away from his face for the first time and sat down rather heavily in the chair.

In the lobby, Stella Donner entered the Family Consultation room and removed a piece of folded paper from her purse and laid it on the table and dialed Operator on one of the white Trimline phones. Why was everything in a hospital white? Was it supposed to convey a feeling of cleanliness, of purity? Maggots were white. So were the worms in apples. "Operator," she began, "I need to make a number of long-distance calls. Four of them. They're to be charged to my home phone in Viroqua. That's in Vernon County," and she gave her home number. Then she said, "Operator, I'll give you the individual names and the numbers first, all of them, and then I'd like you to place the calls in that same order." She waited, listening. "No, I prefer to do it this way, if you don't mind," and she read the following names and cities to the operator, together with the telephone numbers and the area codes:

(*10*)

Tess (Mrs. David) Wilson, Tucson, Arizona,
Donna Jean (Mrs. Richard) Kelley,
    Chatsworth, California,
Mr. Stewart Donner, Seattle, Washington,
Mr. Wallace Donner, Denver, Colorado.

"I appreciate this, operator. Thank you."

TWO

GRANDPA HAD called Tess Potato Sack. He would sling her over his shoulder and carry her out of the house and around the yard and sometimes to the barn, then back into the house again, announcing that he had acquired potatoes for sale by the sack, in excellent condition and at a fair price. Her sister and two brothers, as one by one they made their appearance in the family and began to talk, tried to pronounce the name, but it came out Po' Sack in every instance. Mattie would have nothing to do with the name because she thought it too common for her daughter, and Irv didn't use it because he didn't use names when he addressed his children—a cough followed by a glare, steely and unassailable until he was finished with it, usually sufficed. In talking to people outside the family about a particular child, it was always "my oldest girl" or "my second son," that sort of cold chronological reference.

Potato Sack lasted until Grandpa died when she was eight, Po' Sack a few years longer, until even the youngest family member, Stewart, threatened to let it die from disuse. Oh, occasionally, as the years passed, the name would reappear, made more acceptable by time than by familiarity, for it was still instant recognition, a password to the unique clubhouse of shared history that siblings know. It would sometimes pop up when one of them sent a Christmas card or wrote a letter to her, which was rare, or when she called them, usually on a birthday. "Hi, this is Po' Sack, thought I'd say hello on your special day." But even that usage eventually declined. Now it was just Tess—"Hello, this is Tess in Tucson"—as though she needed not only to remind them what her real name was but also where she lived, as last night when she'd called each of them—DeeJay in California and Stewart in Washington and Doc in Colorado— "Hello, this is Tess in Tucson. Did Stella call you about Irv's stroke?"

They'd each answered yes and she'd said, "All right, now listen to me," first to Stew and then to DeeJay. "About going to La Crosse . . . I won't fly, not even for this. You understand what I'm saying? You'll just have to go on ahead and wail till I get there. Or maybe I can work something out with Doc, some other way. I'll let you know. Stay loose on plans until I can talk to Doc."

Doc was Wallace, who'd carried his own nickname out of their childhood, one that had stuck, and she'd phoned him immediately and suggested an alternate plan. Doc had always been the one in the old days who would at least listen to options, and perhaps he was still the only one, she wasn't sure. "Doc, listen, I'm going to have to drive to Wisconsin, okay? Certain things remain constant in life, elephants don't grow wings, pigs can't talk, and I won't get on an airplane. But I'm a genuine Mario Andretti when it comes to getting behind the wheel of a car. No, hear me out, let me finish. I'll leave Tucson at dawn tomorrow and take Interstate 10 through Lordsburg to Las Cruces and then up I-25 through Albuquerque and into Denver that way, from the south. This is Sunday night, so that would put me in Denver Tuesday noon. I can really move on the interstate, Doc. There's actually fewer state patrol in evidence there than on a regular highway, and it's much safer."

"So?"

"So here's the plan. If Stew and DeeJay will fly into Denver and if you've got an automobile with at least three wheels—"

"I've got one with four," Doc broke in, and she heard his spurt of a laugh, "and there's plenty of room in the back. It's called a station wagon—you've probably never seen one."

"I saw a picture of one once. It was painted on the wall of a cave."

"Good, then you won't be frightened when you see me drive up. If everyone brings minimum luggage we should have plenty of room. It's what, a thousand miles from Denver to La Crosse?" He didn't wait for an answer. "If the weather's decent we should be able to make good time and not get too tired either."

"Great idea you've got there, mister."

"If it suits you, Tess, it suits me."

Doc had always deferred to her. They all had, actually, all the kids. It was because she was the oldest and remembered the most, Wisconsin, Montana, even the Depresh. It was a natural thing for her to be the leader, they didn't fight it. Stew maybe, whenever he wanted his own way, which was most of the time, or used to be. And DeeJay too, she could get on a rumble real quick, at least she had on that last visit to Tucson. "But I'm sure the others will go along, Doc," is what she was concentrating on now, "so

(*14*)

you wait there in Denver for me. I'll call you from the edge of town."

"Tess."

"Yes?"

"There is no edge of town anymore. Denver started spilling out of its saucer several years ago and just kept on going. I can't even remember what the original looked like."

"Will Lil be going with us?" Lil was Doc's wife.

"No."

"Good. I'm not bringing Dave either. He didn't know Irv. Never met him. And he'd never consent to drive that far. He'd fly just like that," and Doc heard her snap her fingers, "but not drive. He loves to fly. He'd fly to work every day if he could land and take off in the parking lot. Besides, an old desert rat like Dave couldn't handle the cold in Wisconsin. I assume the weather's cold there now. Lord, I've forgotten, too many centuries have passed since I was there. I never went back, you know, not since we left that time with Mattie."

"I did. Once." He waited, and then he said, "Are you going to be able to get a week off from school to make this trip?"

"I don't teach school anymore, Doc. Haven't for three years."

"What happened, you get too old? Couldn't hold chalk? Couldn't see the blackboard?"

"All those. You won't tell, will you?"

"That depends. Maybe we can work something out." Again he paused. "Well, you should have good weather for driving, at least at your end. The desert end."

"Right. The weather's been perfect here. Heat finally broke a couple weeks ago."

"Man, I can remember that heat. It's something you don't forget."

(15)

"Is it ever like that in Denver? I've never been there. I would imagine—"

"Oh no, it's not that hot here. Thank God."

"Doc, do you remember when Mattie first brought us to Tucson from Montana?" She waited for him to acknowledge that he did, and went on. "Remember how we used to try to escape the heat by wrapping wet towels around our heads?"

"Never forget it. I think some of that lint is still trapped in my sinuses."

"That's nothing, I've still got the original heat rash on my eyelids. It's like I've been permanently tattooed. Everything here is refrigeration now. You can actually survive the summers."

"If you want to, that is," Doc muttered, and then he changed the subject with the same fluidity with which he used to roll a baseball up one arm and across his shoulders and down the other arm without ever touching it with his hand. He could do the same with a basketball. "Tess, do you remember the two of us shooting baskets when we lived in that house off North Stone that had a garage instead of a carport? I think it was on Adams Street."

"I remember the game but I've forgotten the name of it."

"Horse. One person has to match the other person's exact shot, one point for a layup, two for a set. I play it with William now. William's my son."

"Do you beat him?"

"I beat everybody. I'm pretty damned good, you know."

"You used to beat me, I remember that. Twenty-one to nothing every time. I don't think I ever scored a point against you."

"I didn't even give you a free throw once in a while?"

"What you gave me is similar in nature to what the

pigeon dropped on the statue. Or as Irv used to say, what the bull left at the fair."

"Did he? I don't remember that. Irv was never what you might call a salty talker."

"You're right, he wasn't."

"He could imitate some of the talk he heard on the radio, like that corny Pa Kettle stuff, or Mr. Feeney or Tweedy or something like that on *Allen's Alley*. But he never originated any of his own, not that I remember."

"You're right, he didn't."

"Listen, Tess," he began, and again she knew a change was coming, not out of lack of interest but out of logic. With Doc one thing came to an end and another started, that's how his mind worked. "Would you mind calling the other kids and telling them about the new plans? They'll more or less expect you to call the plays."

"Right. I'll say we're all going to meet in Denver around noon Tuesday and then drive on to La Crosse in your car. And that they should schedule their flights accordingly."

"Sounds like a W to me."

"W?"

"For win. Winner. Sounds like a winner."

"Right. So I'll see you Tuesday then, won't I? Bye for now. I love you."

"Love you too."

Then, almost too late, she thought for a second he might have started to hang up, she said, "Are you sad about Irv, Doc?"

But he hadn't hung up, he was there. "I don't know," he answered. "I had some mixed feelings right after Stella called. I didn't think I would. The man is such a stranger. I'm not sure what I think." He paused. "One question does keep popping up, however."

"What?"

(*17*)

"If it were one of us that had been stricken, would he come?" He waited for her, she could hear him, hear the silence; it was like the interior of a house in summer when the front door is standing open.

"Look, Doc, I've got to hang up and call the others, okay? See you in Denver. I'll be the big broad with the gray hair."

"You mean the broad with the sad eyes and the great legs, don't you?"

"Oh, Doctor Doc, it'll be so good to see you," and she immediately felt a choking sensation in her throat as though her words had jammed up there and wouldn't let her go on. And because it frightened her, she hung up.

When she first left Tucson there was a moon overhead, huge and white and seductively low in the sky, flooding the desert with an opalescence that she had never seen anywhere else, but then it was gone and there was only the normal predawn darkness to drive in. She couldn't see anything, so she concentrated on what could be remembered rather than seen. She remembered the series of phone calls the night before and the false excitement they had engendered, remembered the reaction of her husband when he realized she would be absent for several days (an agonizing thing to witness in an inarticulate man), but oddly enough it was something Doc had mentioned on the phone that she zeroed in on. It was the house with an attached garage instead of a carport. Garages were rare in southern Arizona. And he was right about its being on Adams, but it wasn't their first house in Tucson. Had he said it was? Their first house was on Helen and Tess could remember it perfectly, an adobe house, squat and white and flat-roofed with thick walls and dark heavy ceiling beams. It was the first adobe house she'd ever lived in, ever been inside of for that matter. They'd gotten off the bus from Montana that morning, four kids and Mattie, with not the slightest idea of what part of town was best to live in or what was available, or how much rents would be. Some lady on the bus had said that rents were high in Tucson because it was a university town and university towns were basically for rich people. The news bothered Mattie, Tess remembered. Normally quiet in any kind of public situation, she had grown even quieter.

Tess tried to remember how much the rent was on the Helen Street house. Had she known? Had she even cared? At fourteen you didn't care a whole lot about things other than yourself, didn't know a whole lot, especially how much money was in your mother's purse. The house obviously rented furnished because they had no furniture of their own, just six suitcases and a couple of tied-up boxes. Mattie had bought a newspaper in the Greyhound terminal the minute they got off the bus, and they drank milk and coffee while Mattie read the classifieds and asked questions of the waitress. Then she phoned someone and they walked all the way out to Helen Street from downtown, carrying the suitcase and those dumb boxes. It took them hours with the heat piling up every minute, not Wisconsin or Montana heat but the kind an oven blasts at you when you open the door. It had a peculiar burned smell, Tess remembered, and a sweetness that was new to her.

They met a man at the house on Helen, the owner or the manager probably, a seedy-looking man with sweat darkening the crotch of his pants. Mattie obviously rented the place immediately, because the next thing she did was give her and Doc some money and tell them to go back to the little grocery store they'd passed and buy some bread, onions, skim milk, white potatoes, peanut butter, and dark

Karo syrup. That was all, no candy and no gum, if they bought junk they'd have to answer. That in itself was worth remembering, for Mattie had never been one to threaten.

The kitchen on Helen was the biggest room in the house, Tess remembered, and the only one with linoleum on the floor. The rest of the floors were cement, or tile or something similar to that. There was no icebox in the house, just a spot by the kitchen sink with warped linoleum and curled-up edges to show where an icebox had stood. She remembered that Mattie had to make a deal with the man on an icebox. There was a gas stove, and cupboards that held a few plates and cups and some plastic glasses. In the oven were a skillet and two aluminum pans so flimsy that they toppled over if there was nothing in them. One of the windows in the dining room was fitted with a boxlike affair that none of them had ever seen before. There was an electric fan inside the box surrounded on three sides by a straw packing through which water dripped steadily. The box was rusted in the corners and over the years a lot of the water had obviously seeped out because most of the adobe in the windowsill was crumbling. "Must be a cooling contraption of some kind," said Doc, who was the inquisitive one, and he flipped a switch on the wall next to the box.

A cloud of dust and dead flies blew out and enveloped him, in addition to which the unit shook so badly that Dee-Jay was afraid it would shoot backward out of the window like the Fourth of July rocket that Tom Antelope brought to school one day in Montana. But later, after they had eaten the bread with a mixture of the Karo and peanut butter on it, and the potatoes (they always had to save the water the potatoes boiled in so Mattie could make onion soup later), they all went back into the dining room and stood in front of the window box and let the air blow on them for a long time. "Yeah, it's a cooler, all right," Doc declared. "I guess we're going to need it down here."

Before they moved out of that house the adobe window-sill rotted completely away and the cooler fell onto the dining-room floor, sparks flying and water running everywhere. Stewart carried on something awful, Tess remembered. "When you gonna get us a *nice* house to live in?" he screamed at Mattie. "One that isn't falling down!" But Mattie was worried about having to pay for the cooler, so she and Tess and Doc fixed it with friction tape and wire and stuck it back up. In another window.

There were a lot of things they needed in those days besides new coolers, things like dresses and shoes and medicine, but didn't get. About all they got was a different house to live in every year, sometimes bigger, sometimes not. Mattie went to work without knowing she had to have a Social Security number, and her first check was delayed. She took a job as a clerk in a laundry over on Speedway, and when she finished there in the evenings she would work a couple hours in the grocery store. Eventually she got a job at St. Mary's Hospital, which seemed to pay a little better, but she had to take the bus and was gone from home more. She seemed tired all the time, Tess remembered. She never laughed. Tess would hear her walking through the house at night and some nights she could see her sitting in the single upholstered chair in the front room, that eerie desert moonlight at the window. She'd be leaning forward holding her head in her hands. Tess supposed she was crying but she couldn't tell for sure because the window cooler made so much noise.

But things got better. As DeeJay said that time they were all sitting out in the double swing Doc had rigged in the palo verde, "Of course it'll get better. You don't think it could get worse, do you?" DeeJay was always coming up with remarks like that, half flippant, half disgusted, and even when you looked straight at her you couldn't tell how she meant them. Doc managed to borrow a bicycle from a friend so he could get a paper route, and Tess got more and more baby-sitting jobs, building up a good neighborhood reputation in the process. They both brought their money home and gave it to Mattie, and one time, on a chilly Sunday in winter when they didn't have to run the cooler, she gave some of the money back to them for candy and gum. Yes, things had gotten considerably better.

Eventually they moved to a house that had cactus in the front yard. Tess remembered that Mattie began to take care of the cactus in the evenings when she got home, no matter how tired she was, but that was also the house that had the garage instead of a carport, and the basketball hoop, and she didn't pay a lot of attention to what Mattie did because she and Doc usually played Horse in the evenings.

My God, how long had it been since she'd seen Doc? She had a moment of genuine panic. How could *any* amount of time have gone by without seeing that big, string bean of a brother with the thick neck and the feet slightly toed in when he walked, like an athlete? Of course he would walk like an athlete, you simp, that's what he was! Or at least he had been. Right after high school, where he'd made All-State in baseball, as well as basketball, he'd been assigned to a Triple A team in Evansville, Indiana. He played there two years and then got traded to Waterloo, where he played for three. But for some reason he never got called up to the majors. She remembered how anguished Doc's voice sounded the time he'd called from spring training camp in St. Petersburg and told her he was being reassigned to Triple A again. "This team's got one first baseman too many," he told her, "and I guess I'm it. Of course I can play third base too and I told them that but . . ."

Doc quit baseball for good that summer and went to

Colorado and started college. She assumed he'd gotten over his baseball hurt, but she wasn't sure. A part of her earlier panic had come from not actually knowing Doc that well anymore. You grew up in the center of your brothers' and sister's lives and one morning you woke up and realized you weren't even sure what they were doing anymore. Was that the price you paid for getting older, becoming "middle-aged"? Did you trade a beloved younger brother in on some questionable wisdom, a few lines of "character" and some gray hair? Dave thought the world of Doc, he was Dave's favorite in the family, and he was immensely proud when Doc graduated and also later when he was appointed Director of Purchasing at the brewery there in Denver. She remembered Dave's recent judgment of her family, startling to her, rare for him; he was not given to the profound analysis of human relationships. He could live them, yes, explain them, no. "DeeJay was lots of fun," Dave announced one afternoon driving back from Tombstone, "but she went to California and got married. Or got married and went to California, one. Your brother Stewart is spoiled rotten. Your dad I don't know, but from what little you've said I don't believe I'd like him too much. And your mother . . . your mother's strange the way she . . . clings to things . . . throws herself into them."

"Strange?" They saw Mattie only every fourth year when it was their turn to host her June-to-June visit. "What do you mean, strange?"

Dave laughed at her intensity, which was his traditional way of circumventing it, and he never answered the question, saying instead, "But that Doc, he's your winner. A great guy even if he is a little pussy-whipped." Again he'd laughed, this time out of a brief flare of embarrassment for having used that term in front of her.

Tess had contemplated that judgment then and she did so now. Perhaps Doc was pussy-whipped, but apart from what the term actually meant, what difference did it make? It wasn't the ominous condition men assumed it was. If Lil had subdued Doc with a good steady supply of domestic pussy it was probably the best thing that ever happened to him. She wondered if he still "cut up" like he used to. His humor had always been of a physical kind, nothing sophisticated. She remembered in the old days whenever they moved into a new neighborhood how he would meet people for the first time. Tall and gangly, he would stand there in a knock-kneed stance and then push one corner of his mouth down, close the opposite eye completely shut, and tell the people he was afflicted with ankylosing spondylitis, a disease he knew absolutely nothing about, just how to pronounce. He was tall still but not gangly, not anymore. An image of him flashed across her mind at that moment, big, soft-footed, elegant-looking in an outdoorsy way, and she thought immediately of the Robinson poem. *Clean favored* . . . how did it go? . . . *A gentleman from sole to crown, clean favored and imperially slim.* And only fourteen months younger than she was, so much a part of her growing up, an inseparable part really. Oh Doc, how could we have become strangers like this? When her throat suddenly tightened she thought, you simp, don't start crying about your brother or you'll have to pull off the highway and you haven't got time! Think of something else. Concentrate!

She did. She concentrated on trying to recall when was the last time she'd seen each of the kids, and to help herself she began a mental list and pinned it up in her mind as though it were something physical that she could write on.

But it took her all the way to dawn to do it, dawn and the New Mexico state line. In summer the dawns ordinarily exploded into the day like dry tumbleweed in a barrow-pit fire, but in November they held back. The truth was, she didn't know about dawns anymore, she never got up early enough to step out onto the patio and watch them. She hadn't seen a dawn, a real live sunrise, for years. But in order to welcome this one, now that it was there in front of her, she rolled down the window of the car and looked out.

It was as though she had let the dawn in. The odors came first, the peculiar sweet smell of desert plants that grow without much water, the clean carbolic smell of creosote bush that the night's dampness had released upon the air. Sand too had its smell, a smell of heat first trapped and then let go, every day, endlessly, making it nearly pure. The light of dawn followed the smells but it brought the lesser faces of the desert, the asymmetrical billboards, the progression of signs announcing SEE THE THING FIVE MILES CAN YOU TAKE IT???, the scorched riverbeds where the Indians dumped their junk cars. Lesser faces were better unseen.

But what she had accomplished in that span of time and highway between the moon's death in Arizona and the sun's birth in New Mexico was that in the case of Wallace "Doc" Donner it had been twelve years since she'd last seen him. She computed bits of related chronology in her memory and concluded that it was the year Dave opened the second restaurant. Doc and Lil had flown down from Denver for a week's visit that year and the four of them had spent half their time playing poker in the cabin on Mount Lemmon and the other half across the line in Nogales buying baskets and hats and top-grade Mexican tequila for Doc to take back to Denver for gifts.

And Stewart, what about him? It must have been the time he stopped over in Tucson while on a flight from Seattle to El Paso for an engineers' conference. That was the year *after* Lil and Doc's visit, so it was eleven years for the old Stewball. Old stinky Stewball, the youngest of the four, the beautiful baby who had grown seemingly overnight into a chunky thirty-six-year-old. No, not thirty-six anymore but forty. No . . . *forty-one!* Was it possible she had forgotten the foolproof way to determine the family's ages? It was simple enough, but you had to think back to the very beginning. There was exactly two years between each child in the family and since she was forty-seven, Doc would consequently be forty-five, DeeJay forty-three and Stew forty-one. Irv and Mattie had apparently believed that babies were an alternate crop, benefiting from a fallow period of precisely two years, and had bred accordingly. Sow, lie fallow, reap. Sow, lie fallow, reap. That was a fine system, it even had a certain mathematical rhythm, but why hadn't these particular harvesters enjoyed the harvest? Wasn't there supposed to be pleasure in harvest? Oktoberfest, Oktobertanz, weren't those harvest festivals?

Stewart's name got crossed off her "Completed" list and it was DeeJay's turn next. Remembering was easier now because DeeJay had not only come to Tucson the same year as Stew, she had come in the summer. No one in possession of his wits came to southern Arizona in the summer. It began with a nearly incoherent phone call from Chatsworth one evening that announced a forthcoming arrival on United Airlines, but with no accompanying reason for the arrival. The following morning, taking no chances, Tess had stationed herself outside Baggage Claim at Tucson International and the next thing she knew here was DeeJay Kelley stomping out onto the sidewalk flipping her pink-blond hair and clutching an elegant overnight bag in both hands.

She stayed two days, sleeping through the balance of the first, yawning and combing her hair and staring into space the second. "Why?" That was the question Tess finally threw at her in the last hour before driving her to the airport for the return flight. "Here you come, no husband, no kids, just you getting off an airplane looking like you'd killed the stewardess. And not half a hundred words to me or any of mine since that time, certainly not anything in the way of an explanation. Did you come five hundred miles just to sleep? To see the Old Pueblo again? Sweat some desert sweat? What? *Why did you come?*"

DeeJay's cinder-black eyes narrowed. "What bothers you most, sister, my being here or my not talking about it? Your inquiry isn't clear on that point." Her hair, after all the combing, shone like something Marco Polo might have brought back from Far Cathay to show the peasants. As if to exhibit it now for Tess, she flipped a rich bolt from off one shoulder. "Has my visit been better or worse, would you say, than fresh shit on a newly waxed floor? Can you scale it for me numerically?"

Tess coughed patiently. "Your visit? You call this a visit, kiddo?"

"Kiddo?" The tone was superior. "I believe that went out with Spanky McFarland."

"Spanky didn't go out. If you watched Saturday-morning TV with your kids you'd know that." She waited. "Or are you too busy combing your hair to watch TV?"

In response to this thrust, DeeJay parried with her haughty, above-it-all look, the one she'd inherited from Mattie. But Tess wouldn't be put off. "You were running from something, young lady," she said, refusing to make it a question, preferring to leave the end open.

It worked. DeeJay's eyes returned to the present, and one hand lifted tiredly from her lap, then sagged back. That gesture was likewise pure Mattie, but at least she answered. "That woman," she said, squeezing the words almost painfully, "that woman . . . smothers."

Tess swallowed, then said in the quietest voice she possessed, "Smothers? What does that mean, DeeJay?"

Her head lifted. "Does it really matter?" She had

switched to impatience, her eyes showing it clearly as though some dull apprentice had failed to comprehend a nuance.

"Oh shit!" Tess hissed finally, but her explanation to Dave that evening when he came home from the restaurant had no disgust in it, only amusement. "I'm sorry you missed DeeJay's performance," is how she presented it to Dave. "She played all the parts herself, as usual, but I couldn't tell if the play was a tragedy or a comedy. Whichever it was, I missed the plot. Probably because I missed the beginning."

Tess. A sweet simpering cuddly name when attached to a petite body, but when you were two inches short of six feet tall and hovered consistently at 155 pounds, the name could be thought of as misconceived. And young, old, short, tall, it had always been confusing. "Bess?" is how new girls at school had greeted her. "Is that really your name? Or did you say Dess?"

"*Tess!*"

"What's it short for? Tessandra? Tessopolis? Tessine?" They had a great time with this part of it.

"It's not short for anything. It's a full name."

The boys had the most fun. "Tess is short for mess, 'cuz she's made of watercress!"

She didn't mind now, the name was almost fun. She loved to announce it to strangers and then watch their faces. They would invariably pause before repeating it back, and some would say, most of them in fact, "What an odd name. So different. And lovely too. You're lucky."

But not when she was a child; the name had hurt then. To be different among your peers in childhood was to be scarred for life, a pathetic outcast. Uniformity was all. When she could, in class, in Sunday school, to the *new*, she said she was Mary. There were no warts on the name Mary, it was safe, saintly almost. But the deception never lasted long; by midterm, on school papers, at PTA, she was undone. "Mama, why why why did you give me a stupid name like *Tess*?"

She couldn't remember all of Mattie's answer. It wasn't saccharine, this she knew, but it would have been romantic, secret. Mattie loved secrecy the way a cat loved comfort, and if a story lacked it, or excitement or drama or suspense, Mattie was sure to put some in. "It happened this way," was probably the way Mattie began, in that mellifluous, deep-soft voice that had been hers so uniquely. "When I was a little girl I lived with my parents and my brothers in the city of Madison. We lived in a big house with a library. My papa loved books and was a great reader. One of the books he had in his library was a novel called *Tess of the d'Urbervilles*. I can't remember who wrote it but in the evenings Papa would take the book down from the shelf and read to me about Tess, the poor country girl in long-ago England who discovered too late that she was descended from an aristocratic family by the name of d'Urberville. Oh, I loved that name so! I loved the story! I loved the book itself, it was so . . . exquisite, so grand. Papa would let me hold the book sometimes. The cover was a dark rich color like the wood of mahogany and the individual pages felt fine and silky like the cigarette papers my brother Frank carried in a sheaf in his shirt pocket. And Papa would explain to me about Tess and her family, how bright and true they were, even for country folk, and how they were betrayed by their new kinspeople and had their hearts broken in the end by those they loved."

"But when—"

"So I promised myself that when I grew up and had a little girl of my own I would call her Tess. She would be beautiful and sweet and way down deep in her secret heart she would feel that she too was of the aristocracy."

"But how—"

"I kept my promise. I grew up and had that little girl and I named her Tess, after the original Tess of the d'Urbervilles." Mattie stood her on the floor and smoothed her dress and straightened her hair. "So . . . what gown would you like to wear today, Tess of the d'Urbervilles? What kind of cakes would you like with your tea?"

"Oh Mama!"

They had countless tea parties, just the two of them (no one else in the family even knew about the d'Urbervilles; Mattie said it was their secret), and not on cheap tin sets either, but real china. Mattie smoked in those days and had to buy cigarettes out of her "cream-and-egg" money in order to keep the expense hidden from Irv, and it was out of that same secret fund that she bought the china cups and saucers and smuggled them into the house. They were a dove color with dainty blue flowers painted on them. They were heavy too, Tess remembered, not like the flimsy tin settings that some of the girls at school had. "And how many lumps of sugar would you like in your tea this morning, Tess of the d'Urbervilles?"

"Oh, Mama, this is so much fun!"

A road sign announced Lordsburg, New Mexico, and Tess said aloud, blurting it deliberately, anything to break the stillness, "My God, I was married in this town!" She began an immediate search for landmarks, for a familiar street or a building from twenty-five years before, perhaps even a sign reading Justice of the Peace Next Exit. But she could recognize nothing, it had been too long, the whole approach to Lordsburg had been altered by construction of the interstate. She didn't need mementos anyway. She and Dave had driven over from Tucson in his Chevy coupe, marrying out of state for no other reason than that it was romantic. And a little wicked. Wicked because shacking up in a motor court the night before didn't count because in a matter of hours you would be a married woman with a new name. What Tess got for a name was Mrs. David Wilson (it beat Donner, Donner sounded so harsh, so Teutonic) and for a husband an authentic, drawling, boots-and-Stetson Arizona native. Dave had been in the army in Europe in World War Two. He had come home to part-nership in a restaurant with an older brother who had spent the war years making piles of money providing food and drink to the hordes of airmen stationed at Davis-Monthan Field east of town. Tess had done part-time waitress work at the restaurant while attending college, had met Dave and eventually married him. Now, after twenty-five years, he was still the dearest thing in her life.

The more she left her home state behind the more she began to feel like a long-distance traveler, and consequently she began to refer to the map more often. Just now it indi-cated that at Deming a motorist could turn northeast onto New Mexico 26 and avoid having to drive all the way to Las Cruces before turning north. It looked on the map like a whole pie wedge of country could be cut out of the trip by such a detour, perhaps as many as fifty miles' worth, not to mention the time. So she did exactly what the map sug-gested, she turned off at Deming.

State 26 was an unimaginative route for something truly imaginative to happen on, yet it did. Perhaps twenty miles after leaving Deming the mountains on the right side of the road began to pull back and leave huge, empty flats in their place, and the imaginative thing was that although it was no longer summer, nor even hot, a mirage began to appear on those flats. As quick as it took to look, the empty basin on that side of the road, and only that side, began to fill with what one would have sworn was water, and when it was full the ends turned up like a canoe as though to keep the water from escaping. Staring at this magic lake, Tess could see trees and islands standing in the center of it, and she realized that it was hard sometimes to tell what was real and what was make-believe. And no matter how many times she turned her attention to the road, when she glanced back at the flats the lake was still there, dotted with those same mystical islands of trees. Highway 26 had become an endless, shimmering fairyland, not a shortcut through dull, high-desert country. It was hard to fix reality in a fairyland, now or then, present or past. "I'll take two lumps of sugar in my tea, thank you, madam."

The shortcut ended at Hatch, a shriveled adobe oasis on the west bank of the Rio Grande, famous for its chilies. Tess stopped at the Cotton Patch Cafe downtown and ordered enchiladas and coffee, and when she had finished she crossed the river and turned north onto Interstate 25.

It wasn't the same desert here as the one at dawn, it was not as flat and the saguaros were gone. And there was the river. No dried-up Indian junkyard this, but the *great river*, the Rio Grande. The highway clung to it stubbornly, hugging the tenuous green littoral of the riverbed like a wandering animal afraid to leave its source of drinking water.

What a magnificent waste a desert was, Tess thought, watching it stretch away on all sides, and how helpless, how truly stricken and helpless. It reminded her of a lizard sprawled on a rock, unable to come to life until the morning sun warmed it and then growing so swollen with heat that it couldn't escape and was forced to wait until night came and saved it. The desert waited for everything, for life and for death. Its only true redemption lay in the late winter storms when great armies of cloud rumbled in from the vast reaches, darkening the brittle hills, shutting out the sun. The rain was merely a probe at first, an advance scout stalking the parched arroyos, leaving cautious foot-prints in the sand. Finally the full attack came, launched in a merciless onslaught of water, water as swift and ter-rible as a *penitente*'s tears.

But in the exhausted aftermath of a storm, birth. Some-where a cactus plant trapped a drop of the water and nur-tured it, mated it with time and heat and fashioned a desert flower, the red, yellow, pink-purple harvest of forgotten thorns. From ugliness, beauty. Out of desolation and space and Biblical deluge, the one true miracle of the desert.

Tess knew the highway would lead her out of the desert. As trapped as it appeared now, still it would climb even-tually into gray-blue foothills of juniper and pine, onto the high mountain-rimmed steppes of Colorado. Then the great western plains, endless and still, and finally Wisconsin.

Wisconsin was where it all started, for her, for the rest of the kids, for all of them. It was where Irvin Donner and Mathilda Elmor had met, in a Methodist Bible camp in Madison, the city of lakes. Tess thought immediately of the picture she had of the two of them, a small snapshot that the years had faded into a cracked sepia print. They had posed themselves against a clot of lilac bushes in that camp, he a blocky figure in a white shirt and patent-leather bow tie with his sleeves rolled to the elbow, dark hair cut short, arms folded in front, Son of the Middle Border. She equally tall, the long hair and faintly lidded eyes and the olive skin creating a curiously Mediterranean image, Daugh-ter of the Wine-Dark Sea. She had her hands folded demurely and yet provocatively around both Bibles, hold-ing them against her thighs. They were alone in the picture, close but not touching. They looked unbelievably young, and one suspected they had just suppressed a giggle and would explode into another as soon as the shutter clicked, that they would push at each other playfully, she turning slightly away in a vague coquetry. Their loins pulsed, Tess knew. You couldn't see it in the picture but you knew it was there, the need to know the physical, to experience the man-woman mystery, craving it with a kind of cold nervous fever.

It was soon theirs. They were married in La Crosse the end of that summer, in the week following Labor Day, merging their youth and their hunger into a legal entity known and entered as Mr. and Mrs. Irvin Donner. Tess wondered if her parents had had a honeymoon. Had they slipped away after the ceremony to a motor court outside of town? Did they place their Bibles on the dresser and remove their clothes and lie together on the bed? Had they been shy? Had Mattie been a virgin? As Irv's thick body pressed her down had Mattie wept for her tall, elegant papa who had read romantic novels to her in a faraway library room? Tess tried to picture her parents in the act of sex, the moaning and clutching, and she could not. It was a picture destined to remain forever undeveloped.

Irv took his bride home to his parents' farm in Vernon County, where they lived through Tess's birth and Wallace's. It was the very heart of the Depression by then and farm after farm was being lost to the banks. Through alertness and a bit of luck, Irv was able to rent one of those repossessed places for "not much more than taxes," as the bank people said. It was a valley farm with mucky ground and the barn in better condition than the house. In the first year Irv got together a team of horses and some used farm machinery, plus a dozen milk cows borrowed from his father, and in the second he put up a shed and filled it with chick incubators whose lights glowed an eerie blue night and day. Irv was tenacious if he was anything, and he wanted desperately to make a good start.

But his chickens got infested with some kind of disease, possibly black wattle, and began dying off faster than he could bury them. He finally left that bottom place and rented a ridge farm that was bigger and had a considerable amount of timber on it. It also had a well so defective that he and Mattie were forced to carry water from a spring more than halfway down the hill. Irv simply didn't have the resources to put down a new well or pay for repairs. He wanted to conserve what little money he had so he could buy the land he lived on. He wanted his growing family to survive.

They did, through DeeJay's birth the following year and finally Stewart's, and it was the timber that turned Irvin Donner from a renter to a landowner. He sold off all but three of his Holstein cows to make a down payment on a saw rig, and he began to clear the ridge of trees and saw the logs into rough boards which he sold to neighboring farms and in the nearby towns such as Viroqua and Viola. Many of the farmers were forced to pay him in beef sides and leghorn eggs instead of cash, and although Irv grumbled about it, it was in truth precisely what he needed to make it through the hard times.

All this while, Mattie was becoming the perfect helpmate to her industrious husband, or so Tess believed. She saw her mother in those years as the quintessential farm wife, cooking big hearty meals in heavy iron skillets on huge kitchen ranges, planting, harvesting, canning, washing every Monday with the black electric cord reaching from the generator in the cellar to the Maytag washer just outside the back porch, the galvanized rinse tubs sitting on tables that Irv had made for her out of sawhorses and old shed doors.

But something happened between her parents about that time, with the war and Lend Lease looming and shoving the Depresh slowly aside, and Tess was never to know what it was. Her parents had done as Irv's Calvinistic God had commanded, they had sought grace through atonement of original sin, they had been fruitful and multiplied; why had it culminated in disunion and despair? That Wisconsin ridge farm was locked in Tess's memory, for it was where the fury began, where the beatings started. That wind-haunted ridge house she would never forget.

She pushed that remembrance aside, as she had learned long ago to do, and traded it for a better. There had been a barn on that farm, and she thought of the times she and Doc had played a follow-the-leader game of climbing out onto the rafters in the mow and dropping into the hay below. In summer the hay level would be low and the fall was longer and more frightening, more exciting too. But they never got hurt, nor broke any of the bones the adults positively guaranteed they would. More important, they managed to keep the two younger kids out of their game. The haymow belonged to her and Doc, it was their hide-away, their secret place. They could give their dreams voice there, make up poems, recite others they had memorized for school, all this after they had wearied of plummeting into the hay. There was a big door near the peak of the barn through which the hay fork lifted the hay from the wagon into the mow, and she and Doc would many times lie back in the sweet dead flowers of alfalfa and watch the sky through the door. It was a beautiful square of blue, calm and uneventful, and what she remembered most about it was how terribly important a cloud or a bird or an airplane became when it chanced to pass across.

But the days on that farm, whether brutal or idyllic, were numbered. At some point that year they left and moved to the town of Viroqua. Not Irv. Just Mattie and four kids and Mickey the dog. It was unexpected. "Tess, I have a special job for you," Mattie whispered to her one morning after breakfast when Irv was outside in the toilet. "I want you to bring the kids straight home after school today, understand? No dawdling, no stops, just come

(*36*)

straight home. It's very important, Tess. Will you do that for your mother, please?"

She managed it perfectly (unquestioning too, she had always been the loyal one), and the result was to find a strange car in the lane and suitcases stacked on the porch steps, along with pillowcases full of heavier stuff like Stewart's tin soldiers and DeeJay's dolls, and Mickey on a rope leash. They drove straight into Viroqua with the strange man and unloaded everything back out of the car into an apartment that made up exactly one half of a house on a street that Tess recalled had a number rather than a name. She'd never known streets had numbers.

It was a nice enough apartment, almost unbelievably small, with a furnace under a grate in the floor and tan shades at the windows instead of the old cracked green ones on the ridge place. Her only question of Mattie was, "What are we living here for?"

"The war will be over soon," her mother answered, and the words sounded as though they had weights hanging on them, probably because the rooms were small and the ceilings so low. "We'll be able to get tires and buy all the gasoline we want. We won't be trapped anymore."

"What do tires and gasoline have to do with it? We don't even have our own car!" But she knew before the words were out that she wasn't going to get an answer. Mattie was a master at going quiet, and this was no exception; she immediately turned away and started unpacking suitcases.

Mickey hadn't liked the new place, Tess recalled. He had to stay in the backyard and he howled all the time, nights especially. Tess remembered too that she'd finished out that year in a school she didn't like, it was too big, there were too many students and she had to go through the *Tess* inquisition again. She kept to herself most of the time.

Then one day Mattie called her aside and told her to get the kids ready because they were going to move to Custer City, where two of her brothers lived.

"Where's Custer City?"

"In Montana."

"Can Mickey go too?"

"Mickey goes in a crate that will fit in a compartment on the outside of the bus. In the back. The weather is nice, summer is coming, and the man promised me the dog would make the trip just fine."

"Will he need his own ticket?"

"Never mind about that, Tess. Just keep the kids together and see that the packing gets done. Can you do that for your mother, please?"

She could. She was the loyal one.

Mattie's two brothers turned out to be Uncle Frank and Uncle Willard. They were both Methodist ministers, whatever kind that was, probably named after a man named Method, like the Lutherans were named after Luther. Method sounded English to Tess and that made sense because Mattie and her two brothers were English, although Mattie had told her on the bus coming out that her family was actually French and that their true name was d'Elmore. An Immigration official had gotten the name garbled when the original ancestor landed in America, and wrote it down as Elmor. It was sort of a secret, which is why Mattie asked her not to talk about the name in front of others, especially her brothers, who were sensitive men. But it was a pretty name nevertheless, even if Tess couldn't use it. D'Elmore. Like d'Urberville.

Mattie split the family up as soon as they reached Custer City, going with the boys to live in town with Uncle Willard and Aunt May, sending Mickey and Tess and DeeJay to Uncle Frank and Aunt Ida's place in the country.

Then one day Mattie disappeared.

DeeJay insisted she'd been kidnapped by Indians, and for the first few days she would sneak out to the ditch along the road and spy on the cars driving past, especially those with their rear shades pulled down.

But she never saw Mattie. None of the kids did. Mattie was gone. The telephone never rang, no letters came, and after several weeks had passed Aunt Ida announced that even if Mattie did come back she wouldn't be allowed in *her* house. "May and Willard's maybe," Aunt Ida huffed, her neck turning red as a rooster's wattle, "but not mine!"

Uncle Frank's was not a happy place that year, but it was a busy one. Naturally, being a minister, Uncle Frank had a lot of God-type plaques and framed samplers hanging on the walls throughout the house. The biggest, and obviously his favorite, was *Go Ye into All Nations, Jesus said, and Teach the Word of God.* Uncle Frank must have been very devout, because that is exactly what he'd done. The nation he'd selected was the Crow nation, which must have occupied the same area as Custer County because there was, as DeeJay was constantly declaiming in her new Western talk, "a wealth of Injuns hereabouts." Uncle Frank referred to the Indians as Our Red Brothers, whereas Uncle Willard called them The Heathen. The two men argued continually over terminology, with even their wives joining the battle from time to time.

Uncle Frank, a tall thin man with sour eyes and an Andy Gump Adam's apple, took his ministry seriously. He was absolutely committed to spreading the gospel among that part of his congregation that consisted of Red Brothers, and he tried ever so hard to help them in every way possible. That is the reason he initiated his Bible Call Program.

"Call God for an answer," was the way it began. Uncle Frank was walking through the house rehearsing his Sunday sermon, stopping occasionally to try the phrase out on a sofa or a chair or a closet door. "Call God for help." Next he began putting his ideas on paper, "giving the program a text" he called it, and then one night at supper, in that severe voice he ordinarily saved for the pulpit, he declared that his Bible Call Program was ready. He seemed excited, as did Aunt Ida. Even DeeJay was impressed; she thought the title catchy.

The Bible Call Program, simply put, was a way for any member of the congregation seeking spiritual guidance to get it by calling Pastor Frank Elmor at his home. There were several options available the moment the phone rang. The caller could be directed by the pastor to helpful areas of Bible study, or counseled on matters of Christian faith such as Salvation, Worship, Morality, Family Life, Eternity, and so on. Personal problems, regardless of their intimate nature, could likewise be discussed, usually at the price of "a little something extra" in the collection plate on Sunday.

Being prepared for every conceivable request from a parishioner was of paramount importance to Uncle Frank because he'd always had a fear of being caught, as they said, "without his collar on," and to protect himself he initiated two precautionary measures. The first, before the program was officially announced in church and in the printed fliers mailed to the homes, was to catalog all the possible areas of discussion and assign them a number. The second contingency was to have all incoming calls answered by someone other than himself. That person would identify the subject of the call, look up its number, and announce the number to the waiting Pastor Frank, who could then have his response well in hand, so to speak, by the time he picked up the phone.

The first procedure presented no problem, for it was apparent that Frank Elmor had a gift for organization. Guidance subjects he numbered and placed on 3 × 5 cards. Under "Salvation," for example, the topic *Who Must Be Baptized* was assigned number 4. *Heaven Described* was 13. *On the Cross With Jesus* got number 25. Under "Family Life," number 8 addressed itself to *When A Son Marries*, and 19 looked at *Being A Stepmother*. *When Whiskey Wins*, always popular among the Crows, was covered by number 20. A master list of these topics was typed on a sheet of paper and placed next to the telephone.

The second procedure, assigning Aunt Ida to answer the phone, ran into immediate difficulty. In addition to her other failings, Aunt Ida wasn't good on the phone, in fact, she was so timid and bumbling the instant she picked up the receiver that Uncle Frank was forced to change the assignment. He gave it to Tess. For Tess it was a break in the tedium of the days and also clear proof that she shared her uncle's gift for organization and logistics. She had memorized the entire pack of 3 × 5 cards, their subjects and corresponding numbers, by the end of her second day on the job. And she was possessed of a strong assertive voice. The phone would ring, she would answer and listen and identify (many times the caller would be drunk and this slowed the process), then she'd cover the mouthpiece with her hand and sing out, "Number nine, Uncle Frank!" Or another time, "Uncle Frank, take a seventeen please!"

She grew so adept at her duties that she would call out the subject *in addition to* its number. "Fourteen, *Who Goes to Heaven?*, is on the phone, Uncle Frank." And again, "Can you take a twenty-six please, Uncle Frank, *Does It Really Matter What Church We Attend?*" And on occasion she'd call out, just like in a Bingo game, "On the

Morality Card, number eleven, *God's Thoughts on Adultery*. Take it, Uncle Frank!"

DeeJay, indifferent as she was, got caught up occasionally in the fervor of Bible Call. When Tess retired to their upstairs bedroom after working the phone all evening, DeeJay would often insist on being included. "The third call was a twelve and that last one was a twenty-six, wasn't it, Tess? Wasn't it?"

"No, it was a twenty-seven. *Wrongs Made Right by Jesus' Love.*"

But the job eventually grew tiresome, if not frightening. For one thing, Tess began to see in Frank Elmor a tendency to abuse the power that his program afforded him. Around the house his pronouncements became more and more righteous, and he often grew blatantly hostile on the phone. For another thing, the excluded Aunt Ida grew increasingly more jealous of Tess's importance to the program. Most of the downstairs rooms in her house had linoleum on the floors, some in pattern but mostly plain white, and she began to blame Tess for the scuff marks that appeared there, accusing her of playing jacks or skipping rope in the house, both expressly forbidden. More and more she ordered Tess to get the bucket and the brush and the Kitchen Kleanser and scrub her linoleums clean.

Winter swept down from the north and still Mattie didn't return. The prairie stretched away cold and empty in every direction, the wind was a mournful crying that night after night, in her darkened room, Tess tried hard not to listen to.

Near Santa Fe she pulled off the interstate. It was nearly four o'clock. She filled the tank with gas and ordered a plate of tacos and a cup of coffee in the adjoining restaurant. Half an hour later, she was back on the highway.

North of Wagon Mound, a picturesque place that had been a landmark on the historic Santa Fe Trail, sunset came, fast, trapping her in the flat open country. There were no people, no ranches, no towns, the earth seemed deserted. The small lumpy hills on the horizon looked like curled-up animals trying to go to sleep before darkness came.

Unbidden, Mickey came back into her thoughts. Uncle Frank hadn't liked Mickey from the beginning, and late one winter afternoon he'd come stomping into the house, announcing in his preacher voice: "I caught that dog of yours in the chicken house sucking eggs."

"Oh no, Uncle Frank, not Mick. He's afraid of chickens. He's afraid of everything. It couldn't be Mick."

"I'm going to have to remedy this situation," he said, a favorite threat of his, whereupon he marched out to one of the sheds and tied Mickey to a pillar and shot him, shot him with the helpless puzzled look still on his face. She and DeeJay buried him where the ground was thawed, laid the burr-eared, still-warm brindle body in the ground wrapped in a flour sack with the sunset coming down cold and bleak all around.

Oh Mickey dog, you've been gone so long! Won't you come back and sit with me for a while? It's so lonely here in the sunset.

THREE

STEW HATED IT that morning when the alarm
clock first buzzed. He wanted to stay where he was on the
rich green lawn with the sun blazing down and the flowers
pooling at his feet like colored water. His father was there,
that was the reason, the young father of his earliest memory,
the big, black-haired man with the sleeves of his shirt rolled
to the elbow, smiling, waving from the edge of the lawn. . . .

He got up at the second buzz of the alarm. He had no
choice, the day was scheduled, filled from the beginning
with timed events, a six-thirty shower and shave, breakfast
with the kids before they left for school at seven-twenty,
some appropriate parting remark to Mattie and then a dash
to the station wagon (*dash* because it would almost certainly be raining), which Bev would have already backed
out of the garage in anticipation of the drive to the airport
to make the nine-fifteen flight.

It all went off as scheduled (which proved again the

efficacy of good planning, a virtue he constantly expounded to his department at work) and he was finally on his way. Bev was driving, and when Stew cracked his side window the wet air hit him and reactivated the scent of face powder his mother had left on his cheek when she kissed him. He'd said his goodbye in the hallway leading to the side door. "Well, Mother, this is it. I'll probably be seeing my father for the last time." She had ignored it with a look of frosty dignity, her usual, and tilted her face for the kiss. It wasn't much of a tilt, for she was only an inch shorter than he. "Goodbye, Stewart. Tell Wallace when you see him in Denver that I know I owe him a letter. I haven't forgotten. I'll write soon." There was nothing additional from her, no theatrics. He'd expected theatrics—the moment held some dramatic potential, farewells usually did, at least with Mattie—but for all her concern he might have been leaving for work. Then at the last minute she called after him, "Tell Donna Jean I'll be at her place in June as planned."

It stopped him. He turned. "You do that purposely, don't you, Mother?"

"Do what?"

"Call DeeJay by her real name."

"It is her real name, Stewart. I know because I gave it to her myself."

"She hates it."

"That would have to be something you remember from childhood. You haven't seen each other for so many years—"

"Why can't you call her DeeJay like the rest of us?"

A slight flare then, very nearly concealed but not quite. "Because *DeeJay* sounds like the initials of one of those racecar drivers. It's what a disk jockey might call himself, like that disgusting Wolfman Jack the twins listen to."

"Who did you listen to in your day, Mother? A Yale preppie with a head cold wheezing into a megaphone?"

(*45*)

She sniffed audibly. "You can be so pompous, Stewart."

He left the house then, feeling somewhat better despite the failure of his goodbye. Mattie hadn't picked up on the *last time* reference to his father, which he had inserted expressly for her. The only thing accomplished was that the kiss had imprinted him once again with her smell, that familiar, old-fashioned rouge and powder scent that was as changelessly his mother as a photograph.

It was raining as they drove through the streets of Bellevue, which was their suburb. Seattle was a city of suburbs, and the rain fell on each equally. You never planned a single event in that country that didn't allow for rain, it was an integral part of life, a subparagraph to every contingency plan ever drawn up, especially now in the fall of the year. The rain seemed merely a drizzle but once Bev turned onto Highway 405 and picked up speed the rain literally flew at them. The roadways in the Seattle area were little more than fire lanes anyway, and the strangest thing was this, that you could see the rain ahead of you on the highway but not when you looked to the side. It was because of the trees, they created a formidable background that hid the rain. Trees were wonderful but there were too many of them in Seattle, too many forevergreens as the twins called them, endless ranks of dense pyramids against which rain did not show well. It wasn't like Montana or Arizona, vast exposed empty places he had lived once. The only exposed places in Seattle were the parking lots. The city was a greenhouse with moss growing on both sides of the glass, but as his boss at Boeing was fond of saying, so it rains here for ten months of the year, so what? What can you do about it?

Touché. You could do nothing about it except adjust and accept and remind the tourists of the innumerable benefits of rain—the bucolic landscapes, the lush foliage,

(*46*)

the absolute Eden the city became when in rare moments the rain stopped and the sun came out. He and his wife gave names to the rain—the Sheik's Revenge, Bev called it, Paul Bunyan's Broken Bladder, said Stew—but their kids didn't seem to mind. Just last Friday night at the football game against Kent the field was practically underwater and yet the twins, both of whom were cheerleaders, hadn't missed a single routine. In the kitchen with their beaux afterward they had prattled on interminably about how cool it was beating Kent for the third straight year but never a word about the virtual lake the game had been played in. They were, after all, natives. Rain was the norm.

Not to Mattie. When she arrived every fourth year for her allotted time with them she made her usual show of accepting the rain—a brave little smile and a stoic toss of the head, probably something from *Mrs. Miniver*—but it was unconvincing, not one of her better performances. Stew would occasionally catch her studying the rain from behind the fogged windows of the house; at other times he could see her fingering the drapes and the bedclothes, rubbing the towels between her fingers, confirming the eternal dampness. Many evenings when the whole family was watching TV he could feel his mother *listening* to the rain, hearing it on the roof, the walks, the porch steps, everywhere. That much rain must have seemed an obscenity to her, remembering Arizona.

In Arizona, rain was rare and momentous. Its fall constituted a special occasion. In fact, a rain in Arizona was the one event in their lives that could push Mattie into even a semblance of levity. Certainly it was the only time she was ever fun. The kids occasionally performed olios, which was Tess's term for a series of comic sketches in costume, but they never included Mattie. She had never been one to laugh easily, not like Irv. No sound of barriers being let down ever emanated from Mattie; she was constantly *on her manners*, fearful of committing some unredeemable breach.

Except when it came to the rains.

The coming of those rains served as a theatrical vehicle for her, and over the years she had worked out a little skit for the occasion. Brief yet dramatic, the performance never varied from year to year. Naturally she was the star, the only other role being that of the straight man, a bare-bones part, no meat at all. A husband would have been ideal for the role but Mattie didn't have one so Tess, being the oldest, usually got to play it. Seldom was it Doc, for he was too critical of make-believe, and never Stew because he was too young. And not DeeJay either, for she would consistently blow her lines each time Tess consented to give her a tryout.

For eleven months of the year the city of Tucson huddled in dusty isolation on the desert floor and then, usually in July, tiny rivulets of cloud began to seep from the horizon and flow toward the city, joining together innocuously until the sky overhead was suddenly a purple-black menace. It was a dramatic moment. All movement of air would cease and the first drops of rain would begin to fall, gouging tiny polyps of red dust out of the yard. The minute they saw the raindrops hit they would run into the house to await Mattie's performance.

She never let them down, she always knew curtain times. She would emerge from the bedroom or the living room or the kitchen, wherever she happened to be, and move fatefully to one of the windows and peer out at the hovering tempest. Then, after an interval which Stew believed was what they called a *dramatic pause*, her body would tense and her eyes would take on a silent-movies look and she would turn to her waiting lackey of the boards and call out in a grim voice: "Get the other children and bring them to the window."

"What is it?" Tess would cry out, for that was her line.

"Hurry. Get the children. I want them to see this."

"But there won't be room enough to see, not if all of us stand at the window."

Mattie would sigh and throw her shoulders back and take on that imperious look, so natural to her. "All right then. I'll give up my place. I've *seen* rain."

Oh, it was splendid, absolutely splendid. Stew could remember how all four of them would hang over their chairs or fall onto the sofa or roll on the floor, regardless of how many times they'd seen the performance, and even Mattie would laugh sometimes, just a little something behind the back of her hand, very dignified. If there was a flaw in the show it was that perhaps she overdid the theatrics, that she tried too hard. She did that with everything, tried too hard, but as long as it was the play and the play was fun, who cared?

It had been fun riding on Daddy's tractor back in Wisconsin, Stew remembered that too. The tractor wasn't fast, that wasn't the fun, but the mixture of gasoline and gear grease smelled so good, and the engine would growl like a dog one minute and purr like a sleepy badger the next, depending on what Daddy was making the tractor do. It could do a lot more than some dumb horse. A horse was always lifting its tail and farting, especially when it was pulling on a grade. A tractor beat a horse all hollow!

But hadn't he ridden in a horse-drawn sleigh once? He saw it in his mind, the whole family in a sort of Currier and Ives winter scene, huddled warmly under blankets, laughing, waving gaily wrapped presents and singing "Over the River and Through the Woods, to Grandmother's House We Go." And there were other memories

(*49*)

of the ridge farm, picking gooseberries and being careful not to impale his thumb on the spears, eating wild grapes on the way to school, hiding in the cow chutes under the road when a storm came up, trying to drink the dew out of the white cuplike morning glory flowers in the ditches, raking up colored leaves that looked like they'd been painted, smelling the corncob-and-green-hickory fires in the smokehouse. Hadn't he done those things? Surely he had.

Easier to remember was the work all four of the kids had done with the books on winter nights. He didn't know where Tess managed to find the books but she'd distribute an equal number to each of them and they'd go upstairs and pencil in all the a's and the o's and e's, page by page. It was hard work, hard on the eyes because the print was small and the light was bad. Tess, who was in charge, called it "doing the vowels," and the four of them would work in the books for hours on end, completing as many pages as they could each night. It must have been important, because Tess insisted that Stew sign his work by writing on the back inside cover when he finished, *This book done by Stewart Donner.* She made the other kids sign their completed books too, after she'd checked their work, of course. DeeJay, being the youngest, was the worst worker on vowels. Her eyes would be the first to get red and at times they looked like they were going to cross; sometimes she'd get sick to her stomach and throw up before she finished her book.

It was fun at Easter when they'd dye the eggs the night before. Mama would set cups of different food colorings on the kitchen table and give them a half-dozen eggs apiece. (There was a time on that farm when they had a lot of chickens. Daddy had the logs and the saws but Mama had the chickens. Stew remembered one of the chickens in particular, the one with the bad eye that looked out at a funny angle all the time.) He and DeeJay and Doc would ordinarily work their eggs with crayons, placing the tip of the crayon into the flame of a candle that Mama set out and then smoothing the hot wax onto the shells before dipping them into the cups. When his eggs dried, Stew would take them into the living room where Daddy was listening to the radio. Daddy would keep a few on the radio stand just to look at, they were so pretty he said.

But Tess had to be different with her eggs. She would bring down from upstairs all the pencils that had erasers left on them and stick straight pins into the erasers. Then she'd dip the pinhead into the hot candle wax and draw fancy designs on the shell of the egg, then dip it into the cool dye. He had to admit that Tess was good. One time she drew an egg so beautiful that he urged her to take it in and show it to Daddy, something she didn't ordinarily do, but Tess said, all right, she would do it this time, and she laid the egg very gently in the palm of her hand and took it into the living room. "Look at my butterfly design, Dad," he heard her say.

There was a silence that followed her words, as when a baby bird falls out of a tree and hits the ground, and then Daddy said, "You're a big girl now, haven't you got anything better to do?"

For a long time afterward, Stew remembered the look on Tess's face when she came back to the kitchen.

Then one day they left Daddy and the tractor and the eggs and moved into that dinky half-house in the town that had a name he couldn't pronounce, the one that was built on top of a hill. He supposed that most of the towns in Wisconsin were built on a hilltop, there were that many hills. Anyway, he hated the half-house for a lot of reasons but mostly because their dog Mickey howled all the time. In fact it was that dumb Mickey who got him into the only bad argument he'd ever had with Tess. It was during the second day of the bus ride to Montana when Mama wouldn't answer any more of his questions and Tess, with whom he was sharing a seat, gave up watching for Burma Shave signs and started talking about Mickey. Everything was Mickey, Mickey, Mickey! Was Mickey scared out there in his special crate on the back of the bus? Was he hungry? Could a dog really make a trip like that safely or had the man lied about it?

"I hope the dumb dog falls off, that's what I hope," Stew snapped at her, finally fed up.

Tess had a big face and it started to go pale when she spoke. "You don't care about Mickey, do you, you spoiled little brat? You never have cared about him. All you care about is those dump trucks and tin soldiers you made Mama bring along even when she told you we didn't have room."

That did it. He kicked Tess in the knee. "And you don't care about Daddy!" he screamed at her. "You never talk about Daddy. You never ask Mama questions about what's going to happen to him. You didn't even cry when we left Wisconsin!"

"It'll be good to see Tess again, won't it, hon?"

Stew shifted in his seat. "I'm sorry, Bev, what did you say?"

She chided him with a soft laugh. "I figured you were miles away. You always get dreamy when you look at the rain."

"Yes."

"I said I know you'll be glad to see Tess again."

"Yes, I will. It's been a long time."

"Did she sound different on the phone the other night?"

"No, just the same. I don't think voices ever change."

. . .

"Stew?" the voice had come Sunday night, just minutes after the call from La Crosse.

"Yes?"

"This is Tess in Tucson."

"Hello." The formality of first words spoken into a telephone mouthpiece. Rote words. "How are you?"

"Fine."

"I knew it was you."

"Did Stella call you about Dad?"

"Just hung up."

"You're going back, I assume."

"Got to. How about you?"

The first pause then, a regrouping, a second start. "Stew, listen, I don't know if you remember but I still can't get up enough nerve to fly through the sky in one of those long painted cylinders with a wing sticking out on each side. I think they're called airplanes. Even knowing that you might have engineered the damned thing doesn't help."

"So?"

"I'm going to have to drive back."

"Hey, that's not good planning, Tess. Not for an emergency. The rest of us will be at the hospital at least two days ahead of you."

"Maybe you guys could wait somewhere for me and we could drive the rest of the way together."

Now came his own pause. "Wait for you? Where?"

"I don't know yet. Denver possibly. It's sort of halfway and it would cut my time in half, my time alone on the road, I mean."

"It'll double mine."

"But it's one way to do it, isn't it?"

"It's a *way*, yes, but it means I'll have to delay my departure until you can reach Denver and I'd rather not do that. I want to get to the La Crosse hospital as quick as I can—"

(53)

"Then do it." Her voice had changed. "No one's stopping you. Fly straight into La Crosse or Minneapolis, whatever, and be the first one there."

He waited for a reassuring laugh, but there was none.

"That way, if Irv's still alive you can sit and hold Stella's hand for two days."

"Tess—"

"And if he's dead you can stay and help her make the funeral arrangements. If she's able to think and talk, that is."

"You're not being fair."

"Is that why we're going back to Wisconsin, Stew, to be fair?"

He flipped the twenty-five-foot telephone cord like a whip. "Why can't you fly, for Pete's sake? Air travel is the safest thing going. Statistics prove that. Why do you want to put this extra burden on the rest of us?"

The reprise was instant. "Don't talk burden to me, little brother! You used to be afraid of frogs, birds, tall grass, lights behind a window shade. I wasn't, but I hid you in my skirts just the same. Now for some reason I'm afraid to fly so you're going to have to hide *me* for a change. And please don't say, 'What, a big girl like you?'"

It was his chance. "What, a big girl like you?" And he laughed just enough for her to hear it. She didn't laugh back but her voice softened. "You can't always have everything your own way, Stewart," is what she said.

He walked the full length of the telephone cord and closed the study door with his foot. "Listen, Tess, what do you say we start over again, okay? You go ahead and discuss your plan with the others and then get back to me. Whatever the decision is, I'll go along with it. But let's make it now, tonight."

She got back to him within the hour, announcing that both he and DeeJay were to wait a day and then fly to

Denver, not Minneapolis, and that she would drive to Denver and meet everyone there.

"So when will you leave Tucson?"

"Tomorrow morning early, what Gary Cooper and John Wayne in their movies called first light."

"Sounds good to me. When will you get to Denver?"

"It's a thousand miles on the interstate, which may not be the shortest way but it's certainly the fastest. I'll set my cruise control on fifty-five and just let her go. I won't get so tired that way. On a regular two-lane, like through the White Mountains, Springerville, Gallup, that way, I'd be constantly fighting the hills and the curves, plus the traffic."

"When will you reach Denver?"

"I told Doc it would be late morning on Tuesday. He said to go straight to the airport, Stapleton I think it is. For your part, you've got to book a flight that will get you into Stapleton no later than noon that day."

"Dave coming with you?"

"No. Is Bev?"

"She can't get away. We never taught our kids how to take care of themselves. They don't even know what being alone means. And Bev didn't know Dad that well."

"I didn't know she'd ever met him."

"Just that once."

"Dave didn't know Irv at all."

"Tess?"

"I'm still here."

"It's really bad with Dad, isn't it?"

"Bad enough. I understand he's practically paralyzed. Lungs will just barely work."

He swore. "I wish we were going now!"

"Stella said that by the time the ambulance got him to the hospital he no longer knew her. He looked right at her but all his faculties were caving in pretty fast. He spoke just one word. He said—"

"I know. Stella told me. I've met her, she's great people. She said Dad called out Mattie's name."

"It was his fear that made him say it. His mind went back. I've heard that grown people when they're badly hurt and going into shock will actually call for their mama and daddy." She stopped abruptly. "Stew, you didn't tell Mattie what Irv said?"

"No."

"Don't, whatever you do. She won't handle it right. She'll make it a two-act drama. Or she'll use it for a laxative."

"What do you mean?"

"Never mind." He heard her take a deep breath. It was meant to complete something. He tried in that moment to recall her face and he could not. "Stewball," she said, and her voice was much softer, more familiar, "it'll be good to see you."

"Same here. I wonder if I'll even know you. It's been a long time."

"You'd better know me. I'll turn you over my knee and spank you right there on the runway."

"Concourse."

"I used to do it, you know. Spank you. Mattie wouldn't, so I had to. I used to change your diapers too."

"What a break for you."

"I even know what your pecker looks like."

"*Looked* like. Past tense. It's grown a lot since you saw it."

"For Bev's sake, I'm glad to hear that."

"I'm quite proud of it now. I can show you guys the new model when we meet in Denver."

"No, we'll take your word for it." She took another breath, louder, different. "Stew?"

"Yes?"

"Are you sad?"

"I guess more than anything I'm surprised. I don't remember Dad ever being sick in his life. Maybe a toothache or two, a little bursitis, that's all. Now he's in real bad trouble. It's hard to absorb. So . . . sudden. Gosh, I just saw him ten years ago."

There was a dead moment then, full of the hollow, empty sound of telephone wires spanning the hollow, empty spaces of night. "I love you," they both blurted at the same time, both hearing the same lonely sound. Then they laughed, both embarrassed. "I'll see you day after tomorrow in the Rocky Mountains," Tess said. "Look for me, I'll be riding Old Paint and leading Old Dan."

"Hey, that's Western lingo, isn't it?"

"So is *adios, muchacho*," she laughed, and hung up.

Through the greasy blur of the car window Stew could see tattered rags of gray mist forming along the road, slinking through the trees like night witches that the daylight had caught, but Bev spoke to him at that moment and broke his concentration. "The twins were so cute Sunday night after your stepmother called."

"Cute?"

"Didn't you notice? They wanted to say the correct thing about your dad, be respectful and polite and all that, but they didn't know how. They've never been involved in any kind of family emergency before."

"They haven't, have they?" It was almost a surprise to him.

"They said to me later, in the kitchen when you were on the phone to your sister, that they hoped Grandpa Donner would get better soon. That was the saddest part, because they don't remember him. He's just a name. They say the words 'Grandpa Donner' as though they were part of a new cheer they hadn't become familiar with yet."

Stew shrugged.

"Dwight didn't say anything, he kept watching the girls to get their reaction. It dawned on me then that he's never even seen your dad. I was pregnant with Dwight when your dad came out here that summer, and that's ten years ago." She waited a moment as though she were preparing a more thorough report on the elapsed time. "Your father's made such a stranger of himself that he's competely missed out on his grandchildren. Now that he's old and can no longer—"

"Dad's not old."

"Not old?" It was more surprise than denial. She took in a breath and let it out in a deliberate way. "Stewart, your father is *seventy-five*."

Bev slowed for the turnoff and Stew was so busy concentrating on the maneuver that by the time she had merged into the new traffic he'd forgotten what his reply was going to be. Perhaps he hadn't had one; his mind was curiously blank. He saw Sea-Tac International Airport loom out of what in any other city in the country would have been the horizon but here in Seattle was merely another bank of mist and fog. The unreality of the scene, plus the swish of the windshield wipers, made him feel unaccountably transient. He had traveled very little in his years at Boeing Engineering and wasn't used to this sort of rushing. What he wanted more than anything was to imagine that he was heading not to the airport but to the coast beaches with the twins whispering in the back seat about boys, and Dwight in the rear deck building a tank from a bagful of Legos, all normal togetherness matters, and his wife turning that full-lipped snow-skinned Liv Ullmann face to him saying, "Oh hon, it's going to be too wet for a picnic today, what do you say we go back home and start a fire in the downstairs fireplace and play a game of Sorry with the kids."

Bev didn't get out of the car when she stopped in front of Passenger Check-In, United, nor did she cut the motor. That wasn't the plan. She leaned across the seat instead and kissed him. "Oh babe," she cried suddenly, and her eyes filled with tears, which wasn't in the plan either, "we never do this, we never say goodbye at airports. That's not our life. I hate it!"

"Me too," he said, and a wave of the identical dismay washed over him. He caught a picture of himself as a harried political figure rushing to some distant corner of the world to confront an issue he knew nothing about. He was ready to get out of the car and not prolong his regret more than was necessary, wondering for God's sake if he was going to choke up and be unable to say a proper goodbye, when Bev broke in with one of her standard mood-breaking last-minute reminders. "Stew, when the four of you get together in Denver and start your trip back, you'll remember to mention what you and I talked about, won't you? About your mother and this schedule thing, I mean."

"It really isn't a schedule, Bev."

"But it's what we decided you would do, right? That you would bring it up for discussion with the others. You will, won't you, Stewart?"

"On the single condition," he came back, grateful for the fact that his throat was abruptly clear again, "that you lean over here and deliver me one of those famous Swedish kisses."

"Norwegian," she corrected him, her face showing her own relief, revealing that married couples are more dual mirrors than anything. "The Swedes never learned how."

But once inside the terminal Stew discovered his departure time had been delayed. His flight had a scheduled stop in Boise but there had been early-morning fog in Boise, now dissipated to such an extent, the agent explained, that the wait should last no more than fifteen or twenty minutes. So he sat and waited, watching his fellow passengers. A nurse caught his eye, tall, blue cape, blue cap, white stockings and shoes, and it reminded him of Mattie in Tucson. She'd struggled through a series of insignificant jobs in their first years there but had finally landed a decent one that suited her, a nurses' aide job at one of the tuberculosis sanatoriums Tucson had so many of. She had only one uniform, he remembered, and had to wash and iron it every night when she came home.

Later she became a private nurse for wealthy TB patients at one of the exclusive sans, which is what they preferred to call them because the full word *sanatorium* sounded like a place for crazy people. Mattie's patients were primarily Jewish men from the East, and the one Stewart remembered best was named Shulman, Sy Shulman, a dark-skinned man with silver hair and big lips who bought each of Mattie's kids a box of figs whenever there was a holiday, it didn't make any difference which one. Stew didn't know what eventually happened to Mr. Shulman, his lungs either cleared up or got worse, there probably wasn't any middle ground in tuberculosis, even for Jewish people.

Another of Mattie's rich lungers (the kids called them lungers; it didn't have the class of *guests* or *patients* but there was never any question who you were talking about) was a Mr. Rothstein, a short man with a gravelly voice and a belly so big it looked like he had a pillow hidden under the covers of his bed when he lay out on the screened porch of his private cabin. Mr. Rothstein didn't give presents to Mattie's kids, just to Mattie, and he never seemed to waste away from his disease, which Stew determined from the fact that the man's stomach never got any smaller. Another ᵍ‖

oddity was that he never coughed. You'd think lungers would cough. Stew knew they weren't supposed to spit, there were signs all over the city, on benches and sidewalks and against buildings: DO NOT EXPECTORATE. Maybe there were signs about coughing too but he just hadn't seen them. Then again, remembering Mr. Rothstein, maybe you didn't waste away with tuberculosis, maybe lying in bed eating chocolates and fruit and getting bathed and waited on by a private nurse was all the cure you needed. And listening to the radio. There wasn't much TV, it was too new, and unless you had a roof antenna about all you could get was a picture of snow.

The most obvious thing about those rich lungers was that Mattie was their favorite nurse. Perhaps it was her olive skin, or it could have been her eyes, they were distinctive enough, sleepy and piercing at the same time. Or maybe it was because she was so tall and elegant-looking. In her starched white uniform with the perky blue cap she could look very pure and dignified, like that picture of Florence Nightingale among the wounded troops. At other times she looked like she knew secrets and would tell them to the right person. She must have liked her Jewish gentlemen in return, because she came home one night and gathered the kids together (it had to be on the eve of a holiday because she had four boxes of figs with her) and told them that if one of her patients ever asked if she was Jewish they were to answer that they weren't positive but they *guessed* she was, probably one of the nonorthodox kind who never went to church.

"Synagogue," DeeJay corrected her, and Mattie said she knew it was synagogue, she'd just forgotten for a second.

"Shit," Stew said when Mattie had left the room. (He'd learned to swear a little by that time but nothing compared to some of the boys he played with.) "What is this Jewish business, a new play she's worked out or something?"

(*61*)

DeeJay said, "Maybe Jewish is better than Methodist, you ever think of that?"

"Well, goddam," he said, for he was momentarily stopped and could think of nothing better. But with the extra time he finally came up with, "Why does Mama always pretend to be someone else? Couldn't she just be herself for once, a farm woman from Wisconsin?"

Doc said, "Is that what she is?" It sounded disgusted, although it could easily have been bored. Doc got bored with anything that wasn't baseball or basketball.

Then Tess stepped in, you could always bank on Tess having something to say before a thing went too far. "Mama wasn't asking us if we liked it, she was just telling us the way she wanted it to be. If she needs our help, maybe we should go along with her." Tess almost never defended Mama anymore and this surprised Stew. "What difference does it make," she went on, "as long as we have nice clothes for school and there's food in the icebox?"

Icebox! Tess was forever saying things like that, either using the wrong word or giving it the wrong pronunciation. Iceboxes were completely out of style, what the hell! Maybe the first houses they'd lived in in Tucson had iceboxes but the later ones had refrigerators. Refrigerators made a lot of noise and Mama said they ran up the electric bill something awful, especially if one of them forgot to close the door, but at least they didn't have a melt pan setting underneath that had to be dumped two or three times a day, which was usually his job. Ordering ice too, that was another job he had. If he forgot to order ice the milk turned to cottage cheese and the butter looked like a saucer of yellow paint. He had to stick the order card in the front window every other day with the number of pounds of ice he wanted facing out so the iceman could read it. In the summer it was fifty pounds and sometimes even that wasn't enough. It was goddamed hot in Tucson in the summer!

Boarding was announced and the airplane taxied out and took off but it seemed it couldn't break free of the rain and mist. The sleek tube that Boeing called the 727 might as well have been a submarine trying to rise from the bottom of the sea. "Take her up!" ordered the captain, and the sub's bow tilted upward with a surge of power. But it never reached the surface, it couldn't break through the gray-black waters of the ocean any more than the 727 could break through the gray-black mist of the sky. "Up!" the captain cried. "Up I say!" But to no avail. There was no longer any surface to reach, there were no angles anywhere that the vessel could seek, the top was the same as the bottom and the sides were gone.

Stew leaned back in his seat and closed his eyes and thought of Bev. Was she home yet? Was it still raining? He snorted softly. Of course it was still raining, this was coastal Washington, wasn't it? He thought of their house sitting in the rain, made smaller by it, its colors blurring into those of the earth. The rain did that, it altered and converted things. It hated buildings and stone, loved slopes, soils, lawns, all permeable things it could soften and work in. It had worked his lawns, an entire acre of them, sides, front, back, into a veritable jungle of bushes and shrubbery and vines, every plant known to man except one. The cactus. Never, never had it produced a cactus. He smiled to himself. Poor Mattie, how hard she tried every fourth year to start a cactus garden in that Puget Sound rain forest. He had to give credit to her ingenuity, she picked a different spot on the grounds each time she came, once under the rear deck of the house, another time in the front section of the blackberry patch and this year in a border along the left walk, next to the bamboo. The bamboo would be the lucky charm, the guardian angel, she told him. "This could be the year the garden will take hold."

"That'll be a change, won't it, Mother?"

All her previous failures paraded through his mind with the chronological relevance of national wars. The War of 1962, the War of 1966, '70, '74, and so on up the drumroll of the years.

He remembered the '66 war in particular. Mattie had arrived in early June as usual and immediately suggested that the entire family drive over to the Pacific beaches for the weekend so they could box up a hundred pounds of beach sand and bring it back. Stew announced the project and they drove in high excitement to Copalis and everyone pitched in, even the twins, who were only five (and who also added a few sand dollars and a starfish or two to the boxed sand). When they got home Sunday night, Stew began clearing off a strip of ground at the edge of the patio deck approximately six feet long by five wide, and by the following weekend Mattie had transplanted a dozen fat healthy cacti from the nursery pots to the new rectangle of beach sand. He recognized most of the plants from his Arizona days. There were two golden barrels, a pink nymph, a bishop's cap, some pincushion and a bunch of green thimble, a pair of painted ladies, and finally, guarding the ends of the strip like tiny scarecrows, a pair of *Euphorbia submammillaris*, or corncob.

The following Saturday Mattie filled in around the new plantings with a neat top dressing of pea gravel she had asked Stew to pick up from the local nursery, and Sunday she gave the plot its first watering, a gentle but precise irrigation with the garden hose.

That was late June. By late July the tips of the cacti had begun to turn brown, and by the first week in Septem-

(64)

ber, when the twins started school for the first time, the barrels were lank and floppy, the bishop's cap had deflated, the pink nymphs looked like binder weed, and the proud apple-green sentries at each end of the plot had sagged into discolored sponges.

A month later, when the winter rains began in earnest, Mattie asked him to bring home a fifty-pound bag of perlite, which she carefully mixed in with the pea gravel and the sand. It didn't work. The root rot was so far advanced by then that when any member of the family, including the dog, so much as glanced at one of the plants it would immediately fall over. By Christmas, every cactus plant on the premises was dead, and Stew raked them up and threw them out with the Christmas wrapping paper.

Let's see, did the cold frame belong to the War of 1970 or was it 1974? Yes, it was '70. When Mattie came that year (again in June, always in June) she selected an area almost fifty feet square directly in front of the currant bushes at the back of the yard, dispensing with pea gravel and beach sand this time and concentrating instead on mounding each individual plant with nests of sponge rock. Her plants were bigger that year, more ambitious, they included the ever-present golden barrel as well as a blue agave, from which they would be able to make tequila, Mattie explained, as soon as the plant reached maturity.

"How long does that take?" Stew asked.

"About twelve years. Sometimes fourteen."

He cleared his throat. "I never cared for tequila anyway. Burns my tongue."

1970 was an especially pleasant summer, Stew remembered, and the cacti retained their glaucous green plumpness right through Labor Day, but in an attempt to thwart the inevitable winter rains Mattie asked him to build a cold frame and place it over the cactus patch. "That should protect the plants," she said.

(65)

The coldframe was an elaborate structure, Stew remembered. He had performed his very best carpentry on it, roofing the rectangular structure with corrugated tin and installing a glass door in front. It kept out the rain admirably, which wasn't as heavy that winter for some reason, but it also kept out the sun, of which, just as mysteriously, there was an abundance. On Valentine's Day, when the twins insisted on picking one of the cactus flowers that Mattie had been promising would be ready by mid-February, Stew went out to the backyard and dismantled the cold frame.

The blast of sour air that rose from the plants nearly gagged him. Instead of a phalanx of cheery blooms that had successfully withstood a Seattle winter, he found only a troop of limp shriveled stalks the color of old straw.

In the next war, the War of 1974, Mattie mixed up her selection of plants a little better, assigning to the area left of the patio a generous planting of beavertails and cow horns, while to the right she installed a neat circle of teddybear cholla and owl eyes, which the twins laughed at each time they ran out to check the garden, for the owl eyes were truly comical.

And let's see, did '74 also feature the battle of the compost? The answer again was yes. The way he remembered the compost was that during the winter Mattie had written from Doc's place in Denver and asked the twins to start a compost pile so that when she got there in June it would be ready for her.

The girls threw themselves into the task, raking up the few tree leaves that were still caught in the lawn from the previous fall, saving the grass clippings when spring came, plus all the vegetable waste from the kitchen that could possibly qualify for "Grandma's compost pile." Deciding to do his part as well, Stew picked up new cactus plants at the nursery and had them waiting for her.

Upon arrival, Mattie planted the cacti in the patio plot and immediately buried them in compost. Following this, she initiated a sophisticated overhead watering program, her intention being, she announced, "to allow the rich organic material in the compost to leach down into the soil and spur the cactus plants into vigorous growth." Mattie was good at pronouncements such as that, especially after memorizing the product brochures. To her, they were scripts.

The summer came in hot. An excessive amount of rain fell, turning their lawn in the lush Clyde Hill area into what Bev called Amazon Basin North. The rotting compost turned rancid, and the stench filled the lawn and the patio and the entire house. By Columbus Day, Bev could stand it no longer, neither the neighbor's complaints nor her own almost constant nausea, and on the first day following the holiday she ordered a truck to come and remove every last shred of compost from the place. "Cactus plants too!" she commanded, and when the truck people had completed their job and left, Bev drove to the nursery and bought a beautiful prize-winning *Sedum morganianum*, or donkey tail, and hung it just to the left of the arch in the family room as a sort of laboratory example of what plants worked best where.

Mattie was incensed at the removal of her plants and wouldn't look at the sedum, however magnificent, for its being there seemed not so much an option of modern husbandry as a violation of deep-seated belief. "Under no circumstances," she announced theatrically when Stew arrived home that evening, the twins and the overwhelmed Dwight in rapt audience, "would I hang a donkey tail in a pot inside a house!"

Several responses to Mattie's pronouncement coursed through Stew's mind, but he let them all go by. The children were disappointed but sensed his adult wisdom nonetheless—he had saved them from having to pick sides in public.

Through January and February and into that tortured season that a late spring can become in that part of the state, all dialogue between Bev and Mattie was a concession to civility, nothing more. Like a gene-trapped lemming, when the Memorial Day weekend was over Mattie headed straight for DeeJay's in southern California.

Yet four years later here she was, arriving in the first week of June as usual, insisting in that flush of optimism which characterized the beginnings of all her projects that the new site adjacent to the bamboo would prove ideal for the plants, that it would utilize the very best elements of time and climate and produce a hardy catcus garden.

And once again the early optimism waned. As a guardian spirit the bamboo was proving woefully inadequate, for now in November, five months after her arrival and on the very eve of his trip to La Crosse, Mattie's cacti looked sadly spiritless. The War of 1978 was about to settle into the customary winter pattern of attrition and despair.

When he sensed the sudden brightness, Stew opened his eyes and saw the interior of the plane flooding with sunshine. He expelled a breath of relief and leaned his head back against the seat and closed his eyes, savoring the moment. It would be better now, they had risen from the dark ocean into light, he would see his father and it would be good. Irvin Donner would throw off the shock of the stroke and regain full use of his body. He would walk and talk again, laugh in the peculiar way he had, his shoulders shaking out of all proportion to the volume of his laughter. He would become the familiar Irv Donner of the Viroqua sawmill business, the brusque hardworking father of long ago who had stood beside Stew's car smiling in at him as he prepared to drive back to the campus in Madison after spending the weekend in Viroqua with him and Stella. "Listen, Stewart, I'm gonna get down there and see you one of these days, okay? We'll spend a weekend together, take in a Badger game, why don't we? Maybe catch the Golden Gophers or the Ohio State Buckeyes, how about it? I'll buy the tickets," and he punched Stew's shoulder through the car window. "I've got this deal coming up I have to take care of but then we'll be all set. Got a buyer coming in from Minneapolis–St. Paul, what you call your Twin Cities, to look at my hickory. Hickory's your best for furniture and the like, and that's what this gent is starting up, a furniture business along custom-made lines. Kitchen chairs, cabinets, that sort of thing. Could be a big contract for me, but I need to get some finished boards ready for him. It's like the old philosopher says, 'The man who rolls up his sleeve seldom loses his shirt.'" Another pop on the arm. "But listen, Stewart, we'll do it, okay? We'll get together down there in Madison for a good old-fashioned Badger weekend, just you and me."

It would have been great fun, but something always came up . . .

FOUR

EVEN AS THEY taxied out, DeeJay asked the stewardess for a Scotch and water. "Cutty Sark if you have it, otherwise, Chivas Regal."

"I'm sorry, we don't serve those brands on the airplane."

"I've changed my mind," DeeJay said. "Make it a bourbon and water," and the reason she said this was not that she had changed her mind or that she preferred bourbon, but that she couldn't allow this sap-eyed twit of a stewardess to go one up on her before they even left the ground.

"Any particular brand of bourbon?" asked the stewardess, whose every snide feature revealed the hope that Dee-Jay would again ask for a brand they didn't serve on the plane. "Sorry," she could then reply, "we don't serve that brand on this flight either," and the victory would be hers.

But not today. Not on Continental Flight 218, nonstop to Denver. DeeJay Kelley, who had never been a stewardess and never taken an order for drinks in her life, but who knew about overconfidence and its place in the histories of defeat, looked up and smiled sweetly and said, "Why . . . whatever you're pouring, dear." She was old enough to say *dear* and young enough to feel vengeful about it, and with that she wet the tip of one finger and marked *victory number one* on an imaginary scorecard, then turned to her window and watched the takeoff.

She had flown out of Los Angeles several times, primarily for CPA seminars or conventions, and mainly it was a beautiful sight. When you took off from LAX you flew out over the ocean first and then circled back toward the east, and the city turned under your eyes into a gigantic canvas, what DeeJay called a Paint-by-Shape. She even had her own set of directions. Paint all the small ovals blue, for they are swimming pools full of water and water is blue. All squares must be painted green, they are lawns and parks. The narrow straight lines are streets, the wider oblique lines are freeways, and both take the color Cream-Gray, but be careful, don't confuse this with White, which is used exclusively for buildings. When you come to the borders and circles and arcs, *all* your paints must be used, all the different colors contained in your kit plus whatever new tints you can mix and create, for the borders and circles and arcs are California flowers!

A few times there had been smog at takeoff. Smog was the enemy of Paint-by-Shape, distorting the buildings, running together the precise blues and reds and greens, reducing the entire canvas to an insane urban Rorschach.

She could imagine what her suburb of Chatsworth should be colored this time of year, now that the Santa Ana winds had finished blowing in from the Mojave and making crispy critters out of everything that grew. Seen from the air, beige would be the dominant color of her town, beige fields and beige lawns all crumpled together into tiny beige hills.

Actually they were more hummocks than hills, like ancient lavas that had gotten trapped in an area too small to level out. Chatsworth was typical of that strip of earth just in from the coast, growing up half town and half country, every block a paradise for kids with coaster wagons or teenagers with trail bikes. Their own home, hers and Kell's, was probably the perfect example, one hummock formed the front yard and another the back, while a third tried to intimidate the house from the north. All beige now in this beige season of November. Other than that, California stayed the same year-round. It was Mediterranea come to Pacific Shores with every other town a Vista—Monte Vista, Mar Vista, Hi Vista, Chula Vista—and every other house your basic Happy Hacienda in the Hills . . . three-level Spanish with Aztec White walls and red tile roofs, black ironwork balustrades looking down on an interior court where a mossy fountain splashed lazily onto lush green plants. . . .

Well, not totally lush perhaps. The jades and ferns, yes, but how about the four-foot saguaro that Mattie had planted on one visit and that had toppled over prior to the next? It had fallen like a condemned building in an inner-city renewal program. When Kell dug for the roots he couldn't find them. "How can a plant grow that way?" he demanded, scratching his head, pointing. "You see that? The thing was just setting there on the ground all this time with no roots! How can a plant do that? Tell me!" Kell was originally from Long Island and his study of succulent culture had been understandably neglected, although he was right about the roots, they should have been there. A lot of his concern was actually for Mattie, it was her saguaro, she had planted it. Kell tried always to be nice, he lived by the book and the book said you were nice to your mother-in-law and appreciative of her efforts in your behalf. "I'll tell her one of the boys ran into it with his bike," he said to DeeJay. They had two boys, both careless bike riders. "Or maybe I can replace it before her next—"

"No, Kell, tell her the truth. Tell her the cactus bombed because she blew the transplant. Tell her it should have been planted in that big area behind the house instead of here in this little sand border next to the fountain. Pretty, oh my, yes, but stupid. Tell her that the reason she can't do anything right stems from two principal causes. One, she doesn't know what she's doing, and two, she tries too hard to do what she doesn't know how. Kapeesh?"

The stewardess brought the bourbon and water.

The failure of the saguaro was ironic because the slopes on the west and south sides of the house were purely and simply Lawn Beautiful. When she and Kell first bought the property—four acres lying directly west of the To-panga Canyon Road where it wound down to the ocean—they immediately began improvements. They put in a winding flagstone walk and flanked it with oleander hedges and rose espaliers that arched over the walk at select intervals. New redwood benches were placed in the rose quartz borders of the walk as though to tempt the tired stroller, and in addition to the trees already growing on the grounds they planted others—deodar, bottlebrush, blue gum eucalyptus and madrone, canyon live oak, California bay—so that as a result of all this labor and landscaping their home became a sort of orchard-park. The trees pleased DeeJay the most. She could never have enough trees. She supposed it was the year she'd spent in Montana that was responsible. Just to have *one* tree would have been heaven then, one tree to walk to and stand by, to throw her arms around. To have anything of her own on that desolate prairie would have been enough, it didn't have to be a tree. . . .

"We'll go to my brothers," Mattie told them when they

left Wisconsin, and as the bus growled its way across Minnesota and one of the Dakotas, she explained the wonderful welcome awaiting them. "Your uncles are missionaries. God-fearing men, both of them. They'll be kind to us."

The first thing the uncles did when the bus got there was split the family up, and the kindness of that act escaped DeeJay completely. Mattie and the two boys stayed in town while she and Tess and Mickey went to Uncle Frank's farm out on the edge of town. It wasn't actually a farm, just a dumpy square house with a few outlying sheds. Uncle Frank said it was a parsonage, entrusted to their use by the church as long as he was there "in the service of the Lord." He had eyes the color of maple tree sap and a long gaunt face like a church painting of the dying Jesus, and he rubbed his hands a lot. So did Aunt Ida, except hers were blunt and square and didn't have a lot of finger to them. She wasn't tall like Mattie and in the looks department she'd had the door slammed on her; there was a smudge of hair on her upper lip that showed either faint or dark, depending on how the light hit. She wore dark clothes that were too big for her, and ankle-top shoes that looked as if they belonged to Uncle Frank and she'd put them on that morning by mistake. On the bus coming out, Mama said, "You'll find Aunt Ida a little fusty." That was understated. Tess did better when she described Ida as one of those old-fashioned stoves with the damper set wrong.

Mattie never explained why the four kids had to be separated. All four of them living in town one month, all on the farm the next, would have been a better arrangement. But then Montana hadn't been much good for anything. Shortly after all four kids got enrolled in school for the coming term, the girls in the country and the boys in town, Mattie left. She just took off. She didn't say anything to anyone either, because the way they found out was Uncle Willard and Aunt May and the boys came barreling down Uncle Frank's lane one afternoon in the black car and Willard jumped out and began screaming to Frank, "Mattie's gone! She's run off! She's run off and left these hell-burned, misbegotten children with *us!*"

DeeJay remembered it perfectly because she'd never heard those particular cusswords before. They didn't sound like your general run, but you can tell a real cussword more by the way it comes out than by what it says. Almost anything can be a cussword in the right mouth. Another thing she remembered about that day was how Doc and Stewart kept staring through the window of the car, their faces so grainy and colorless it was hard to tell them apart.

Everything changed after that. The world became full of different ways to live. DeeJay began studying the cars that drove by the house, the ones that slowed down, the ones that speeded up. She'd hardly ever looked at cars before. There weren't a lot of cars in that country, people said there'd be more cars as soon as the war was over. Another thing she did was check the mailbox a lot. A letter, especially a little one, could easily be overlooked by someone reaching in for the mail. That wasn't all she did. She listened for the front door of the schoolhouse to open during class, for Uncle Frank's phone to ring in the middle of the night, for a knock to come on the door at the odd hour.

Eventually she quit doing these things. She didn't know when she quit exactly, she just did. There are some things you stop doing simply because they no longer make sense.

Nothing ever comes of them.

If Montana wasn't blessed with trees, it at least had Indians. The state was full of Indians. Crows. Saturday mornings they were shuffling figures hitching a ride into town, fat women in moccasins and clove-colored gowns, big-bellied men in black Stetsons. Saturday nights they were motion-less blobs on the corners of the downtown streets, looking like horses standing at a fence in twilight. Sunday they were stuffed figures in church, the women in flowing, purple dresses and the men in shirts and suits so shrunken and ill-fitting that they looked like effigies someone had propped up in the pews to fool Uncle Frank. Sometimes they were soldiers in khaki uniforms milling around the bus station or drinking out of pint bottles in the alley in back.

At school the Crows were chubby moon-faced kids whose skin was the color of cocoa that didn't have enough milk in it. Their clothes were clean but never pressed. The Indian girls were sullen, and DeeJay decided it was because the Indian boys pinched the white girls' behinds instead of theirs. But neither the girls or the boys ever made a fuss, not even when they fell off the highest part of the slide, or when one of the white kids dumped their lunch pails into the dirt.

To Uncle Willard and Uncle Frank, who talked about them constantly, the Crow people were their "charge here on earth." Being ministers, they naturally had to raise money in order to more thoroughly spread the gospel and in all other ways administer to the spiritual needs of their flock, which is how Uncle Frank expressed it. And raising money had a good side too, because that's how the four kids got their chance to be together. It wasn't on Friday nights when Uncle Willard ran Bingo games in the base-ment of his church, and it wasn't on Sunday. Sunday, Uncle Frank served Methodist League dinners on the lawn of his church. The cost was a dollar a plate for the white families and, although he never said it at the picnics, "fifty cents a throw for the red." But Stewart and Doc could never make it out to the dinners, being too busy with their own church doings in town.

The day they got together was Saturday.

Saturday was what Uncle Willard called punch board day, and it was always the first Saturday in the month, regardless of the weather. Both families met at eight o'clock Saturday morning at Uncle Willard's house, where Aunt May formed the kids into teams (the two boys in one team, the two girls in the other, it never varied) and distributed to each team what she referred to as "the goods." The goods consisted of a punchboard, a rack of perfume vials, and a little drawstring bag, similar to the kind that boys used for marbles, with the words NEW ZION stenciled on both sides. Aunt May also assigned territories, again invariable: boys on the east side of town, girls on the west.

The purpose of all this was to raise money by selling chances on the punchboard. Twenty-five cents a chance, and if the man (it was always the husband who came to the door) punched out a lucky number he won a vial of perfume. He got to pick the vial himself, because each one had a lady's name attached to it on a little white tag. Dorothy. Alice. Mildred. Patrice. (They didn't sell a lot of Patrice in Custer City.) Each team used a special sales pitch that Uncle Willard had worked up: "Good morning, sir, we're from the New Zion Methodist Church, Missionary Section, and we'd like to ask you a question this fine morning, sir. The question is, what's your wife's name? Is it Edith? Mary? Perhaps it's Margaret, sir. If you punch out the lucky number on this board you can win a beautiful vial of perfume with your wife's name on it. And every vial has a different scent because every lady is different, isn't that right, sir? Would you like to take a chance on the board? It's only twenty-five cents. One fourth part of a dollar. The small part, ha, ha, ha. It goes to help the Crow Indian children, who are less fortunate than we."

At that point Tess, who always gave the spiel because she was the biggest and had this marvelous speaking voice, would present the punchboard to the man standing in the door, and at the same moment, DeeJay would hold up the rack of vials.

Occasionally a man would pop the lucky number and they would have to stand there on the porch while he searched for his wife's name among all those tiny white tags. Tough, especially on a cold morning. She and Tess had to be on guard too that the man wouldn't slip out of giving them the quarter. Uncle Willard was very insistent on this; he said it was sad to report but there were some people, even churchgoers, who would try to con you. Once Tess got the money, however, she spent the rest of the time trying to persuade the man not to open the vial there in the door. It wouldn't be fair, she would tell him, a lady should have the pleasure of opening a gift in the privacy of her own bedroom, "Isn't that right, sir?" Then too, that perfume smelled real bad.

But if the man couldn't be persuaded to buy a chance on the board with a normal pitch, Tess would fall back on what Uncle Willard called the Sally Sad close. Tess would smile wanly and flutter her eyelids and grab DeeJay's hand and say, "Come, little sister, we've still got a lot of doorbells to ring if we're ever going to help our little Red Brothers." Then she would glance up at the man and sigh heavily. "But thank you anyway, sir, for giving us a moment out of your busy life. We know your heart's in the right place so we'll take our leave of you now on this day so near the Lord's day, the Sabbath, and wend our weary way along the streets and byways of life's never-ending stream. . . ."

It could have been an effective close, but Tess always got so overwhelmed with emotion at this point that her throat tightened and the words came out so squeaky and incoherent that the man would end up laughing instead of

(78)

forking over a quarter for a chance to win a vial of that godawful perfume.

Those punchboard Saturdays were long. There were a lot of streets in Custer City, a lot of houses, and when it began to grow dark the teams would leave their territories and troop back to Uncle Willard's house. Aunt Ida and Aunt May would inventory the goods and then start the counting, sitting at the kitchen table with their pinched pink faces and flabby arms, tallying what Uncle Willard called "the take."

Yet those Saturdays were the only opportunity the kids had to be together. While the tallying was taking place the four of them would slip out onto the lawn and start talking to each other all at once.

Have you heard from Mama?

Do you like your teacher? What's her name?

Is that a new sweater? Did Aunt Ida buy you a sweater?

Do you ever get ice cream or anything?

I thought I saw Mama in a green car but it must not have been her.

How's Mickey? Does he still howl at night?

The sweater came from the Pass Me Down box at church.

I can't call you. Uncle Frank's got this church program going and he needs to keep the phone open.

Tom Antelope brought a rattlesnake to school. Longer than me.

Oh the wind comes right through the walls.

Do you think Mama remembers us?

The goodbyes that followed really hurt. They would hug each other and Tess and Stewart would cry so loud the adults would come out of the house and scold them for not being responsible young grown-ups. "Will you continually drown yourselves in the dark waters of childish despair? We are engaged in Larger Work here. You'd see that if your faith was strong enough. You need more faith!"

The Montana winter was grim, its light that of a guttering candle threatening forever to go out. The prairie hemmed them in on all sides, and DeeJay came to realize that a place can be menacing simply by reason of its vastness.

She wound up wearing other people's clothes because her own wore out and were not replaced. There was a sweater of Aunt Ida's that had a hole in both elbows and a pair of galoshes with half the buckles gone that had been left in the Crow box at church. The bedroom upstairs where she and Tess slept was achingly cold, but Uncle Frank wouldn't waste the wood to heat the top part of the house. "We'll leave the stairway door open at night," he told them. "That will give you more than enough warmth." It didn't. There was a night pot under their bed but it was so cold in their room that DeeJay ended up holding her urine until morning. A lot of times it didn't work. She would dream she was using a pot in a nice warm closet in a nice warm house but actually she was wetting the bed. It was the dream's fault, she would have sworn she was on the pot, and although Tess's nightgown got soaked as well, for they slept cuddled together, Tess never scolded her for wetting the bed.

Uncle Frank did. The first time he found out about it he rubbed his hands together more than usual, and the second time (Aunt Ida always told him; she would be waiting in the hall when they first got out of bed and she'd go in and feel the sheet) he lectured her severely and the third time he explained in his tremulous preacher's voice that he would be forced to "remedy the situation." Thereafter, he was the one who checked the bed and if it was wet he'd make DeeJay stand outside in the backyard and hold the sheet up in the wind until it dried. The *redress of incontinence* is what he called it. DeeJay hadn't the slightest idea what it meant but she knew she was being punished, and she knew also that Tess couldn't go on trying to take the blame. "Gosh, I think it was *me* who wet the bed this time, Uncle Frank," Tess would say. "I have weak kidneys too. I just couldn't control myself." But he wouldn't listen. He knew. And he wouldn't consent to heat the upstairs either.

DeeJay could remember how tired her arms got from holding the sheet, how cold and cramped, how the wind blew and blew and wouldn't stop. She realized that the wind was the thing that dried the sheet but that didn't ease the sting. And she could remember how Uncle Frank would watch through the window until he figured the sheet was dry and then come out and march her upstairs so she could make the bed before she went to school.

Aunt Ida remained as pure as Caesar's wife. She spoke not a single word, neither to shame nor to sympathize nor to defend.

Tess was powerless to help. She'd stand with DeeJay in the yard, clenching her fists, her shoulders trembling and her face fiery red, but she never made a sound.

One Saturday morning she did. DeeJay was holding a sodden sheet up to the wind and Uncle Frank was watching from his customary spot behind the window. Tess was standing in the yard a few feet away when suddenly she ran to the porch door and began pounding on it, shouting at Uncle Frank that he had to stop doing this. Then abruptly, she turned from the porch and ran across the yard and out the lane, screaming at the top of her voice, "Mama! Make him stop, Mama! Come back and make him stop!"

. . .

One day, in the spring DeeJay thought it was, Mama did come back. Uncle Willard's big black car stopped in the lane one afternoon and there she was getting out of the front with Stewart hanging onto her leg and Doc right behind, rubbing his eyes and swallowing real fast. They all crowded around and hugged her, all except Tess, she didn't join in, she just stood back by herself. Then Uncle Frank and Uncle Willard grabbed Mama's arms and swept her into the house so fast her hat fell off (a small blue hat with a piece of black net hanging down in front) and left the rest of them standing there in the lane staring at the open door of the car. The boys had forgotten to close it when they got out.

Perhaps a week or maybe a month later, DeeJay couldn't be sure, Mama called them together and said she was going to take them away from Custer City. "As soon as the school term ends," she said. "I don't want you children missing school," and when the day came and they were waiting for the bus at the Greyhound terminal that had candy-bar wrappers all over the floor and huge, symbolic Crow drawings on the walls, she told them they were going to Arizona.

Stewart said, "Arizona, what's that?"

"Do we have uncles there too?" DeeJay wanted to know.

"You'll like Arizona," Mattie told them. "It'll be warm there. There's sand, mountains. We'll be out of the cold and snow for good."

Tess said, "Have you been in the cold and snow, Mama?" and nobody said anything.

It was good to leave Montana, but traveling south through the sage and yellow clover of Wyoming, DeeJay realized it was goodbye forever to Wisconsin, goodbye to the green fields and the creeks and the green hills, to the trees and even the big house on the ridge where Daddy probably still lived, although she had trouble remembering it now. Sometimes memories were like clothes, they eventually got so worn and faded you couldn't tell what the original color had been. Already, after the year in Montana, she'd forgotten what Dad's face looked like. She had no snapshots of him and she suspected that Mama didn't have either. Her best memory was the smell of his mackinaw jacket when he came into the house for supper. The cold air would cling to it for a while, as well as the smell of the sawdust from the big lean-to shed where the saws were. Sometimes she would see a tiny woodchip stuck in his jacket and wonder if the chip would hurt if he were to bend down and hug her. She never found out. She hadn't thought of it then exactly, but he wasn't a man to hug.

"Another bourbon, please, stewardess."

So . . . now . . . they would be together again, all four kids, and it would happen in Denver, of all places. She'd never been to Denver, never been inside any house of Doc's since he'd married Lil, but she remembered that the two of them had come to California once, flying out one summer to visit her and Kell and their first two kids, Peter and Paul. Three kids now, Peter, Paul, and Mary. *Puff, the Magic Dragon . . . Don't Think Twice, It's All Right . . . In the Early Morning Rain. . . .* What was going on here? Was it Growing-Old Time for the Donner bunch? *I take the book and gather to the fire, turning old yellow leaves; minute by minute the clock ticks to my heart. . . .* That was the poem Tess had forced her to memorize in the old days. Forced all of them to memorize. It was in one of the books they had voweled when they'd lived in Wisconsin. My God, that was antiquity! The "less miserables" of the Wisconsin hills (so Tess had labeled the four of them

(*83*)

once, mispronouncing the title of the Victor Hugo novel she had gotten from the library) had grown up and had kids of their own old enough to drive, or beg to drive, whatever. Hard to believe that much time had passed, but she wasn't going to shed any tears over it. Tears were bullshit. *Que sera, será* was more appropriate, it was the California way. Doris Day had said it, hadn't she?

She would see Doc and that was good, maybe the best part of all. Big Doctor Wallace, the graceful slightly stooped figure of the yearly Snapshot and Christmas Card Exchange Club that their relationship had evolved into. Would he be the old Doc, quiet, a shade ploddy, looking perpetually as if he'd been on the verge of saying something really salty until someone beat him to it? Forever arching scraps of paper at imaginary hoops, cocking his arm for a desperate throw to the plate. . . .

Doc hadn't returned to Tucson after his baseball days were over but had gone to Denver instead. After college he had taken a job with a local firm (sugar beets, beer, what?), where she believed he still worked. She remembered that she had asked Doc in those days to come to California to live but he wouldn't do it, he wouldn't join the stampede to paradise, he informed her, wouldn't fly into the neon with the other moths. Nor would he go back to Wisconsin. Somehow she sensed that Wisconsin had been bad for Doc, and she supposed she knew at least some of the reason. For a moment she saw him again as in a set of misprojected slides, throwing a tennis ball (a beatup thing) against the barn pretending it was a game of pepper, kicking a football straight up in the air so he could catch it, shooting a half-deflated basketball (she'd always insisted it was stolen from the school) into a netless barrel hoop nailed to the woodhouse wall, alone, always alone.

She would see Tess. Tess was the only one who stayed in

Tucson, in the city she once, long ago, had called Mattie's Last Stand. Now, this day, two or maybe three hours hence, she would see that tall, square-faced, big sister with the enveloping voice and the monstrously sad eyes. . . .

"DeeJay?"

"Tucson Tess, right? I had a hunch you'd call."

"Obviously, Stella talked to you about Irv's stroke." It was as much question as statement, perhaps because the voice sounded so strange to her.

"Not more than an hour ago. I guess we've got to fly back to Wisconsin."

"Watch that *we*, it's terribly inclusive. There are still some of us who refuse to do it."

"Afraid to fly? You, the original Vitamin Flintheart? You've got to be kidding."

"Backwards, forwards, sideways, my cowardice knows no limits. No direction either, obviously."

"I always had you figured for one of those intrepid souls who are forever bearding the lion in his den."

"You were right, I'm not afraid of lions. It's airplanes."

"Won't this delay things? I mean, isn't there some urgency in getting to the hospital? I assume Irv was calling for us, as hard as that is to believe. Hard, hell," she added, "more like impossible."

"Did Stella tell you he was calling for us?"

"Well . . . now that you ask. . . ."

"All I heard Stella say about names was that Irv called out Mattie's just before he lost consciousness."

"God, he's sicker than I thought!" She took time to light a cigarette and then went on, surprised that Tess hadn't picked up on the tone of her remark. But then, Tess had never been rapier-swift at picking things up. "So where does that leave us tripwise, Madam Chicken? Are you saying you're going out to the corral and select one or two of your hardiest ponies, plus a bag of horseshoes, and gallop straight across country? Arriving La Crosse, say, by Christmas. Or is that too soon?"

"I've talked to the other kids, DeeJay, they know I'm going to drive. It's not really that far from here to Denver, but because I can't do the straight-through, nonstop-express thing it's going to take me a day and a half. Which means I'll be in Denver by Tuesday noon. That's day after tomorrow."

"You always were good at thought problems. If train A leaves station B—"

"Plan your flight into Denver accordingly, then we'll drive the rest of the way with Doc. He's got a wagon with beaucoup de room."

"Translated, you're telling me that brother Wallace has sufficient room in his motor vehicle to accommodate the three of us and our luggage on an extended motor trip to La Crosse."

"The three of us?"

"Oh shit, I forgot Stewart. What about him, anyway?"

"He's coming. He'd walk all the way if he had to, you know him. I understand he'll be landing in Denver around noon Tuesday, which is when you should arrive." She stopped then. It was like gears lining up, seeking their proper niche, nothing random. "No spouses, right, Dee-Jay?"

"We couldn't bring spouses and still be four, could we, big sister?"

"I may be good at thought problems, but you're the math whiz." Again that delay, full of a curious suspense as if she were waiting not to hear something, but to feel it. "You know what?" she said then, and the voice was altered. "It'll be good to see you again. Good to see all you guys. I may not like the reason for the trip but I'm going to love the company."

DeeJay took a slow deliberate drag from her cigarette. "Me too, Tess, I mean it. The four of us together again, it's great. It'll give us a chance to kick the can around a little. I hope we like what comes out."

"What do you mean?" The old uncertainty was suddenly back in the receiver.

"Well, it's been a while for us, hasn't it? We might . . . get into some things."

"What kind of things?"

"Down, King! Down! My God, you've been reading too many mystery novels. These are not *clues!*" This time it was she who paused. "You still read mystery novels, don't you?" She could hear the change in her own voice. Perhaps it was what Tess had been waiting for.

Tess answered, "I read Del Monte can labels mostly. Campbell soups too, they're exciting. When I quit teaching, I quit reading. Finally. My eyes probably thought I'd died."

"You quit teaching?" She waited, not necessarily for a reply. "God, I don't know any of you guys anymore. This *will* be a can kicker, won't it?"

"There's one consolation. We won't be bringing Mattie."

"That's a blessing, not a consolation. And it would be up to Stewart to bring her, wouldn't it? She's with him this year, it's his turn in the barrel."

"If there's anything certain in life," Tess laughed, "it's that the old Stewball won't bring her."

"I wonder how that little fart's doing, anyway. Kell's disappointed that he won't get to see him. He likes Stew. Calls him a potential Daddy Warbucks. He even wanted me to invite Stew to join our CPA firm if he ever gets tired of drawing pictures of airplane bodies, or whatever it is he does up there in Rainy Day Land."

"Right."

"I wonder if he's still got those cute little Pillsbury Doughboy buns on him. And that jack-o'-lantern grin."

"We'll find out soon enough, won't we?" Then she coughed and said, "Listen, DeeJay, I've got to hang up now. See you Tuesday at the family reunion."

"Right, see ya!"

"Another bourbon and water, stewardess."

The Little Boy Who Wanted a Lot and Damned Near Got It, that's how she thought of Stewart James Donner. Cute, yes, no doubt about that, so beautiful as a baby that even now, running across the rare picture or remembering him toddling around the house in Wisconsin, it could take her breath away. Mattie's coloring. Eyes the same shade as the blue enamel cooker she'd had in her kitchen. Eyelashes longer than a pony's coat in January. And talented? Intelligent? Oh hell, yes! Quick and successful and well adjusted and happily married and a devoted parent? You betcha you ess, goombah!

And spoiled absolutely rotten. The best tricycle, best bicycle, boxing gloves at Christmas when all the rest of them got was a pair of school shoes. The number-four child had miraculously become number one through very little effort of his own, mostly a matter of physiognomy. And male, a cute male, that was a factor. The only parent-financed education in the family had gone without demurral to Stew. Over the years, quietly, secretly, methodically, Mattie had saved for it. She knew that the "better" families sent their sons to college; her Jewish patients at the san would speak proudly of a son in Columbia or at City College, wherever those places were. "What college do you think you'd like to attend?" Mattie kept asking

Stewart in his senior year at Roskruge High in Tucson. "There are *so many* colleges."

Stewart pretended to agonize over the decision all that year but as soon as his class graduated in the spring he asked Mattie for the tuition money she had saved for him, and flew immediately to Wisconsin. In September she got a letter announcing that he was enrolled at the University of Wisconsin in Madison ("Your old hometown, Mother, isn't that a coincidence?"), even listing the names and catalog numbers of the courses he had selected. It seems that Stewart James had discovered the difference between resident and nonresident tuition fees and had persuaded Irv to attest to the fact that he was not only native-born but a current resident of the state.

It was in this same letter to Mattie that Stew had asked after "the others" and had said "Hi" to them at the end, along with a few other gratuitous droppings. Always the charmer. They weren't to think that he had broken with "the Arizona branch of the family"; he would always "think of them kindly there in Tucson." A warm, feeling child, Stewart James Donner.

DeeJay's first reaction to the letter was anger, and being nearest him in age, as though that conferred a certain responsibility, she asked for a couple of weeks off from work so she could drive to Madison and personally give Horatio Alger a piece of her mind. The leaves would be turning this time of year, there would be a smell in the air. There were other reasons, vague ragtag promptings she couldn't understand that were threatening nevertheless to escape their ancient prison.

Stewart's first official act was to drive her up to Viroqua to meet Irv. He drove his new car, bought, he said, "with the little money that was left after the tuition payment." She found Wisconsin to be what she remembered, a cup-

and-saucer country compared to Arizona, a place of hazy light and soft air, of hills that looked like they were hiding in mounds of scarlet and rust and amber leaves and would, like children, jump out at any moment and want to play. She was nervous, anticipating Irv.

She needn't have been. His greeting recognized neither the passage of ten years nor the novelty of having a grown daughter in his house. His reaction to her peck on the cheek was to grow slightly embarrassed, as if she were actually a girlfriend of Stewart's that he was meeting for the first time, someone "from the campus."

Not once that weekend did he ask her how her life was, whether she was happy, what her career plans might be. She had readied an answer for him—"Well, Dad, I've sort of got my heart set on being an accountant and I'm attending school during the day and working in a restaurant at night so I can pay for everything"—but he never asked. He spoke instead of Stewart's having decided "not to carry a lunchpail through life" by enrolling himself in "one of the Big Ten schools right there in Madison," and ten minutes into her visit Irv had delivered himself of his first apothegm: "An investment in knowledge pays the best interest."

He didn't stop there. Over the next two days he produced apothegms for every conceivable situation. That they were often forced or nonparallel was of no importance; their pithiness was what mattered. She sat on the lumpy thirties-style sofa and watched her father talk and *saw* his intelligence for the first time in her life. It was a borrowed thing, having more to do with anthology than intuition. It sprang from *Poor Richard's Almanack* and *The Book of Practical Homilies* by Edgar A. Guest, from a lifetime of committing to rote the encapsulated wisdom of *The Old Farmer's Almanack*. Sitting there listening to him she remembered that the closets in the old house on the ridge had been nothing more than archives, for her father never threw anything away. Papers, old letters, photo albums, the almanacs, none were ever discarded. She hadn't made a judgment on his hoardings in those early days, it was simply *Daddy's way*. "Daddy saves things," she would say, and close the closet doors.

But that weekend she opened an upstairs room by mistake and there they were, in boxes, in stacks, in rows, the same poignant accumulation of the years. Staring in at the clutter she realized that her father saved things because he was unable to determine their worth. He would, therefore, commit them all to memory, store them up against the inevitable day when their use would be appropriate and his wisdom might be revealed.

She and Stew left Irv's house late Sunday afternoon and drove back to Madison. The parting had been awkward for her, not for Irv. He had shaken hands and then stood on the porch with his arm around his new wife's shoulder and waved her and Stew out of sight down the street. It was an amenity, a social observance. "The kids were up from the city for the weekend," he would tell people at the mill the next day. "You know how kids are, they like to come home. As the wise man says, 'That host is best who opens the door to his Heart along with the door to his Home.'"

The following morning, after Stew left the apartment for classes, DeeJay started back to Tucson. On the way she stopped at a hotel bar in downtown Omaha and got loaded. It was legal, it was her twenty-first birthday.

She remained in college, continued to stay with Mattie because it was rent-free, but gradually she became tired of Tucson and the succession of dowdy houses they lived in. Nothing in the West is as ugly as the dirt lawn of a house at the edge of town right next to the open desert. She feared for a time that her life might be drifting, but then enter one Richard Francis Kelley, Lieutenant, United States Air Force, whom the fates had temporarily assigned to Davis-Monthan Field. "I can't stand all this sun and sand," he kept saying, those crisp Irish blue eyes crackling over her like ice. "Let's live in California by the ocean. I love the ocean. I need it. I need you."

"Ye Olde Nuptials first," she countered, "then paradise by the sea. I prefer it that way."

That's the way they did it. *Mi casa, su casa.* Life became flower gardens in the morning full of dew and perfume, the honey-beige of coastal hummocks and the camphor smell of bay trees when the ocean winds blew over them in the lavender evenings. . . .

Then years later, after their three children had reached double-digit ages, a letter came from Irv. He was planning a trip. "West," he wrote, using caps like some ancient Saxon scribe, "going West to see my Children. Dear Grandchildren too, that I have Never seen. For as the Wise Man says," he added didactically (does anyone ever really change?), 'a baby is God's decision that the World should go on.' "

Shit, some trip! "Stewardess, another bourbon!"

Irv had failed to lay out any kind of itinerary, but after a phone call to Stew a rough plan did show itself. Irv would visit all four of his children, practically in reverse order of their birth, that is, Stewart first and DeeJay in Chatsworth second, then over to Tucson and up to Denver and then finally home to Wisconsin.

Irv got to Stewart's on schedule. They were having a nice visit, Stew reported to her on the phone, a little stiff at first perhaps but what the hell, it had been a while between visits, right? In any event, Stew told her, Dad would be leaving for her place the following Monday as planned.

At precisely that same time, California's infamous Santa Ana decided to cause some trouble. It came roaring in off the desert and knocked a camper's night lantern off its stand in the Encino Recreation Area southeast of Chatsworth. The tinder-dry chaparral blazed up like a satanic arrow pointing straight toward the city. She and Kell and a dozen threatened neighbors hosed roofs and walls, dug fire trenches, lugged water, felled trees, singed their hair and blistered their hands, side by side, night and day. Finally, with the help of both County Fire and Volunteer Fire, they got the conflagration first slowed and then stopped. Following that, the Kelley family spent two days putting their house and grounds in presentable condition for Irv's visit. First visit ever.

But when he left Stew's, Irv went straight home to Wisconsin without a word to her.

Jesus Christ, what kind of a world was this, anyway? Wasn't there a law that said parents couldn't go on forever hurting their children? She turned to the man sitting next to her. "I mean it! There's got to be an end somewhere. Scared kids in a ridge house and grimy bus rides and Crow clothes because you had to leave yours in the last town and Margaret Dorothy Alice perfume and pissy sheets and all for one and none for all and I mean it, so help me, where does it all stop?"

The man in the seat beside her dropped his magazine and his mouth flew open.

She stood up and faced him. "Don't parents have a responsibility, will you tell me that? Doesn't decency and respect apply to parents and children alike? Isn't that a two-way street? I want to know who made the rules so one-sided!"

Someone in the aisle was reaching for her.

"What's the price of a phone call? What does it cost to say to a child, 'I love you'? To say you're mine and you're not perfect but then neither am I and maybe we can get through this life with that? Perhaps we can be friends but if nothing else we can at least extend some common courtesy to each other."

It was the stewardess who was grabbing for her, trying to push her down into the seat. "Stop this at once! You've got to stop this screaming and shouting!"

"All right! I hear you!" And suddenly she was back in her seat, sitting there voluntarily, not pushed. "I'm in my seat now, okay? My God, cut me some slack, will you?" She tried to make it sound indignant. "Better yet," she said, "cut me a new bourbon."

"Absolutely not!" The stewardess was bent over her, red-faced and breathing hard as though she had been running, and there was a man wearing a uniform cap standing directly behind her. "You're not getting another thing to drink and that's final!"

"I'm not drunk, you twit! I'm mad!"

"You either sit here and behave yourself or you have my solemn promise that the captain will hold you for the authorities when we land!"

DeeJay sat back hard against her seat, gripped the arms, looked up at the stewardess, and said, "I'll tell you what, little Miss Bird Princess of the azure blue, how would you like to stick a vial of original New Zion perfume right up where not even the angels can find it? Would you like that?"

FIVE

A MAN OF HAIR his father was. Tufts and whorls and clots of hair. It was in his nostrils, his ears, it protruded from beneath the collar of his shirt, and with his shirt off his chest was a thick curly mat of the stuff. It grew on his back, spread the length of his arms and crept down onto the backs of his hands, clumping finally between the knuckles of his fingers like the dull obsidian rings that gypsies wore.

Doc remembered the time he actually made a remark to his father about the hair. It was when they lived on the ridge place and all four kids had raced into their parents' bedroom one Sunday morning and jumped on the bed, yanking at the covers, wanting to play, and in the excitement Doc had cried out to his father, who wasn't wearing a pajama top, "Daddy, if you had one more hair you'd be a monkey!"

The other kids froze instantly, even Stewart, young as

he was, and Mattie drew a startled apologetic breath. "Wallace, you mustn't say that to your father, even if you're joking!"

Doc glanced at Irv and saw his face turn darkly angular the way it did when he hadn't decided whether to give vent to the anger or let it pass. *Let it pass* was a possibility in those first few seconds; there was a chance that the potential victim might insinuate a laugh or a disarming smile and divert the wrath, which meant that the entire family could break its frieze of terror and return to normal. But nothing was certain with Irv. The hair-choked nostrils *could* flare and the full lips *could* pinch down to a cold line and the chin could begin to quiver, all because some thoughtless happy child had said the wrong thing. In the bed, the kitchen, the yard, the barn, it didn't matter, Irv loved to explode. Rage was his principal weapon in life. Lacking patience or even a modicum of understanding of all those shorter, weaker, younger, smaller than he, Irv Donner ruled with rage. With only women and children facing him, it was an incredibly easy reign.

Unfortunately, it wasn't merely women and children who peopled Irv Donner's kingdom, it was animals as well. Another of Doc's memories (and he didn't know why he was thinking of these things; he was driving to the Tech Center to meet Tess, thinking of Tess, and the memories just came flooding in) was of the time their collie dog, Starter, had inadvertently been left inside the house while the family ate supper. Starter had always been a notorious beggar, and he immediately began begging handouts between Tess's chair and Irv's. Without a word of warning Irv raised his fist shoulder-high and brought it down on Starter's head. The blow floored the dog instantly. After a moment he got to his feet and crawled around behind the range. Later, when Doc and Tess were completing their last chore of the day, which was to fill the woodbox, they found Starter still hiding amid the gloves and galoshes.

Then there was the episode of the yearling cow that Irv had sold to a neighbor. The neighbor drove into the lot one Saturday morning and backed his trailer up to the barn. Irv was trying to guide the heifer through the door and up the ramp into the trailer, but she chose not to go, being stubborn and unpredictable in the way of heifers. After repeated attempts and a lot of shouting—"You, cow, get in there!"—Irv lost patience and made a fist and swung at the frightened animal.

The blow struck the heifer between the eyes, and she went down. And before the sound of her fall had died away, the grunt, the belch of startled air, Irv kicked her in the throat. The heifer lurched to her feet with her eyes rolling white and ran off through the barn while the neighbor slammed his trailer gate shut and drove off without a word. Doc couldn't remember which way *he* ran, but he certainly didn't look back. A short time later he heard the truck drive out the lane, and it wasn't until afternoon that Irv returned, wearing a cast on his hand bigger than a head of cabbage.

Germans are like that, people said. Germans are mean and have bad tempers.

Bullshit! Bullshit to the Germans being anything simply because they came from a particular spot on the map of Europe. Place could bestow no excuse for cruelty. And to this day he hated the German language, the *ich und glanz mit bloock* guttural of their talk. And their names! Helmut Klump and Brunhilde Statschneider and Wolfgang Potz. God, how ugly!

Yet, in a bewildering paradox, the Irv Donner who was always erupting in anger could just as quickly cry at a movie. Doc could recall times when Irv accompanied him and Tess and the younger kids to a show in Viroqua. (It was always those times when the admission was a dime plus one can of vegetables. The Depression was still on and the food was for the poor people.) One particular movie Doc remembered had a scene in which Jackie Cooper was saying goodbye to his grandfather for the last time. Irv sat with his eyes riveted to the screen and when the critical moment arrived, where Jackie ran across the cabin and threw himself into his grandfather's arms, Irv coughed a couple times and cleared his throat and then his eyes misted over. Doc could see them glisten in the light from the screen.

Al Jolson singing "Sonny Boy" on the radio could produce tears in Irv. The fatal illness of a friend could do it, a farmer gored by a bull or run down by a tractor, some old woman dead out on Bauer Ridge or Kleinst Ridge (it was a land of ridges, they stretched away into the distance like the spines of resting cattle) could start him off. "I know this," he would say, his eyes going moist and his lips starting to quiver, "I know there's a special crown in heaven for a Christian soul like her." Even his recitation of a favorite homily could elicit wet eyes and a trembling chin. It wasn't sympathy that birthed such reactions. Sympathy was not at the core of his makeup, what little he had was peripheral, off to one side like a coat sleeve. It was emotion that did it. Emotion was to Irv Donner as strong drink to a drunkard. He couldn't handle it.

As the years passed, Doc began to wonder how his father fit into life away from the ridge farm. Obviously he was not "one of the boys"; he didn't huddle with assorted cronies in dank roadside taverns as some men did, nor did he give autumn weekends over to hunting with friends. There were times when Doc questioned if Irv had friends. Wherever they happened to meet him, church or lumberyard or sidewalk, men were respectful, nodding or speaking his name, but they never kidded with him. They didn't rap him on the arm or call out any of the customary greetings—"Hello, you old shit, how they hanging?" or "Hey, Double Ugly, when did the missus start letting you out?"— none of that rough badinage that serves to reveal one man's genuine liking of another. But was it because Doc, a child, was always present? The closest Doc came to an answer, and he thought more about it in later years than he did then, was the time he hitched a ride to the County Co-op in Viroqua so he could sell his monthly catch of mole's feet. He exchanged his twelve pair of front feet for sixty cents in cash and was standing outside counting the money when he heard several men talking on the dock and realized his father was one of them. For no reason that he could ever identify, Doc didn't step forward and join his father but stepped back into the shadows and watched. What he saw was a man ill at ease to the point of misery, unable to join what even Doc in his youth could tell was the most bantering kind of conversation. His father spoke only in shallow spurts of interest, laughed too quickly and without real mirth, asked no questions, called none of the men by name. He was, in short, unable to involve himself.

"Are you sad about Irv?" Tess had asked on the phone Sunday night, and he'd answered that he didn't know, he wasn't sure, he said he thought he should be feeling more than he was but perhaps it hadn't sunk in yet.

But what was his father feeling? If he was conscious where he lay in that hospital bed a thousand miles away, the emotion for Irv Donner would almost certainly be fear. Fear had been one of the dominant themes of his life, fear of injury, fear of pain, of death. He lived in absolute dread of mortuaries and dentist's offices and hospitals, and it stemmed, Doc knew, from a lifetime of believing the horror stories told about such places, stories that he himself retold without judgment or thought.

"Yes sir, they went to embalm the corpse and darned if it didn't sit up on the table and start screaming at them."

"When they opened the coffin they found the woman with her hair grown long and lying on her face. She'd come alive in the grave and tried to get out!"

"They put such a hole in old Bill's jaw when they pulled his teeth that they couldn't get it sewed up again and he bled to death right there in the dentist's chair."

"They didn't have to operate on Oscar. I know that for a fact. But they went ahead anyway and of course he got an infection out of it and died."

"Well, I got the straight of it from Sadie, that's Tom's wife. Seems they were supposed to feed Tom this sugar water through his veins but they gave him iodine by mistake. Sadie said when they showed her Tom's body it was red all over like a ripe tomato."

In the summary that inevitably followed, Irv would promise his listeners that they could bet their last acre of ground *he* would never allow anything like that to happen to *him*. "I can guarantee you they'll never get me"—and here you had to pick a particular fate, depending on the story he'd just told—in that chair, on that table, under that knife, into one of those contraptions.

Now they had him at last, those faceless institutional fiends he had managed to elude for three-quarters of a century.

Doc tried to remember when he had seen his father last. He supposed it was when he went back to Waterloo, Iowa, for the Warriors' reunion. Vern Harris, the Warriors' coach, lived in Waterloo and had kept in touch with most of the players over the years, mainly through Christmas cards, and he'd gotten the idea one summer of holding a team reunion. Doc had taken Lil and the kids and gone back. They'd had a super time (everyone still pretty much in shape, seven innings' worth at least, and the wives were all beautiful) and had promised each other to do it again sometime.

But Lil had an additional idea. "Hon, as long as we're this close why don't we drive up to Wisconsin and see your dad? We'll never get a better chance. And I'll bet the river is beautiful in summer."

There was logic in her argument, and they went. From Waterloo they angled across the northeast corner of Iowa and picked up the river road and followed the Mississippi all the way to La Crosse.

It *was* beautiful. Lil, who was a Denver native, kept insisting that she'd never seen so many trees on level ground, had never seen a river that *wide*. "The green is *so* green it looks like moss growing on the earth." And the bluffs of the river! Mesas and buttes she knew, but not river bluffs. And the hills when they turned from the river at La Crosse and went "inland" as she called it, to Viroqua. She'd never *seen* hills so wooded and dense and jumbled, like Sleepy Hollow, she joked excitedly, and told little William to keep his eyes peeled for Rip Van Winkle.

"I think Rip's still sleeping," Doc told her, and they giggled about that, even William. It was a wonderful trip.

The stay at Irv's was not. It was dismal. There were problems from the beginning, two of them. The first was that his father didn't know what to say. It wasn't that the Coloradans were intruding; unexpected guests had never been a pet peeve of Irv's. In fact, he bought a carful of groceries that first morning, as well as a box of toys for the kids and a whole case of Old Style Lager for Doc.

"I don't drink beer," Irv said, "but I understand Old Style's the best there is. Bottled right there on the Big Muddy, at La Crosse." He laughed and his shoulders shook. "I call the Mississippi the Big Muddy."

Irv never held any of the kids, not even William, who had expected to sit on his grandpa's lap for most of the visit. He didn't mention Tess or DeeJay or even Stew, who at that time had graduated from Madison only a few years earlier. He didn't offer to drive Doc out to the old ridge place, or to the bottom farm where Doc was born. And he wouldn't call him Doc, not once, although if memory served correctly it was Irv who had hung the nickname on him when he'd had to wear the corrective glasses for a couple of years as a little boy. Irv called him Wallace, as if he were talking to a salesman who was calling on him for the first time, and like the remote stranger of the long-ago Co-op dock, he spoke in bursts of partial involvement, laughed too loudly and at the wrong time, and never once referred to Lil by name, nor any of the children. Neither did he ask questions. Are you still working at the brewery, Wallace? Isn't that where you worked? Do you ever play baseball anymore? How was your trip out? None of those. And especially he didn't ask, *How are you, son? How's your life? Are you happy?*

The second problem was that Doc didn't know what to say, and consequently they left Viroqua after only one day, left that deep-set, tree-besieged house and drove back over the roller-coaster hills to the Mississippi and turned south. It was good to be near the water again, to drive along under the comfortable loom of the bluffs, to see the locks and the islands and the endlessly confusing, ever-changing channels of the great river. Lil got into a game of counting barges with William, she the northbound, he the south.

Doc never did determine who won the game because he couldn't stop thinking of his father, about the physical man he had seen for the first time in nearly two decades. He hadn't looked any heavier, wasn't "big at the belt" as the saying went, but his hair had been something of a shock, not the old full pompadour but a cropped, dirty-looking gray that was thin enough at the top to show his skull. It was easier for Doc to picture a dark head bent in attention to the Philco radio that sat in the living room of the ridge house. Irv loved listening to the radio. He liked the Eddie Cantor show, especially the Greek restaurant owner, Mr. Park Your Carcass. "We gotta four kinds pie," Park Your Carcass managed to announce every week, "We gotta mimce, we gotta stromberree . . ." and sitting with his elbows on his knees and his hands clasped together and his ear close to the crackling speaker, Irv would laugh in that soundless way he had, his head bobbing and his shoulders shaking in a mimelike syncopation.

Sports were Irv's weakest area. He simply wasn't interested. When Doc made the church baseball team he would announce to his father each week, "I'm playing this Friday night." Or Saturday, or Sunday, whatever the schedule read.

"Oh, is that right?" his father would say, and his head would lift from the radio or the almanac and his eyes would blur with a painful attempt at concern. "What team are you playing, Wallace?"

"Jimtown Methodist." Or Viola United Brethren or Westby Lutheran, whatever the schedule.

"Where?"

"Viroqua park."

"What time?"

"Two o'clock sharp." Or six-thirty. Or eight o'clock.

"Listen, Wallace, by golly I'm going to try to get to town and see the game, okay?"

At the park, Doc would do his best to extend pregame practice as long as he could, keeping one eye on the bleachers even after the game had reached the middle innings. One Sunday afternoon against La Farge Baptist he

(*103*)

hit two homers, the last a grand slam in the ninth to win the game, and as he circled the bases he thought he saw Irv standing at the far end of the bleachers. He hurried home immediately after the game to share his excitement with Irv, but when he spotted his father asleep in front of the Philco he realized he hadn't left the house all afternoon.

It wasn't just the sports that slipped by without being shared. Earlier, long before the baseball, there was the bus trip the two of them made in January to the funeral of Irv's uncle in the eastern part of the state. Coming back, they missed a bus connection in some city somewhere and had to wait until after midnight for the next one. The bus station was deserted and miserably cold. They sat side by side on one of the benches and Doc kept waiting for Irv to reach out and hold him, perhaps drape part of his overcoat across his shoulders to keep him warm. He didn't, he just sat there shivering, staring out the window into the dark empty street. "I understand," he said to Doc at one point, "that in cold weather the shivering helps keep us warm. Funny thing, the body, how it works."

Mattie was always there in their lives, of course, yet glimpsed across the curious refraction of time she seemed the one who slipped most easily out of focus, more so than Irv. She was an edge-of-the-circle person, working at the far end of gardens and lawns, moving in rooms of the house that were more private than central. In contrast to Irv there was no authority in her; in the face of conflict, or the threat of it, she would step aside rather than stand. She called down no lightning upon herself, drew no metals to her core. Doc supposed that his father saw her that way as well; the strong naturally would, blinded as they are by their own powerful lights.

Her attempts at disciplining her children were oblique—

"You wouldn't want me to tell your father, would you?"—
and she had only one admonition that Doc could remember: "Do not spit, child! It shows a lack of breeding."

She worked hard, relying a great deal on pattern and
schedule. Monday she washed clothes, heating the water
on the kitchen stove and asking Doc to help her carry it out
to the tubs in the backyard. The tubs sat on a spot on the
lawn that had been scalded into virtual cement by years
of wash-water dumpings. Tuesdays she ironed, Wednes-
days she sewed and darned, Thursday she cleaned the
house, upstairs and down, plus both porches. Fridays were
bake days. On Saturdays she gardened and tended baby
livestock, shopping in town when she needed to. Sunday
was church and it was here, oddly, that his mother stood
out. She was tall, much taller than the other women, and
wore a different kind of hat. Instead of a prim straw or one
of the popular, tight-fitting cloches, Mattie's hat was big
with a floppy brim that seemed to draw the eye. Maybe it
was her smile, flashing as it did out of the shadow of her
face.

Monday was washday again. Season after season. Year
after year.

It was about that time in Doc's life that the trouble started.
Lying in his bed upstairs at night he began to hear the
sounds of argument rising from below, doors slammed and
chairs pushed roughly aside, voices swelling up in a sort of
wave. Occasionally a single word would fly up out of the
mass and he would hear it perfectly. *You* or *why?* or *no*,
sometimes a *yes* so violent that it might have been an *Ah!*
But whose voice was it? Mattie's in a deep shriek? Irv's
in a thin, high bellow? Then the waves would subside, the
house would grow broodingly silent, and in the morning
when he went downstairs Doc would search for telltale

signs of violence and there would be none. Lamps still stood, chairs sat neatly in place, no shards or rendings of that midnight tempest lay anywhere in sight.

Yet he thought that something of this began to show in Mattie's face. Or was it that something was gone? On Sundays at church her smile no longer flashed, and there were times during the week when her involvement in family affairs became infuriatingly abstract. She grew silent, but because silence had always been the principal measure of her, it elicited only more frustration. He remembered that she began to stand in an unusual way whenever she talked to them, her arms not drawn in close to her body but held out, akimbo. It made her look less whole, more assailable. He believed she was doing it deliberately, drawing attention to her own vulnerability, practically *offering* it. In the evenings after supper it was Tess's company she sought, no other, as though she had secretly made Tess her confidante.

Then, abruptly, his mother became bribable. Doc stumbled onto it, it wasn't planned, he wasn't even sure when he knew. It may have been the Saturday she left for town earlier than usual and he said to her, almost on a whim, not expecting a reply, "Mama, how about buying me a baseball?"

"Yes, of course I will."

"You will? Really? A glove too? Would you buy me a baseball glove?"

"Certainly, Wallace, just don't make a fuss if I'm a little late getting back, all right?"

One day he stayed home from school sick and was lying on the daybed in the spare bedroom upstairs instead of in his own, and Mattie came in. She didn't see him, the room was large and made extra-shadowy by the window shade always being drawn. His mother crossed the room to the window and pulled up the shade and lit a cigarette from a pack she had obviously hidden on the windowsill. Next she went to the bureau and took from a drawer a pair of silk stockings and a pair of high-heeled shoes with a strap around the ankle. She sat on a chair and very carefully put on the stockings and the shoes, then stood up and looked out the window while she smoked her cigarette, the smoke curling insolently about her face. At one point she let the cigarette dangle from her lips and smoked without touching it. When she had finished smoking she sat down again, pulled her skirt up, removed the stockings and the shoes, and returned them to the bureau drawer. Then she pulled down the window shade and left the room.

He saw his mother do the same thing on several occasions after they moved to the apartment in Viroqua. Once, with the high-heeled shoes still on, she lifted her skirt and rolled the silk stockings all the way down to her ankles, and when she had finished the cigarette she rolled them back up again. Doc sensed even then that there was something sleek and voluptuous about his mother's legs, especially naked like that. She never spoke during any of this, never cried or patted her hair or put her hands on herself anywhere, she just stood there tall and quiet behind the curtain in her bedroom, smoking and looking down the street.

What did you see, Mama? What was it you were looking for?

Custer City sprawled. It resembled the contents of a crate that had dropped from a passing freight train and been left where it fell as not worth going back for. There were only a few trees in the town, very little ground that showed a genuine green, no softness anywhere. The wind blew incessantly and there was too much sky all around. Sky was no good for stopping the wind.

Mattie stayed with the boys at Uncle Willard's while the girls and Mickey were the lucky ones who got to live out in the country with Uncle Frank. The two men were Mattie's brothers, shorter than she but more talkative, and they wore the same shiny blue suits every day, the same kind that church ushers wear. The only thing that set them apart was the snappy straw hats they wore whenever they went out "among the faithful." The hats made them look like the booth salesmen you see at carnivals, although Doc wouldn't have dared say that. They ignored Stewart and Doc but were nice to Mattie, they made a show of seeking her advice on "practical" things and took her for drives on Sunday afternoons, and called her "sister." It was very sweet and gentle and religious-sounding.

But it didn't last. Mattie wasn't there long enough. One day Uncle Willard met him in the hall when he came in from practicing dropkicks and told him his mother was gone. Willard had big protruding eyes that never blinked.

"Gone? Mama?"

"Took off. Ran away."

"Where?"

"Never you mind."

"Maybe she's with the girls out at Uncle Frank's. Can you call Uncle Frank and ask him? I'll bet Mama's there. She can't be gone. *We're* here."

"Your mother isn't at Frank and Ida's, boy."

"Well, where then? She's got to be somewhere."

Uncle Willard didn't answer, he was a man who answered only a small percentage of questions from children. In a few minutes they all got in the car and drove out to Uncle Frank's. Mattie wasn't there. The adults went into the house and closed the door and left the kids outside. Stewart cried and DeeJay kept saying, "There's a note from Mama somewhere. I know it. They just haven't found it." Tess just stared off into the prairie and didn't say a word.

"A cross," Uncle Willard announced to him and Stew at the supper table a few nights later. "You children are a cross that He has decreed we bear during our period of service here on earth."

"Praise Jesus," exclaimed Aunt May, looking at her plate. Her skin was so blue-white it looked like skim milk. Add to that a puffy face with the eyes sunken in, like raisins in dough, plus fiery red hair and baggy arms and you had an aunt you didn't run to for comfort and understanding.

"You boys are secretive, lazy, and you cry altogether too much," Uncle Willard went on.

"Praise His name," Aunt May said.

"We can hear you in the night," Uncle Willard continued, not looking at his plate but at the two of them seated across the table. As if his words were a reminder, Stewart put his hands to his eyes and began to cry. "It is the melancholy," Uncle Willard said, "the manifestation of the early workings of the devil, stemming from excessive masturbation."

Doc stared first at his uncle and then at his aunt, and Stewart began to bawl even louder.

The summer passed and school started. Stewart was as big a baby there as he was at home. At recess he pouted and kicked stones if he didn't get to be first down the slide, and he screamed like a lynx if he fell off the gym bars, insisting that someone had pushed him. And there was an extracurricular problem with Stewart as well. He was so pretty, his skin so fair and scrubbed-looking, that the little Indian girls were forever running up to him at school and kissing him on the face. The problem came after school when the brothers of these Crow girls would try to avenge their sisters by isolating Stewart with the purpose of beating him up. Doc managed to blunt their attacks but he usually got knocked down for his efforts, and some of the blows from those swarming, rose-brown fists really stung.

What stung more was Aunt May's reception when the two of them got home. From the porch she would watch them cross the lawn and when they got inside the house she would bend down to Stewart and hold him to her heart as if he were an old wedding picture. "Look at this little boy," she'd croon, peering into his face, "such a perfect gentleman." Then she'd turn to Wallace. "But look at you! Face smeared, hands banged up, dirt all over your clothes. Shame! Do you think I have nothing to do but clean up after you, Wallace Donner?"

Autumn came. The leaves of the giant cottonwood in the yard turned to gold, and when the leaves fell they looked as big as pie pans. He and Stewart saw the girls only once a month now, on the Saturday the four of them peddled punchboard perfume for the spiritual betterment of the Crows. It was a dismal job, and saying goodbye at the end of the day was even worse. Stew would cry and Dee-Jay would get mad and Doc would do his best not to look at any of them, especially Tess. Tess always stood off to one side of the lawn, a strangled look on her face as though she were drowning.

Uncle Willard, if he happened to be around, never interceded. He didn't concern himself with the details of child-rearing nor with the day-to-day management of the Elmor household. He was too busy raising money for the church. It was his gift, his "true calling." He had all sorts of revenue programs going, some of which were genuine money-makers. Friday-night Bingo was highly successful, fifty cents a card, no limit on the number of cards. A chain letter was in circulation "across the membership," supervised by certain select elders of the church. There was a lottery in operation which keyed on the numbers of the hymns scheduled to be sung at Sunday-morning worship service. Other numbers mentioned by Pastor Elmor in his Bible lesson reading, preceding the sermon, were also factored in.

"Today's Bible lesson is found in second Samuel, chapter eighteen, verses thirty-one through thirty-three," Uncle Willard would announce from the pulpit, whereupon he would read these passages aloud. When he finished—"So ends the Bible lesson for today"—and closed the Bible, two ushers would immediately disappear from the rear of the church and head for the basement, where a parlay would be made from the combination of numbers, in this case 2-18-31-32-33. When the services were concluded, Pastor Elmor would slip the prize money to the lucky winner as he paused in the front door to shake hands with the pastor. There was a lot of handshaking at New Zion Methodist, which spoke well of Uncle Willard's efforts among the heathen.

Nor was Willard one to let a Christmas holiday go by without initiating what he called a Special Blessings Program. Doc volunteered to help by cutting a stencil on the old Underwood typewriter that sat in the church office, along with an ancient A. B. Dick mimeograph drum. "It's thankless work," Uncle Willard told him, "but it must be done. After all, it's not for us, is it? It's for our Red Brothers. They will be the infinite gainers."

Working off Willard's abysmal handwritten original, it took Doc one whole Saturday to prepare the stencil and the following Saturday (a non-punchboard Saturday, luckily) to mimeograph the entire batch of solicitation letters for mailing to membership. He stuffed envelopes every night after school, and the one he picked to proofread for Uncle Willard happened to be addressed to a Mr. Harold Bobtail Horse, Rural Route 3, Custer City, Montana.

NEW ZION METHODIST CHURCH
My sheep hear My voice, and I know them,
and they follow me.
(John 10-27,28)

Dear member in Christ's love:

Christmas will soon be upon us and I wanted to send you this invitation to honor our Lord and Saviour on His birthday. I hope that you will include Him on your Christmas shopping list with a gift amount that reflects your love for Him!

As you probably are aware, the needs for this Special Christmas Offering are the greatest your church has ever faced. First, we must pay for our roof repairs from last winter's heavy snowfall at a cost of $1,250. We need to make the final payment on our new church organ ($500), in addition to which we must regravel our church parking lot or see it taken over next spring by erosion and binder weed.

We also need to finish the sanctuary remodeling that was approved last year by the Council of Elders but held undone for lack of funds. That cost was an estimated $10,000 of which we have less than $2,500 in hand to provide for new rugs, curtains and et cetera. So you can see our desperate need.

In closing, I wish to say that the Holiday season traditionally awakens special feelings of thankfulness and generosity in God's children. I have always found you, as a member of God's family in Custer County, to be a most loving and warm-hearted person.

Please pray over this letter and bring your special gift with you to place in the manger at worship service on December 25th. If you are unable to be present

you can insert either bills or a check in the enclosed
envelope and mail it to the church office.

Yours in Christ,

W ILLARD T. EL MOR
Pastor

Enclosure

"Did you remember to put a return envelope in each of the
mailings?" Uncle Willard asked him. "Without these—"

"I did, yes," Doc broke in. "But one thing—" He stopped
to clear his throat. "One thing bothers me about this letter."

"Oh?" Uncle Willard usually went into a peculiar stare
whenever he was taken by surprise, a blank fractured look
that resembled an owl fixing on a field mouse. "What is it
that troubles you, Wallace?"

"It's this last paragraph," and he held Bobtail Horse's
letter up in his hand, "this part where you ask them to
pray over the letter."

"Yes?"

"You said once that you'd been trying to get the Crows
to stop praying to the wind and the birds and the larger
animals. Now you're asking them to pray over a letter.
Isn't that taking a step backward?"

"Wallace—"

"If you keep asking these people for money every time
they turn around they'll end up being infinite *givers* instead of infinite *gainers*."

The complaint proved ill-considered. Uncle Willard
raced to his retribution like a hungry dog to a buried bone.
"Wallace," he announced in his most reproachful voice,
"you are a bad seed. Mischief flows from you as growth
from a root. You cause dissension wherever you go and

whatever you do, just like your mother. She, too, was a bad seed."

Doc paid for his heresy. Nothing was expressly mentioned concerning it, but he participated in no further church programs, nor was he allowed to buy a lottery ticket at discount. At home, all attempts to attain a special "grace through good works" were turned aside. He was no longer permitted to clean the cellar and the attic, to polish the furniture or glue down the heat-loosened corners of wallpaper. His new work station was not inside the house, it was *out*.

The woodpile.

The woodpile sat in the rear of Willard Elmor's house on the alley, the alley lay at the edge of town next to the prairie. It was an inordinately big woodpile, and Doc quickly discovered the reason. The entire New Zion congregation was expected to tithe a certain portion of their yearly income to the church and were issued color-coded envelopes accordingly, but there were those who couldn't fulfill a pledge of money and consequently were asked to give what the church liked to call "other goods and/or materials."

In Custer City, Montana, that meant *wood*. A dozen leghorn eggs would occasionally be accepted, a sack of uncarded wool, a quarter of a possibly rustled beef, but mostly it was wood.

For a state that wasn't supposed to have a lot of trees in its eastern section, Montana produced a lot of wood. Cottonwood mainly, although there was a scattering of pine and spruce and alder saplings. And the "unworthy" who brought the wood were as rich in ingenuity as they were poor in finances, for they would go to any lengths to meet their substitute obligations. The number of torn-down sheds and barns and corrals in the area must have totaled in the hundreds, nor could there have been a single rural bus shelter or gatepost or road sign still standing in Custer County. They were all in Pastor Elmor's woodpile in Custer City.

These "woodsmen" obviously dumped their loads during the day, because when Doc got home from school and changed clothes and went out to the pile he could see that it had been replenished. It certainly hadn't gone down. It never went down. He carried cords of wood to the porch, a porch that sagged toward the lawn under its mounting burden, and still the pile would not go down. The stoves of the Elmor house roared night and day, but the pile never diminished.

The only gesture of assistance Aunt May made was to buy Stewart a little saw of his own at Christmas, a toylike affair less than a foot long. The idea was, possibly, that Stewart might be induced to help his brother, but it didn't work. His best production, accomplished on a rare warm day between Christmas and New Years, was a pile of twigs perhaps eighteen inches long and twelve high. Stewart wouldn't carry them to the kindling section of the porch however, so nothing was accomplished. The only blessing associated with the toy saw was that Stewart broke it on a board nail the very next day and went into the house to pout and never came back.

Doc worked on alone, resigned to the certainty that he would never be finished, that regardless of how well he organized his work or how good he got at it, he would never see the bottom of that pile.

"Chores are never completed in this life," his uncle announced one night at supper, his voice as righteous as ever, his eyes the dull gray of snow clouds. "Labor is the sweat of the brow the Bible speaks of. The atonement of Sin. The curse of the Fall. Woman has her burden, man has his."

Apparently, Willard's burden was to sit at the kitchen table and match names with amounts in a gilt-lettered Book of Accounts while the stove blew heat at him like a bellows. Uncle Frank came in from the country once a week and the two of them would huddle at the table with the coffeepot bubbling on the stove, plotting their everlasting salvation of the Crows.

Winter descended on the prairie, locking them to the earth. The sky was an ice lake, it had no shore, no reef of hills that would stop the cold. Some days the chimneys of the town smoldered in the frozen air like ghostly punk sticks, on other days the wind blew snow in off the prairie as dry and hard as a harvest of oats.

Doc's wrists, where they lay exposed between his worn-out gloves and the cuffs of his jacket, became so chapped they looked like red bracelets he had taken to wearing on his arms. His mouth grew raw and cracked and the girls at school called him Cherry Lips. His fingers festered from wood slivers, blisters turned to ulcers in the palms of his hands. In the fickle days of late March the woodpile thawed and froze, thawed and froze, but would not shrink. Beyond the alley the prairie lay as white and lifeless as a body in a coffin.

Then one day he came home from school and went upstairs to his room to change clothes, and Mattie was there.

She was sitting on the edge of his bed, her face in that first moment looking old and unfamiliar. She spoke his name, just that single word, and held out her hands to him, very slowly, as though there was something she wasn't sure of.

He stepped forward and put his hands in hers, reluctantly, for he too was unsure.

She turned his hands over and looked at them, and gave a tiny cry. "Oh, Wallace!"

"It's the wood, Mama. Will you tell Uncle Willard I can't do the wood anymore?" He lowered his head and his mother reached out and held his face between her hands. Her hands were unbelievably soft, but the strangest thing was how clearly he could smell her face powder.

The four of them didn't peddle a single vial of perfume after that day, didn't perform even the remotest kind of church business or household chores. The girls came into town every weekend, or the boys and Mattie went out there, whatever, the five of them managed to do something together. Picnics, walks, gathering wildflowers, it didn't matter, it was all fun, all exciting, all blurred like something passing real fast. "Soon," Mattie said to him one day, whispering it fiercely as though she were angry. She'd always had a distant look in her eyes, a gaze that traded the near thing, the immediate, for something far away. Now it was gone. "Soon. When school is out."

He assumed she meant that was when they would leave Custer City, and he didn't mind waiting. It was easy, it was like saying to a snow-buried rose bush in the dead of winter, "Hey, you'll be all right, I'll see you in the spring!"

The last day of school finally came and Mattie, true to her word, told them to get ready to leave. The boys emptied their dresser drawer into a suitcase and the girls came in from the country with their suitcase packed as well. Everyone seemed excited. Uncle Frank and Uncle Willard hugged Mattie and called her "sister" again, and both Aunt Ida and Aunt May gave the kids a sack of oatmeal cookies for the trip. Funny they would both make oatmeal, everyone laughed about that. Then all of them

(*117*)

together, kids and adults alike, locked arms on Uncle Willard's lawn and sang that beloved Methodist hymn, led by Uncle Frank, who was far and away the best singer in the family, "Where Will You Be When Jesus Comes?"

Whereupon Uncle Willard, laughing happily, drove them in his big black car to the Greyhound bus station.

Rumbling south out of town, Doc sat back in his seat and thought about the winter, and the church, and about Mattie. She had kept her word, and as surprised as he was at that, he was also pleased, pleased with everything. But he began to suspect that leaving Custer City was more difficult for her than staying would have been, even if she could have stayed. Moving four kids and paying for five bus tickets (just one of which, he supposed, would probably cost as much as a baseball glove) was no small task. And now the cost of rent would have to be added, since they didn't know anyone where they were going and obviously couldn't stay anywhere rent-free. He reflected on all this expense for several minutes, trying to think of it as his mother would, and for the first time he realized that responsibility could be a difficult thing, like a big boulder in your path, like a terrible pain that you would run away from if you could.

Then he gave that up and concentrated on the kids. Stewart, who was sharing a seat with DeeJay, had managed to pick four White Owl cigar bands off the bus-station floor. He had them on the fingers of one hand and was holding the hand up in the air, admiring it. Beside him, DeeJay was sulking over the fact that they weren't going back to Wisconsin to see Dad, and then she switched from that and started being hateful. It was easy for DeeJay, she loved being hateful, she loved a good scrap. Now, here in the bus heading for Wyoming, she started scrapping with

Stewart, working *through* Stewart rather, as though he were some kind of medium, telling him over and over that the name of the town they were going to in Arizona was pronounced "Tuck-sawn" and not "Too-sonn" the way he said it, and he wasn't so smart after all, was he? Little dummy!

It worked. It always did with Stew, he couldn't see through anything. He argued with DeeJay about the pronunciation until he got so mad his face swelled up like a sage hen's. He kicked DeeJay's seat then threw himself onto the rubber carpet in the aisle and started screaming, pretending she had thrown him there. Everyone was impressed except the driver, who stopped the bus and threatened Mattie with revocation of ticket without refund, or something like that, whatever the penalty was on Greyhound for allowing bratty kids to create a nuisance.

"It's like we're pioneers going to a new land, isn't it, Mom?" crooned DeeJay in the respectful silence that followed the driver's ultimatum. DeeJay was good even then at absolving herself.

Doc didn't remember Mattie's answer, or even if there'd been one, for he was sitting with Tess in the seat ahead. "Arizona must be a beautiful state," she announced quietly, making it a private matter between the two of them and yet still watching out the window for Burma Shave signs. "Arizona was the last of the forty-eight states to be admitted to the Union," she told him.

"In 1912. Thirty-three years ago."

"Thirty-four."

"Right, thirty-four."

The bus stopped in Sheridan and Tess got off and bought a can of Cuticura salve so she could soften Doc's sores, for the chap still banded his wrists like a pair of rusted handcuffs. He was convinced he would suffer permanent scars and told everyone so; he even looked forward to having them. In Cheyenne, Tess got off the bus again, and this time she bought a styptic pencil and wet the tip of it and worked it into the blisters on his hands, some of which were still suppurating. He remembered it perfectly because Tess had started having her menstrual periods that same year and she was having one now, here on the bus, he could smell it on her. It wasn't a bad smell, more like wet graham crackers. She kept switching from his hands to the window and suddenly she saw the signs beside the road and cried out, " 'Well, shiver my timbers, cried Captain Mac, I'm ten miles out but I'm turning back, I forgot my Burma Shave.' "

Now she was here in the Tech Center parking lot in southeast Denver getting out of her car, dressed in a dark-ish, slightly rumpled two-piece suit. Hair medium long with considerable gray in it. Tall. God, he'd forgotten how marvelously tall she was, a big woman really without being the least bit fat. And with those big sad eyes.

He got out of the station wagon and walked to meet her, but when he was a few feet away he stopped. "I remember you," he said, smiling, making sure she saw it. "You're Tess of the d'Urbervilles. I knew you once."

"Yes," she answered quietly, "and I knew you."

"It was in another land."

"And another time."

"Yes."

They stepped close and hugged then, not speaking but merely holding each other, the sun warm but not terribly bright, not intrusive, with a November wind blowing old October leaves across their feet.

SIX

Doc DROVE STRAIGHT from the Tech Center parking lot to the airport, and as he listened to his older sister tell about her trip he thought her voice sounded more timid than it once had, that she seemed preoccupied, uncomfortable, that she was too much in herself and couldn't get out. He waited for her to finish her account and then asked about Dave, who was fine, and she asked about Lil, who was equally fine, then they both dropped into long monologues about their children, full of lists of accomplishments so intermixed with lists of goals that neither had a clear picture of where the children actually stood. They listened to the words with one part of their attention and with the other they wondered why they were having trouble connecting the kids' faces to sizes, sizes to ages, ages to names that had once been more familiar than now.

Yet by the time Doc managed to find a parking place at Stapleton and they got out of the car and headed for Passenger Pickup, Tess's voice had begun changing back to the one he thought he remembered. Her manner seemed less tentative, her stride was no longer the choppy anxious thing he'd first suspected, and he couldn't figure out why he'd thought her hair had a lot of gray in it. "Hell," he said abruptly, "you're no grayer than I am."

"Should I be?"

He eyed her with a grin. "I'd better be careful with this, otherwise you'll take me down and spit in my face like you used to."

"I can still do it," she said, but her smile was the real answer, smoothing out what remarkably little hard edge might have been lurking at the mouth, making the smoke-dark eyes somewhat less wistful. She reached out and touched his arm as if to say she knew his appraisal hadn't been too harsh, that she might at any moment go silent and make her own. Then she said, "What's Stew's arrival time again?"

"Eleven-twenty."

"And DeeJay's?"

"Eleven forty-five."

"My God, those two kids learned how to tell time after all, didn't they?" They laughed and a sudden arc of warmth leaped the space between them. "Just think," she said to him, "the four of us together again. No children, no parents, no mates, just the original Donner gang. Should be fun."

"Will be."

People swarm at airports as though they were bees trying to find the entrance to the hive. Stewart Donner was one of these. He came floating out of the deboarding pod and into the passenger lobby with a welcoming grin already on his face. Obviously, by some opportune magic, he had spotted them first. But as Stew came nearer, Doc realized that what he was seeing on Stew's face was not a grin of recognition but a feature. It was the way he'd always looked, it was the Stewart Donner of album snapshots and of memory books that now were being thumbed too swiftly. The grin on Stew's face was endemic, forming his whole mouth, shaping permanence there like a dimple. He looked as if he'd heard a joke on the plane (or in study hall, the locker room, the pro shop, the sales meeting) and the enjoyment of it was still on his face. It explained why people were so expectant around Stew, they were waiting for him to tell them the joke.

When he finally spotted Tess and Doc standing in the swarm waiting for him, waving their arms to get his attention, Stew's face didn't change. The grin remained. Then he was among them, jostling a little, switching a thin brief-case to his left hand so he could stick out his right and shake Doc's hand. "Here's a pair to draw to," he said, and his voice sounded higher than the memory album had tricked Doc into remembering, and he looked like he'd gained weight. Still, he'd always been something of a chunk, hadn't he? He'd simply forgotten that Stew was built more like their father than the rest of them.

"Hello, Stewart," Doc said, shaking the outstretched hand and wondering in the same instant why he had been so formal. But before he could add something familiar Stew had reached past him to hug Tess. She did better, calling him Stewball, and this time when he smiled he showed his teeth. My God, Doc thought, he looks like a jack-o'-lantern!

"It would appear you're here to sell something," Tess said to him, backing out of the hug and nodding at the briefcase.

"I'm selling rain. You interested?"

"Skip me," Doc put in. "I've seen rain."

They laughed at that, it was a tame, relaxing burst of a thing. Then they moved by unspoken accord away from the United gate and melted into the flow of the concourse. "Gate 17 A is the one we want," Doc announced before anyone could ask him. "Continental Flight 218. It should be on time."

It was. There was new ejecta from yet another airline cocoon, eggs spilling from a queen bee's sac, and in the spill rode DeeJay Kelley. Doc spotted her immediately, slim, tall, perhaps medium-tall but at least taller than those around her at that moment. She broke out of the pack easily, walking in that brisk impulsive way that young girls walk, her hair a blond waterfall drenching her shoulders and her eyes in that lifting face magnificently black. God, he thought, that's what aristocratic Castilian women must look like. And then the reality came, no, not this one, this is plain Donna Jean Donner from Vernon County whose eyes were once unshadowed and whose original hair was brown. And who now was carrying fatigue in her face, the kind that fades under the traveler's phony perkiness but will not go away.

When she reached them where they waited expectant and isolated just off the main stream of people, DeeJay pecked at Tess's face like a hurried hen at a pebble, pecked a second kiss at Stew, not seeking any sort of embrace from either of them, then lifted her head and looked directly at Doc. She didn't speak and neither did he, but in the next moment she took a mincing step toward him, shifted her feet so that she stood slightly sideways, placed her hands on her hips, pushed her mouth into a wet red pout, winked sulkily and whispered in a throaty sigh, "Hello . . . sailor."

SEVEN

THERE WAS SOMETHING about the time of day that made the earth look discarded. It was probably the light, it was too flat, too honest, it didn't accentuate anything, didn't lend depth where it was needed. There was a strip of blue sky hugging the top of the mountains to the west but it wasn't going anywhere, it was just waiting for tomorrow.

Tess, who was driving and could see what lay on both sides of the highway, didn't know exactly what to expect. The country was getting steadily more level as they got away from the mountains, that was to be expected, but did it look like this because it was Colorado or because it was the middle of November? She hoped the latter, because she wanted to like Colorado for Doc's sake, after all, it was his state. He wasn't making any apologies for the country but as the minutes passed and the miles went by he appeared reluctant to look out at it, as if doing so would attract more attention. He stared straight ahead as though he were looking for holes in the cement. Finally he couldn't stand it any longer, their silence too accusative. "Colorado *can* be pretty." His voice was half miserable, half indifferent. "I've seen it so green and alive it would take your breath away."

Tess was the first who tried to ease his distress, perhaps being the driver gave an added sense of responsibility. "Don't you think it's the time of year?" she said, trying to match Doc's earlier tone. "Everything dying and going brown? Getting ready for winter? Don't you think that's it?"

"Oh, I'm sure that's the case," Stew put in from the back seat; it was quick and firm, obviously, he wanted to like Colorado too. The truth is, they all did. They wanted to like *something*, the station wagon, their luggage, the engineering brilliance of Interstate 76, something that would center them, provide an arms-locked, all-together breakthrough of the stifling formality that was riding in the car with them like an unwelcome fifth passenger.

In an effort to lessen the strain, Stewart asked if they'd heard any good jokes lately, and then tendered one about a Polack soccer player. It was good, and he decided to follow up with a Rastus and Liza, which proved to be old and rambling. They'd all heard it but didn't stop him. Tess, aware that she told jokes badly, felt compelled to make an attempt with an equally ancient Pancho Villa. It failed, its reception as polite as the one given Stewart. They waited for Doc to keep things going but he coughed self-consciously and said, "I know it's dumb but the really funny things that stick with you over the years are not jokes at all but the true stories, the things that actually happened."

Concurrence was immediate. "Yes, that's true," they said, pretty much in unison, but it was only in Tess that the remark triggered any vocal proof. "Remember Smitty?"

she began, already starting to snicker, trying to coax their memory, "Smitty, you're so good to me—"

"Oh shit," DeeJay bleated in her smoker's voice, "I'd forgotten that! Tell us about Smitty."

"Let Doc do it," Tess countered, whereupon Doc turned in his seat and faced them, grateful for the switch from outside the car to inside. "Well . . . you remember . . . it was when Tess first went to work at the restaurant where she met Dave." Everyone said "Right" to the time and place and then allowed him to continue. "There was this waitress who worked the counter at the restaurant and her name was . . . Mary Beth, right, Tess? Right. Mary Beth was a cute little thing and naturally got a lot of attention from the guys who came there to eat. One of them was named Smitty and he fell head over heels in love with her. Brought her little surprises every day. Offered her the use of his car whenever she wanted it. Gave her tips on the quarter-horse races at Rillito. Bought rodeo tickets for her. You name it, he did it for her. Unfortunately, Smitty had been pretty much left out in the looks department and Mary Beth didn't care snap for him, with the result that all the attention he was lavishing on her got to be a real drag. The last straw was when he came in one day carrying a box and plops himself down on a stool and says, 'Mary Beth, honey, I got a nice present for you,' and proceeds to open the box and take out this blouse, all lacy and intimate, and gives it to her right there at the counter in front of all the customers. By this time Mary Beth has had it up to here, I mean, all the way. She puts her hands on her hips and pushes her face into Smitty's and says, 'Smitty, you're so good to me and I'm so goddamned *tired* of it!' "

It did the trick, they laughed, laughed hard, for they honestly remembered. After they'd quieted down, Tess told the family story of when DeeJay was a little girl and accidentally broke wind at a dinner table full of guests, one of whom happened to be the minister. "She got so embarrassed she had to leave the table, but as she was getting out of her chair she inadvertently let another one go. Irv was convinced she'd done it on purpose and demanded that she come back to the table and apologize. She did, but she was so mortified at having to show her face to the company again that she let go a third fart, the loudest one of all!"

They pounded their knees at that one, for they remembered the incident perfectly now, even if they hadn't before, and then Doc told how Stewart had come home from a little buddy's house one day pulling a wagon full of brand-new toys. Mattie naturally figured that Stew had copped them from this kid, which he had, but she wanted to handle the situation in a delicate way so she asked Stew very politely where on earth he'd gotten the lovely toys. "Oh," Stew told her, "on the way home I met Santa Claus and he gave them to me. He said some kids had died that he didn't learn about in time and he had these toys left over in his sack."

This story too got a good response, but they got progressively weaker after that and finally dwindled out altogether. The formality began to creep back in. Outside the windows the country continued to bleed itself of color, and so bleak was it everywhere, sky and earth and now the car itself, that Tess decided she was not going to give in and went quickly to a subject she felt comfortable with. Poetry. " 'O sun and skies and clouds of June, and flowers of June together; ye cannot rival for one hour, October's bright blue weather.' "

"That's beautiful, Tess," DeeJay said in a wilting voice, "and would be meteorologically exact as well, except that this is November."

"I suppose we have to be exact," Tess came back, wanting it to be perky. It wasn't. No one continued the topic or switched to something new, they did nothing to fan the struggling flame of conversation, with the result that Tess drove all the way from the Keenesburg exit to the Roggen exit, a posted distance of eight miles, before anyone uttered another word. And then it was a terribly delayed post-script from Doc, almost confusing in its irrelevance: "Have you considered this? 'The melancholy days are come, the saddest of the year, of wailing winds and naked woods, and meadows brown and sere.' "

"It has the merit of correctness," said DeeJay, less caustically than before, "but no author. We need an author." She sat forward in her seat for the first time since the trip started. "May I have the name of the author, please."

"Your idea," said Doc, "you go first," and DeeJay followed his command with, "It's one of the poems Tess made us learn. It's Longfellow."

"Whittier," put in Stew. "I knew by the end of the first line it was Whittier. Right, Tess?"

Tess asked if there was a prize associated with the correct answer.

"Absolutely," DeeJay replied, staying on the front of her seat. "The winner will receive applause of the accolade type, plus deep personal respect for having sustained literary growth."

Tess said, "Then I'll end the suspense. The author is William Cullen Bryant."

"Hah!" DeeJay snapped. "A teacher of American literature identifying an American poet. Does anyone suspect a rigged contest?"

"Slanted, possibly," replied Tess, "but I'm still the one who had the right answer. Prize, please," and she cupped one ear with her free hand.

They responded by stomping their feet, whistling, clapping boisterously. From the front seat Doc cried, "Hear! Hear!"

"Meadows brown and sere, eh?" put in Stewart when they had finished. "Reminds me of someone I know." His voice was mischievous. "Someone who would try to turn this brown and sere Colorado prairie into a verdant garden."

There was a moment of mass contemplation and then Tess said, "The word *garden*, is it significant? Could it be a part of . . . say . . . *cactus* garden?"

"Oh shit," muttered DeeJay, in a way that said *I know who your someone is.*

Doc said, "The garden in question has carried a lot of hopes over the years but has never been successful, am I right? History records nothing but a series of endless failures, I believe."

DeeJay said, "Make that a double 'Oh shit.' "

Stewart said nothing. There was a new game in progress and he found himself surprisingly in charge of it.

"Your mystery gardener," Tess asked, trying to isolate Stewart in the backseat with her voice alone, "are her initials Mattie Ellen Charlotte Elmor Donner?"

"Damn!" cried Stewart in mock disgust. "Can nothing elude the incisive mind? First she reveals the name of the poet, now the gardener."

"Revealed, yes," said Doc, "saved, no. The story still ends in defeat. There's no way Mattie could make this prairie support a cactus garden unless she got hold of some hybrid stock that didn't require roots."

"You too?" DeeJay asked. "You've encountered Mattie's famous rootless cacti?" She lit a cigarette, elaborately, then blew a long balloon of smoke into the front seat. They all followed it with their eyes as though her impending lines of dialogue could be found there. "Mother planted a saguaro at our place once," the lines said. "It sat there four years and then one day a little sea wren flew in and lighted on top of it and the damned thing fell over. I gave voice to one or two of my favorite expletives, I forget their exact nature now, but the event completely blew my husband's mind. 'Can that be right?' he kept saying. 'A cactus doesn't need *roots*?' "

They all laughed but it was DeeJay's lush bray that dominated. It made Tess think of glutted ashtrays and empty cocktail glasses. Lots of them. Too many.

Stew waited out the laughter and then came in with "It's the same situation in Seattle. We get a hundred inches of rain a year but the first thing Mattie grabs when she gets to our place is the garden hose. She can't seem to grasp the idea that different climates require different approaches."

"As long as it's a plant it needs water, right?" This was Tess.

"Exactly. She drowns everything that grows." He popped a stick of gum in his mouth. "A cactus is a unique plant. It literally thrives on neglect. Leave it alone, forget it's there, and it does beautifully. But not in Mattie's garden. She's got to smother. She had this one cactus, I believe it was a barrel—"

"Ah," Tess interjected, "good old *Echinocactus grusoni*."

"She had that barrel standing in water all summer. It got so swollen with moisture that the pleats actually flattened out."

"Glub, glub, glub," DeeJay mocked, and Doc grunted as if he were reminded of something even more outrageous. But Stew kept on. "Mattie doesn't know what the word *drainage* means. I don't believe it's ever occurred to her that soils have different properties in different parts of the country. Naturally I don't like to play the Dr. Botany role and lecture her all the time. She's with us only one year out—"

"Science is a waste of time with Mattie," said DeeJay, finally managing to interrupt. "She prefers romance. The romance of the unknown."

"Chemicals," Doc blurted, going back to his earlier thought, having waited his turn. He'd always been the polite one.

"Chemicals?" they asked him, and it was a chorus, not just a single voice.

"It's what Mother prefers now. It's her new approach."

"Oh, marvelous!" DeeJay cried, lighting another cigarette.

"It's also the new mortality," Doc kept on. "Whatever survives immersion in water she burns to death with powders. It's called the chemical overdose."

DeeJay laughed so hard she took a fit of coughing. "It sounds," she choked, wiping her eyes, "unbelievably exotic."

"I was thinking more *erotic*," put in Tess.

Stewart said, "What could you do with *neurotic*?"

"Wonderful!" DeeJay cried again. "I love it!"

Stewart then asked Doc, in a serious voice as though he were attempting to return the conversation to a higher plane, what the exact chemicals were that Mattie used. But Doc turned in his seat and eyed Stew suspiciously. "What are you planning to do, start your own cactus patch in those off years when Mattie isn't with you and then overdose them?" He glanced in mock alarm at the others. "What have we got here, a closet cactus killer?"

Laughter again, front seat and back, even from Stew. It was easier for Stew, he had that head start of the incipient grin. Sensing the moment could tolerate even more levity, he put on a leering face and twirled imaginary mustaches. Tess saw him in the rearview mirror and winked. *I remember*, the wink said, *it's your Hairbreath Harry role from the Big Little Books we used to read. I remember.*

Doc took over again. "Actually, Mattie puts a new program into effect each time she comes to Denver. Visit before last she saw the problem as being associated with the sun's rays."

"Sure she did," DeeJay said.

"She became obsessed with the idea that her failure in Denver had to do with a faulty grasp of the correlation between altitude and warmth. Obviously, the lower percentage of oxygen in the air at five thousand feet would have to be compensated for in the future by a higher concentration of sunshine."

"So how did she solve the problem?" Stew asked.

"Aluminum foil. Pieces of cardboard lined with sheets of Reynolds' best aluminum foil." He took a breath and went on. "Positioned in the garden in such a way that the cactus plants would receive maximum sunshine. They would literally be enveloped by it."

"Did you install the foil?"

"I did."

"How'd the cactus do?"

"They burned up. The sun ricocheted off the foil onto the plants and fried them to a crisp. They looked like overdone bacon rind."

Someone snickered. "What did Matti say?"

"What does she always say? Nothing. She'll never admit that a thing has failed. It's like pretending it hasn't."

"And her program on the next visit?"

"Chemicals, like I said."

"How'd *they* do?" The question came from Tess.

"Well," Doc began.

"Details," DeeJay panted heavily from the backseat, "want hear . . . chemical . . . details. . . . ."

"Well," Doc went on, "Mattie hit our place in June and Lil and I immediately started placing bets on what new scheme she'd come up with to make her cactus take hold." He eyed his audience conspiratorially. "Wouldn't that be a real first, for the cactus to actually take hold and survive until her next visit? How'd you like to be the host city for *that* event?"

"Gawd!" DeeJay exclaimed in counterfeit awe.

Doc waited briefly—Tess could see him organizing his story—and then continued. "Mother didn't announce a program right at first like she ordinarily does, but she finally got around to asking me if I wouldn't clear off an area next to the patio on the south side. So I did. Then she planted her patch, a few cane cholla, some ladyfinger and some claret cup, a rose dumpling or two."

"Familiar names, all."

"Unfortunately, the plants didn't grow up into the sky overnight like Jack's beanstalk did. But she didn't panic and grab the garden hose like she usually does, I'll give her credit for that. She just stood back and waited."

"Waited? You're kidding!"

"But before I could comprehend what was happening I came home from work one day and walked out on the patio and what do I see but Mattie bent over one of her cane cholla with my magnifying glass in her hand."

"Your what?"

"That's right, my four-power magnifying glass. I watched her for a few minutes and then she came over to me and announced in that dramatic way she has, 'Red mites, Wallace.'

" 'Red mites, Mother?'

" 'I want you to get me something to kill them with.'

"Which I did. I asked around at some of the stores and finally came up with some Kelthane powder." He glanced almost supplicatingly at each of them. "Believe me, that isn't easy to do. There's a whole bunch of nursery people out there who aren't very expert in succulent diseases, including cactus pests, and they're scared to death to suggest a certain chemical and then have it be responsible for damage to the plant."

"So," Tess questioned after a moment, "did the Kelthane kill the mites?"

"Along with the cholla," groaned Doc. "The poor things turned yellow and then brown and by the end of the week they looked like something I'd burned on the barbecue grill and forgotten to throw out."

"Oh dear," said Tess, and it was less sympathetic than it must have sounded.

"Then about a week later I checked on the patch again and discovered several sheets of white paper spread out under the remaining cactus. Survivors, I should call them. Pretty soon Mattie came out and gave each of the plants a nudge with the toe of her shoe. Then she picked up the sheets of paper and studied them."

"Mites again, huh?" DeeJay said.

"Mealy bugs. I had to go out Monday and pick up some dimethyl propenyl spray—"

"Raid," Stew put in.

"—and those plants never had a chance. She hit them so hard with the Raid they looked like stumps left over from a three-state forest fire. The cat wouldn't even go near them."

After a silence that seemed to convey an inordinate amount of disbelief, Stewart said, "That reminds me of the time at our place when she spotted a couple of slugs at the edge of our lawn and immediately extrapolated that into a *plague* of slugs." He stopped and eyed them. "You know what a slug is? Fat, creepy thing, looks like a white turd. Dwight pours salt on them just to see them disintegrate. Anyway," he went on, "Mother was so panicky she had me bring home half a dozen cans of Slug and Snail Bait. She spread it on some lettuce leaves and put the leaves in

(*135*)

the cactus garden. That was Saturday morning. When we got home from church the next day the lawn was full of slugs. Dozens of them. They'd smelled that bait, I guess. They'd already eaten the lettuce leaves and were starting in on Mattie's cactus. There was nothing we could do but stand around and watch Dwight launch his salt attack. Those slugs really boil away when the salt hits them."

There was a pause and Tess said to Stewart, "Mattie's at your place this year. What did her cactus garden look like when you left this morning?" The question drooped with the nonchalance of one who is not involved.

"Bad," Stew answered, settling in his seat. "It looked like the last act of a Wagnerian opera."

"Which one?" DeeJay asked, taking over. "March of the Dying Toadstools? Death of the Killer Asparagus?"

Tess saw how easily DeeJay had blunted Stew's attempt at cleverness, but before she could offer something divertive, Doc stepped in. "What lucky child gets Mattie next year?" he asked.

"Donna Jean gets her!" blurted Stewart, and there was a drumroll of revenge in it. "Mother asked me to remind *Donna Jean* of that fact when I saw her in Denver."

Tess waited for DeeJay to snap back with something sharp, and she did, but it wasn't directed at Stew. "Bless Mother's heart," was what she said, "bless her for not only remembering my true name, but for reminding me of it. *Donna Donner.*" She repeated it twice with an exaggerated succinctness. "The name has all the nuance of rotting diapers." She sat forward in her seat and lit a cigarette, the streamer of smoke revealing more emotion than any expression on her face. "I've been giving some serious thought," she began carefully, "to some sort of alternative to this every-four-years business with Mother. Her visits are becoming so inescapable, so fixed, they're almost Biblical."

Stewart coughed and said, "You want to hear something ironic?"

"One suggestion at a time, please. Mine was first."

"No it wasn't," Stew persisted. "That's what I mean, someone else beat you to it."

"What someone else?"

"My wife. Bev. She asked me just this morning if I would bring the matter up for discussion when we were all together. She said the trip would be the perfect opportunity to really come up with something concrete. And it is, you know. If we're ever going to . . . make a change. . . ." He trailed off in the same way he had as a boy, hinting at a particular direction and then stepping aside.

But he wasn't alone, no one took the lead. Finally Doc said, "There's a major question here and one of us has to ask it. The question is *why?* Why should we make a change?"

Tess said, "There's one bigger than that. *Where?* Where will Mattie go? Debtor's prison? Skid Row? Or will she sign a lifetime contract with the Golden Years Rest Home and then finalize it with a bad check? She doesn't have a dime of her own, you know. And where will the rest home be located? Tucson, Denver, Los Angeles, Seattle? Talk about host city! Which one of us gets *that* little bonus?"

Stew said, "There's a third question. Who's going to tell her?"

"We'll draw straws," DeeJay said. "Whoever gets the shortest—"

Doc said, glancing at Stew, "It's more curiosity than anything, but what were Bev's reasons for suggesting a change?"

Stew said, "What were DeeJay's? She's the one who brought it up."

Tess said, "Here in the car maybe, but not this morning in Seattle. Doc's question is legitimate."

Stew sat forward and unwrapped a stick of gum. He folded the wrapper, folded it again, then finally a third time. Hearing his actions, not seeing them, Tess remembered that Stewart had always delayed like this when he wanted to attract attention, or avoid it, she'd never been able to tell which it was. His facial expression, half bemused, half superior, only aggravated her confusion. What he said finally was, "Bev claims Mattie's a troublemaker. A bad seed."

Doc moaned. "Bad seed? That sounds familiar."

"Bev may not be very original," Tess said, "but I think she's to the point."

Encouraged by the support, Stew kept on. "Bev says Mattie's a catalyst. Sets kid against kid. Sometimes kid against adult."

DeeJay sat forward in her seat as if to match Stew's position. "Would you believe adult against adult?" She flipped her hair off one shoulder. "Do you guys remember when we lived on East Second Avenue in the old country?" Tess remembered that *old country* had been DeeJay's term for Tucson. "There was this Mexican family living on one side of us and an Italian on the other. They'd lived there for years. Good neighbors. Loved each other. Do you remember it? Mattie moves in and within two months both families are staying up nights trying to decide how to kill each other. I don't know what Mattie did, maybe nothing. I mean, nothing you can put your finger on or take to court. Maybe it's what she *didn't* do. Maybe that's how a catalyst works."

Tess said, "Bev could be right in this case. After all, she's got the youngest kids and young kids live in a world of 'if you'll be my best friend, I'll be yours.' Mattie might have gotten between the twins in some way, maybe with her tea parties or something—"

"She used to have a lot of tea parties with the girls,"

Stew broke in, "but not always with both of them together."

"Kids are sensitive to favoritism," Tess went on, "girls especially. They could have tattled on each other whenever they felt they weren't number one with Grandma. With kids it's number one or nothing. Bev may have waited for a chance to complain to Stew and when this trip came up she took it. I can respect her for that, after all, she's family."

"Oh, I love that!" DeeJay exclaimed, giving a bleat of a laugh. "I just love it when someone *is* family or *isn't* family. You hear people say, 'Well, I didn't think it was any of her business, after all, she's *not family*.' Or they'll tell you, 'We felt we ought to keep it *in the family*.'"

Tess came back quickly, defensively. "Bev *is* family, that's what I'm saying."

"Down, King!" DeeJay snapped. "I'm not picking on you! I'm picking on the way society defines *family*."

"All right, smartie," said Doc, sounding a little smug, "how would you define it?"

"I'm so glad you asked," DeeJay crooned, hugging her knees, "because I'm dying to tell you. Family is when you *cannot be excluded* from sharing the latest calamity to descend upon it. Failure, grief, scandal, shame, you have the right to participate in *every one of them*. No exceptions. You also have an opportunity to share in knowing *who* in the family has the least money, the most debts, whose daughter got caught shoplifting and whose son spent an overnight in jail. An *equal* opportunity, equal being the key word in families. It means that if Jane gets told the dirt, so must Robert and Sally. Have I made myself clear? Being family means you have to eat the shit you would tell everyone else to *stick*!"

At that point, Doc dared to break in and add a qualifier. "A family can share good news too, DeeJay."

DeeJay pounced. "*When?* When was the last time any of us called you to report that we'd finally learned how to tie a bow knot? That we'd gone a whole year without speeding, without stoning the neighbor's dog, without stealing a ream of typing paper from work, being unfair to the kids, starting a fight with our better half? When did we share with you the good news that although Janie spent the school year screwing half the boys in her class, she did *not* get pregnant? Can you remember when it was we told you that, Doc?" She waited, then gave a forgiving laugh when he didn't answer.

So did the others not answer. There were no attempts at rebuttal because they couldn't have overcome the acuity of DeeJay's attack. She'd always been good at the quick hit. She was innovative and wonderfully witty as long as she could start first and stay out in front; in a long race she inevitably fell behind and could never catch up.

"Back to Mattie," Stew reminded them, shifting in his seat. "Has anyone come up with an idea of what to do with her? Something acceptable to all parties?"

"Does that mean the same as fair and considerate?" Doc asked, but it was a stall and they all knew it. Tess was the only one who gave their avoidance a voice. "We actually do have the power to do something with her, don't we? It's almost frightening, power over a parent."

Stewart suggested that they might as well enjoy it.

"Why not?" DeeJay elaborated. "They had it over us when we were little, didn't they? Practically a life-and-death power."

"We don't have life-and-death over Mattie."

"But we could have, that's what I'm saying. It's there for the taking if we want it. Where could she go if we suddenly said, 'All right, Mother, that's it, out you go, make your own way'? What could she do?"

There was a silence. It was like the pause in music,

expectant, profound. Someone in the back shifted feet, another coughed, finally Doc said, "We don't have to decide on anything right this minute. We can look at it again on the way back."

"What we could do," suggested Tess, "is appoint a committee. That's the preferred way, to dilute responsibility by dividing it. It's very American." She glanced at them waggishly. "We're all Americans here, aren't we?"

"Right!" It was an instant chorus, rich with reprieve, and they settled back in their seats and gave themselves over to the mindless activity of watching the flat brown prairie float past the windows of the car.

Their privacy didn't remain intact for long. A large green-and-white sign informed them they were leaving Colorful Colorado, and a short time later an even larger sign announced that they had entered Nebraska, home of the Big Red. As if there truly existed a preternatural recognition of state lines, the sun broke through the bank of clouds behind them, revealing a lake lying perhaps a mile back from the highway. The sun gave a sheen to the surface of the lake as though it had been painted a vivid silver that hadn't dried yet. But the car moved past and the angle of light changed, betraying the lake, turning it back to the dull, unromantic reservoir it had been in the first place. Then the sun disappeared again. The earth took on a new depth, ridges transformed themselves from lines to shapes, isolated trees began to grow tall before their eyes. A dry creek bed wandered out from a low hill as if it had meant to come down to the interstate and watch the cars go by and had gotten trapped beneath an underpass instead.

The altered terrain acted on them like a signal. Stewart opened new gum, DeeJay smoked, Doc stirred from some distant study and said to Tess, "How are we going to do this? Surely we hadn't planned on driving straight through to La Crosse." He turned to the backseat. "Or had we?"

DeeJay shrugged and pretended she was busy putting out her cigarette. Stew said, "We could go straight on through, but then again . . . What do the rest of you think?"

"Well . . ." Tess began.

"We'd probably be smart not to get too tired." This was Doc, who had asked the original question. "I think if we take turns at the wheel during the day and then stop at night to get a good—"

"A good night's sleep certainly won't hurt us."

"—we'll wind up making as good time as if we drove straight through."

"A hot meal at night and a few quiet drinks could be just what the doctor ordered."

"Ogallala," Tess announced, reading a new road sign, "is the next town of any size. How does that sound?"

"Terribly Western," DeeJay said.

"Like a brand of mineral water," said Stew.

Tess said, "Nebraska is beef country, right? Beef becomes steak, right? Medium rare. Salad bar. Glass of burgundy. Maybe two glasses."

Doc preferred a good Rosé. "And blue-cheese dressing on the salad."

"I like the way you guys think."

"I like the way you talk."

"I really don't care what they serve in the restaurants. It'll feel good just to get out of the car and stretch, maybe cut a fart or two."

"Men fart, women break wind. That's what Mattie always said. In fact, those are the only words of wisdom she bequeathed to us."

"No, there was one other deathless bequest."

"What was it?"

"Men shout, women pout."

"You're right. How could we have forgotten?"

(*142*)

"We sort of took Mattie to task on her cactus gardens today, didn't we?"

"Yes, but wasn't it fun?"

Night came quickly when it came. There was an abrupt rush of shadow across the land and then it was black. There was a rush of civilization as well. Lights flicked on, there appeared to be more cars moving. A little town bloomed against what must have been a hillside, another among trees that might have stood beside a quiet river.

EIGHT

THEY DIDN'T GET out of the Holiday Inn until
ten o'clock. They ate in the dining room and then went to
the lounge for drinks. Their waitress, in the process of
serving them a third round (it might have been the fourth),
sought to encourage a healthy tip by asking with a phony
smile, "Are you folks on vacation?"

The question was innocent enough and because it seemed
the easiest thing to do at the moment, they answered
yes. They had been aware from the beginning that the
waitress had mistaken them for two couples, pairing Doc
with Tess and Stewart with DeeJay, which was partly
due to the way they were seated at the table and partly
to her perception of their ages. It was a harmless misjudg-
ment, as innocuous as the next part of her question, which
was delivered with an even more dazzling smile. "And
where are you folks from?"

Pleasantly, they looked at her and answered, "Arizona, Washington, California, Colorado." But all four answers were uttered at the exact same moment so that what came out was a single word, hopelessly unintelligible and terribly suspicious, making the four of them appear more than anything like shack-ups who hadn't taken the time to get their stories straight.

That's the way the waitress saw it, a ludicrous attempt to cover up what was a fairly common transgression in western Nebraska. Then too, it was the dull middle-hours stretch of a dead Tuesday night and the soft drinks she'd been sipping all evening may have contained something a bit stronger than Pepsi. In any event, she exploded into laughter, throwing her torso first backward and then forward, spilling her drink tray so thoroughly that the ice cubes bounced on the table like hailstones, while the coins from her change cup either fell into the spill or rolled across the floor of the lounge. She made no attempt to retrieve any of the material because she couldn't, she was rocking back and forth on her spiked heels, convulsed with laughter.

The four travelers reacted pretty much the same way, but to the waitress, not to what they had said. Tess found herself laughing so hard she had trouble catching her breath. Doc's eyes filled with tears but he was suddenly too weak to get a firm grip on his glasses to take them off. Stew's mouth split so wide with his own shrieks that his upper plate popped loose and shot out onto the table along with the ice cubes and the sodden napkins and the floating stir sticks. The denture resembled nothing so much as a swamped ferry boat, painted pink with a row of ivory chairs on each side, and DeeJay, who hadn't realized that Stewart wore dentures, simply surrendered to helplessness and slid straight down out of her chair and onto the floor.

The bartender scooted out from behind the bar and

grabbed the stricken waitress by the arm and led her away, whereupon several patrons left their tables and took seats at the bar, convinced it would be a much safer place when the four drunks were forcibly evicted from the premises. They weren't evicted. They weren't even asked to leave. DeeJay struggled to her feet, Stew retrieved his uppers, and together the four of them plucked the remaining stir sticks and napkins from their hair and left the lounge of the Holiday Inn.

They weren't staying at the Holiday. The town of Ogallala was full of teachers, it being the second night of a three-day Western Nebraska Teachers Association convention, and since there were no rooms available at the Holiday they were forced to take lesser accommodations at a motel nearer the heart of town, which is to say, at the north end of the railroad bridge. The name of their motel was the Red Crown, and they had visibly despaired when the night clerk showed them the one room still available (two single beds, two cots, shower, no tub, no TV), leaving them with the single condolence that it was "all that's left in this town, due to them teachers," and with the further bad news that the ice machine was down until Saturday. What exaggerated the matter was the fact that the clerk was possessed of a countenance that matched his role perfectly. Dour. Timorous. Unimaginative.

"Did you see that face?" Doc demanded when the clerk had gone. "Is he the original Mr. Milquetoast or isn't he?"

Now, returning to this same room at the far end of the bridge overlooking the Burlington Northern tracks, the laughter and excitement of the lounge incident still coursing in their blood, they remembered the clerk. At least DeeJay did. Her eyebrows arched mischievously. "What do you say we have some fun?"

Stew said, "Wasn't that what we just had in the lounge?"

"I mean with the motel clerk."

"*Ah, le concierge, Monsieur Milquetoast,*" intoned Tess in her smoothest Parisian. "*Que drôle!*"

"Do you remember the vaudeville acts we used to put on when we were kids in Tucson?" DeeJay asked.

Doc remembered. "The famous Donner Olios?"

"Exactly. I'm sure our friend the night clerk would be impressed by a performance. He might even be cheered, God knows he needs to be."

"We've got no script, no lines to memorize."

"We can improvise as we go along."

"How about costumes?"

"We'll have to scrounge for them. It isn't like it's the first time."

"Hell, let's do it!" Doc piped, bouncing up from one of the cots. "How much time do we have?"

"You mean for preliminary costume requisition followed by full cast presentation?"

"My question exactly."

"How's thirty minutes?"

"It's tight. In fact, it's shitty. But we're the Donners, aren't we? That means the show . . . must . . . go . . . on!"

"*Certainement!*" cried Tess, already scanning the hotel room for costume ideas. "*Vive la show!*"

All four were back in the room in twenty minutes, fully costumed and lined up for DeeJay's inspection in another twenty. "Remember earlier when I said we should take not more than thirty minutes?" she asked them, checking makeup and hats.

"We remember."

"Slip of the tongue. I meant forty."

"What a coincidence, that's exactly what it took us. It just proves once again that the Donners have come through."

"Is that like 'The Show Must Go On' and 'Break a Leg'?"

"Similar, yes."

"God," Tess said, "I feel like Judy Garland *and* Mickey Rooney."

"You look like them too, dear," DeeJay said. She passed along the line of them making a last inspection and then, fully satisfied, led them from the room and across the parking lot to a secluded place in the motel office, across the lobby and around the corner from the front desk.

The clerk was seated at the desk reading. He was elderly, a shy colorless man to whom the joys of theater had been forever denied. His face wore a puzzled expression and around the eyes he looked squinty, as though he'd worn glasses all his life and had just taken them off. But he was handed a lifetime supply of storytelling opportunities when he heard the sound and glanced up from his *Mechanics Illustrated* and saw Wallace Donner leaping toward him across the lobby wearing a red union suit, blue gloves, a green stocking cap and cradling a rack of bone-white deer antlers in one arm. "Merry Christmas, my good sir!" he called to the clerk in a booming voice, bounding to a stop in front of the desk. "Donner here!" He studied the night clerk's sagging face. "Donner and Blitzen? Christmas Air Travel? Surely you've heard of us?"

The clerk merely stared open-mouthed.

"Well sir, that most exciting of seasons is upon us once again, as they say, and I've come to the Ogallala area—I hope I'm pronouncing that right, sir—somewhat in advance of my colleagues. Dancer . . . Comet and Vixen . . . you've heard of them, I'm sure." He paused in sudden consternation. "What's that you say? For what purpose am I come this early? Oh, my good sir," and he laughed in a patient and yet jolly way, "my purpose is twofold, as it were. I am compelled, firstly, to check on possible landing sites in the Ogallala area—am I pronouncing that right, sir?—as well as the availability of forage supplies, the existence of snow removal and/or other contingency plans, plus divers matters of a holiday nature. Secondly, I must determine whether those local residents who are making a Christmas list are also, and this is most important, sir, are also . . . *checking . . . it . . . twice!* Do you take my meaning, sir? Good!" Here he glanced at the watch on his wrist. "I've enjoyed our little visit, my dear sir, and would like nothing better than to chat further with you, or to use the vulgate, *chew the fat,*" and he chuckled, again in a cheery manner, "but I've many more stops on my itinerary. I must be off. Up and away, as it were. I fear my flight companions grow restless, I can hear them pawing and stomping even as we talk. So farewell to you, sir!" He gave a jolly wink and laid a finger against his nose. "I don't know why I do this," he said, "but it seems a nice holiday touch." He gave a great leap straight up in the air. "Merry Christmas to all," he cried, "and to all a good night!" and with a last benevolent smile he wheeled from the desk and bounded across the lobby and out of sight around the corner.

DeeJay was the next to appear, popping into view around the identical corner, striding across the shabby carpet wearing a hard hat and Levi's and Russian boots, carrying a single-bitted ax, an empty red bucket, and twenty-five feet of garden hose. "You're probably wondering who I am," she announced to the clerk, who blinked once, no more, "but you must not ask. Under penalty of threat you must not inquire as to my true identity." She leaned her single-bitted ax against the desk and draped the garden hose over it. "However," she said, smiling conspiratorially at the clerk, "I can tell you why I'm here. Isn't that good news?" She waited for some kind of agreement from the clerk, didn't get it, and went on. "I am here in response to an urgent coded message from our agent in this area, Turkey Lurkey, who has reported that the sky is falling. You can understand our concern but let me say right now, up front, that you must not be frightened, sir! We will never, repeat never, allow the sky to fall. At least not until those teachers who took the best motel rooms have left town and are out on the open highway, then we may look at it again." She paused dramatically. "What time will that be, Mr. Clerk of Motel? At precisely what hour will the convention be over?"

The clerk didn't answer. Actually, he hadn't closed his mouth sufficiently to speak. His eyes had turned glassy and fixed like a rodent's at night and his mouth was twisted up on one side as though a bolus of stomach gas was threatening to exit his body.

"But for the moment," DeeJay continued, "I am desperate to get a message to our agent. I've been unable to get in touch with that turkey, I mean Mr. Lurkey, since I arrived. Poor devil's undoubtedly gone underground." She stopped and studied the clerk's face. "You appear to be a responsible person," she told him, "so I'm going to have to enlist your aid. Ask for your assistance too, I might add. Time is of the essence here, I assure you. If Turkey should happen to come into this motel—and I can't for the life of me think of why he would do that—but if he does come in you must give him this message. It's imperative, which is one classification level below important. Tell Agent Lurkey that I brought the wrong gear. Have you got that? *Wrong gear!* My ax is not double-bitted, my bucket's got a hole in it, and my hose is too short. Tell him that this situation forces me to leave the target area and that if he knows what's good for him he'll blow his cover and do the same goddamned thing. Got that? *Same goddamned thing!*" Whereupon she shot the clerk an imperative look, grabbed her ax and her hose, turned from the desk, and stomped off across the lobby.

(*150*)

From that identical area in the very next moment emerged a forlorn female creature dressed in a flowing gown fashioned from a red-and-orange bedspread and complemented at the neck with a white boa, which showed on closer inspection to be a tightly rolled bath towel. On her head she wore a lampshade, which threw her face into shadow, and which was tied under the chin with a length of drape cord. The tragic figure shuffled across the carpet, laid a weary hand on the edge of the desk, and said, "I am fully aware, monsieur, that you have forgotten me. It has been too long and too much has happened. Cruel fate . . ." and here she raised a hand to her mouth to stifle a sob. "Believe me when I say, monsieur," she struggled on, "that I was not always sunk to this low estate. Surely, in your heart of hearts, you can sense that you are in the presence of one who was formerly of greater stature than now. I beseech you, monsieur, if that is truly your name, to look into these eyes and tell me that you do in fact recognize the desolate wretch who stands before you."

Not the least flicker of recognition crossed the face of the night clerk.

"Yes," she sighed, "the terrible secret is finally revealed. Who stands before you now, this tattered Maid of Dairy, this common household drudge, was once none other than the aristocratic . . . the delicate . . ." and here her voice faltered and her hand fluttered weakly about her face, ". . . Tess of the d'Urbervilles. Some use the small d, some the large," she added, coughing piteously into a washcloth, "but in every case it's still a capital U."

The night clerk swallowed in noiseless terror.

"You will understand me, monsieur, when I say to you from the depths of my soul that I sorely miss the palatial estates of my family, where in days of yore I was wont to dance spritelike in sylvan fields, ofttimes with gentle shepherds, ofttimes alone, of course," and there was a strong impression at this point that her eyelids trembled, although it was difficult to see her face in the shadows of the lampshade bonnet. "But alack and aday," she sighed, wringing the washcloth with both hands, "what boots it in this weary world, *n'est-ce pas?* Therefore I must bid you farewell, monsieur, if that is truly your name. Adieu to you . . . adieu. . . ." And with that mournful word of parting the creature's shoulders slumped and she turned from the night clerk and his desk, one hand pressed to her bosom, the other to her forehead, and wound her solitary way back across the faded red-and-orange carpet, which was not unlike her own poor gown, and disappeared into the dark recesses of the lobby.

The eyes of the night clerk did not follow her, they remained fixed on a spot in the lobby ceiling. It was just as well. In a matter of seconds a new apparition materialized at the same far corner and made its way with mincing steps toward the desk. The figure was that of a male oriental. A plastic ice bucket had been placed upside down on his head and several bedsheets were wrapped around his body in such a way as to resemble a caftan, complete with flaring sleeves into which the figure's joined hands had disappeared. The face bore a severe Fu Manchu mustache, which a closer scrutiny would have exposed as no more than a shameless mascara hoax. The eyes had been taped into almond shapes with flesh-colored Band-Aids. The whole mien was inscrutable, down to the incipient grin, and just as the figure reached the desk and bowed obsequiously, the night clerk looked down from the spot on the ceiling.

"I am Ah Fook," the figure declared, "fortune-cookie salesman." The voice was the mysterious silky reed of the Far East. "Am also franchise representative for Call 'Em Like You See 'Em Tea Leaves Reading Shoppees. Am engaged at present in soliciting partnerships in same. If cannot swing price, must not despair. Maybe catchee exclusive correspondence school program about to begin this area. Only requirement, you be able write name on application, enclose stamped self-addressed envelope for mailing diploma. Must write legibly. If home office unable read name, diploma delayed," and here he shrugged with classic oriental stoicism, "two . . . maybe three days."

The clerk's gaze wavered constantly between the upturned ice bucket and the Fu Manchu.

"You needee explanation franchise? Ah, so. You open Tea Leaves Reading Shoppee, serve fortune cookie with tea, read tea leaves for customer . . . allee same makee big spondulicks. Fortune cookie currently enjoying bull market, am able offer you carload price. For carload quantity, yes. So . . . you write name on application? Order fortune cookie?" His grin widened solicitously and his eyelids lifted, at least as much as the Band-Aids allowed.

But the night clerk failed to reply. In fact, he remained motionless. Only his eyes moved, furtively, as if seeking to escape.

The oriental figure's eyes narrowed to tiny slits and its grin faded into the Fu Manchu. "Ah, so," he lisped, "is velly sad. No cookie, no Tea Leaves Shoppee," and with an unfathomable sigh he bowed his head, his hands emerging from the cavernous sleeves of his bedsheet robe only long enough to press together in a conical blessing. Then he turned and glided soundlessly back across the lobby floor and disappeared into the darkened hall from which he had come.

The four of them left the motel office and returned to their room, laughed for thirty minutes, drank their entire breakfast supply of instant coffee, got out of their costumes and washed up and then sprawled across the beds while they relived their performances and the night clerk's un-utterable dismay.

"My neck is sore from trying to hold in the laughs."

"It's a wonder he didn't recognize some of the props and the costume parts and ask what we were doing with them."

"He was too scared to ask anything."

"He'll never forget this night, will he?"

"Never."

"Hell, we probably won't either."

Later, even with the lights out and the room finally quiet, Tess had trouble getting to sleep. It wasn't the Burlington Northern freight trains. The past was on her, the memory of other olios crowding into the present one, returning her to a time she had long since put away. Or thought she had. Eventually she got up and slipped on her housecoat and stepped outside.

There was a new chill in the air. The sky had cleared and the moon was out, not the lush marble moon of summer nor even a harvest moon, all swollen and narcissistic, but skeletal. It rode bonily in the sky, looking stark and aban-doned like a decoration kids had put up for Halloween and forgotten to take down.

NINE

STEWART WAS BEHIND the wheel now and he hadn't gone far from the downtown restaurant where they ate breakfast when an Indian man crossed the street in the middle of the block. There was no mistaking he was Indian —his legs were too bandy, his face too much the color of dull chocolate, his Stetson too black and too canoed not to be. He wore polished boots and there was an immense silver buckle at his waist that was doing its best to hold in his paunch. Turquoise rings flashed from the fingers of both hands. DeeJay, who was riding shotgun, obviously hadn't been paying much attention because the man was practically in front of the car before she saw him. "I'll be damned," she said then, "there's one of our Red Brothers."

"He's not one of ours," Tess said, watching from the backseat as the man took a toothpick from his jacket pocket and stuck it in his mouth. "He's not a Crow."

"How can you tell?"

"Too prosperous."

"You mean the rings?"

"No, rings are standard equipment. It's because his hat's too new, for one thing. He's wearing boots instead of tennis shoes, for another. And he just finished eating a big breakfast. He's probably a Sioux."

"I don't know about the others," DeeJay said, throwing up her hands, "but you've impressed the hell out of me. How do you know this guy's a Sioux?"

"Because I was a schoolteacher for over twenty years and this is Ogallala and there's a tribe called the Ogallala Sioux, and two plus two equals four."

DeeJay whistled.

"Brilliant," said Stew.

Doc said, "Historically speaking, it was the Ogallala band that wiped out our friend George Custer at Little Big Horn."

"Sorry you brought that up," DeeJay said, "because I hate George Custer. Always have." Stew could tell from the snippiness that she was reverting to type, that she would no longer play the pupil to Tess's teacher, a role she had never been comfortable with. "If George had beaten the Sioux maybe we wouldn't have had to put up with all those other Red Brothers in Custer City." She swept the backseat with a disdainful look. "You remember Custer City, certainly."

"I'm not sure," said Tess.

Doc said, "You mean the home of the Friday-night Bingo games in New Zion Methodist?"

"Oh, *that* Custer City," exclaimed Tess, and Stew appreciated the return of that wide-eyed, innocent, *who me?* humor. It was vintage Tess, the Tess he remembered.

"God," DeeJay began, and he knew it was going to be buoyant, "I remember the Crow boys at that school Tess and I went to when we lived with Uncle Frank. In over three decades I still haven't had my ass pinched that many times. It's a wonder I have any left, although Kell keeps telling me that exactly the opposite is true." She delayed a moment, going pensive, not a habit with her. "I was so young in Montana . . ." and she turned to Tess in the backseat. "My God, what was I?" It was an instinctive gesture, asking Tess, the oldest, a subconscious observance of the hierarchy that exists among siblings. Tess answered just as automatically, "You were ten years old."

"I didn't even know grab-ass was naughty in those days," DeeJay went on. "I thought the boys were just being mean."

"Apparently," said Doc, "the natives knew more about the birds and bees than—"

"Good God!" DeeJay shrieked, slapping her knee. "They were also showing me their erections! *That's* what they were doing, the older boys, I mean, the ones who could get one up on a regular basis." She let out a genuine gasp of disbelief. "I didn't know what they were showing me, can you believe that? They'd press their hands against their pants to show me the outline but I thought it was something they were carrying in their pockets, like a jackknife or a bone totem. I remember thinking what a strange custom that was, showing things by hiding them. I thought it was some sort of tribal ritual."

Doc laughed. "The ancient sheathed-pecker ceremony."

"The Crow version of Show and Tell."

"Playing Hide the Weenie with Montana's own."

"Come back, George Custer," DeeJay cried, "and revenge my honor! Massacre the Crows like you should have the Sioux!"

"Massacre Uncle Frank while you're at it, George," Stew put in. He meant it to be part of the fun, but in truth he could barely remember Frank Elmor. The man would surge forward in his memory occasionally, but he was shifting and off-center, he was the figure in the back row of a family snapshot who was always behind someone, his face concealed in shadow or hidden by a hat.

"Do you remember Uncle Frank?" It was DeeJay, staring at Stew across the front seat, her face showing disbelief even if her voice didn't.

"Of course," he lied. "Who could forget Uncle Frank?" She gave up the interrogation. "I can't, for one. Every time I see a sheet hanging on a line in a backyard I think of that sonofabitch!"

No one laughed. The moment called for something, but not laughter. "What Frank did was bad," Doc said, hurrying over the words, "but do you know what was worse? His getting away with it. There were adults who could have stopped him, but they didn't."

"Or they weren't there," Tess said, and in the silence that followed Stew could feel each of them thinking of Mattie.

"I imagine Frank's dead now," Doc put in, trying the aversion again. "Willard too. Does anyone know for sure? Has Mattie ever—"

"I've never heard her mention either one of them," said Tess with the finality of one who was best positioned to know.

Doc moved forward in his seat, his voice going purposely light. "Boy, that Willard," he said, "there's a guy who flat missed his calling. The man was born to be a con artist. He'd have been more at home on a carnival midway barking the Little Egypt Show than in a pulpit. 'See Little Egypt dance! Buy a ticket to our Special Midnight Show and see Little Egypt dance without her veils!' So ends our Bible lesson for today."

"Those two charlatans took in a lot of money for New Zion." This from Tess. "I wonder how much of it found its way to the Crows."

"Most of it," Doc answered, "as hard as that is to believe. Otherwise, where did it go? Neither of them had a pot to piss in. They lived in those old drafty frame houses. They never went to movies. They wore old clothes."

"Except for the straw hats," said Tess. "They weren't old."

Doc kept going. "And look at those cars they drove. The windows wouldn't roll down, windshield wipers didn't work, tires balder than a chicken's beak."

"You couldn't buy new tires during World War Two," said Tess, continuing her correction of his memory.

"Well, if it could have been done," Doc countered, leaning back in his seat, "our dear old Uncle Willard would have found the way. Lottery. Numbers, something." In the rearview mirror Stew could see Doc thinking of the man they had lived with in Montana, making the safe uninvolved judgments he couldn't have risked thirty years before. What did Doc remember? Had Willard been mean to the two of them? His mind flashed a blurred image of a woodpile, a tiny saw. Who had given him the saw? Had Willard made it for him? Was he that kind of man? The remembrance faded and a new one took its place, one of his bedroom in that house and of his crying. He guessed he had cried a lot and knew it had been for Mattie but he couldn't bring back the feeling that went with it. It was like watching someone you didn't know cry over something you had no knowledge of. Doc could probably remember the crying. Stew could see in the mirror that his brother had retreated inside himself, had shut out the voices and the highway noise to fix on the private path that could take him back unimpeded across the years. Perhaps he was seeing the woodpile and the saw and was living them again. Although he couldn't see Tess in the mirror Stew could feel her silence and knew that she too had gone back. She was seeing the sheets perhaps, feeling the wind and the cold and the shame of moments she and DeeJay could recall but he could not. Let them go back, he thought, let them savor or reject, whatever they chose. The memories were theirs, they had earned them.

Instead, he concentrated on his driving. There were only a few cars moving on the interstate, which was Interstate 80 now, but there were a great many trucks. The day seemed strangely suspended, there was no sun visible in the sky to make it age. The prairie stretching away on both sides of the road was merely an extension of the sky, bleak and dreary with no hint of respite anywhere. At one point a TV tower thrust up out of an abandoned field, and sometime later, farther back from the road, he saw a radar mast. The two objects had no lasting identity and yet, like schoolhouse windows in summer, they were vaguely threatening.

Then, out of the stillness choking the car, Tess voiced the question that had been left unspoken earlier, the one that had to do with Mattie and why she hadn't been there in Montana to stop Frank Elmor's act of cruelty to a child. In truth, the question had always been unspoken, it had lain voiceless in the kids' thoughts since the day they heard unfamiliar relatives in an unfamiliar land announce that their mother had run away and left them. The sore of her abandonment had healed long ago but the scar remained, it was an undissolved lump in the flesh of what their lives had gone on to be since that day. All through childhood and into their adult life with new people, with mates and children, careers and acquaintances, they had subverted Mattie's desertion of them by simply not talking about it. Not once had they asked each other why or where or with whom. But now they had. Now they would bring the pain-deadened skeleton forward out of time and speak to it. At last. "I wonder where Mattie went that time?"

The words came from Tess but they could have come from any of them; there was no surprise in the question, just inevitability.

"And why?" DeeJay said with the same blunt acceptance.

"And with whom?" said Doc, and now it was done, the skeleton all unearthed, the bones lying there ready to be kicked aside or picked up and held, whatever they chose.

"Does everyone understand," Stew said with that same serenity the others had shown, "that we will never know the answer to these questions?"

Tess said, "If we did know them, what would we have?"

"And what difference would they make?" asked DeeJay. "If we had Mattie's reasons for deserting us typed out on a master confession with copies for all interested parties, what part of our life would it change? What part of hers?"

Stew coughed in what he hoped was an assertive way. "I think it's time we got a little practical about what happened. For example, what was the guy's name that Mattie went off with? Fred? Bob? Charley? Was it a name she especially liked? What did the guy do for a living? Was he a teacher, a farmer, a salesman? Where did she meet him? Did he have money? I always figured she'd gone for money. She sure didn't have any of her own."

"What always amazed me," Doc put in quietly, "and I mean *always*, was where she got the guts to do it. She never had any that I knew. She was the original country mouse."

"Jesus," DeeJay said, and like the others it was as though she were talking to herself, letting words spill from some long-secluded reservoir of wondering. "Jesus, she must have had the all-time number-one case of hot pants. When you abandon four kids without a word or a kiss goodbye you've got to have a whole army of itch ants crawling through your pubics." She took a deep breath as if she

(*161*)

expected it to replenish her. "I'll admit to slipping into estrus at least once a month but I never traded my kids in on it. I have three kids and not once—"

"We all have three kids," interrupted Tess. "Have you ever thought of that, any of you? We have exactly three kids and that's all, no more. It's as though we'd saved up all our childhood pain and loneliness to give to a last child, that fourth one, and then didn't have him. Purposely. We didn't want the little bugger carrying *our* load through *his* life. I'm no psychologist but I think you could call that a classic case of inhibited transference—"

"The guy had to be someone Mattie met back in Wisconsin," Stew said, as if no one had diverted his original topic. "Maybe he was the hired man." He started to laugh and then stopped and shot a glance at Tess in the backseat. "Did we have a hired man when we lived on that ridge farm?"

"We did," Tess answered. "We actually had two of them. But not at the same time."

"Maybe it was some guy from church," Stew went on, paying no attention to the answer he had requested.

"You think so?"

Doc said, "There was a period in there somewhere when Mattie started going into town by herself. On Saturdays, I think."

DeeJay said, "Are you sure? Are you sure she could drive a car then? If I remember right she didn't learn to drive until Tucson." Her voice quickened. "Don't you remember? She picked that damned Sabino Canyon road to show us how well she'd learned. It was a car that belonged to one of her lungers at the san and she damned near put us in the creek half a dozen times. Don't you remember that? Stewart was cowering in the backseat pleading with her—"

"She got into Viroqua somehow," Doc broke in, "and on

a regular basis. I remember asking her if she'd bring certain things back for me. And she did."

It wasn't intentional but Tess looked at Stewart when she asked, "You remember the man who drove us into Viroqua the day Mattie left the farm? The man with the big car?"

"You asking me?" Stew said, trying to find her in the rearview. "Because if you are, skip it. I don't remember. That day is a blank. I just barely remember living in Viroqua. I know I had to share a bed with Doc. And the dog howled all the time. Mickey, I think it was."

"That could have been the guy," Tess went on, ignoring his contribution. "I remember him picking up our stuff from the front porch and driving us into town, but I can't recall his face, or what Mother called him. She didn't introduce him to us. Why? I've often wondered about that. It would have been good manners and she was always such a sticker for manners. Her *not* doing it was like the Baskerville hound that *didn't* bark."

DeeJay said, "God, how dumb kids are. How innocent. How easy it is to trick them. How easy it was for Mattie."

"The man was tall," Doc said, "that I know. And I remember I didn't recognize him. I'd never seen him before, at church or the Co-op or anywhere. But I didn't dwell on him that day. I never thought of him as possibly someone special to Mattie. Why should I? I was concerned with where we were going, not who was taking us."

"That's what I said earlier, who *was* the guy?"

"He'd have to be tall," DeeJay said, "because Mattie was tall. I can't see her giving up everything—home, children, reputation—for some Mr. Five-by-Five."

"We'll never know," Stew said. "But I won't buy him being the hired man."

"Why not?"

"Because I see him as better than that. Gutsy, lots of

(*163*)

ambition, not afraid to take a chance. He wouldn't be shoveling shit and sawing logs for some farmer in the hills when the war was going full-blast and everybody with any sand at all was working in a defense plant somewhere. No," he added, slowing it down, "I'll buy Mattie being ripe for picking but I won't buy her being dumb. She wouldn't choose some dollar-a-day handyman. I believe she's always known exactly what she was doing. She took the bus to Custer City instead of the train because she had just so much money. She stayed in town with Willard instead of out in the country with Frank because the place was handier for her, easier to come and go from, less obvious. It wasn't because she preferred Willard to Frank. And in Tucson she knew exactly what she was doing with those rich TB patients of hers. You talk about—"

"We talk about why Mother left," Doc broke in; it was emotionless, yet deliberate, "and we talk about who she left with. But no one's ever asked *why she came back.*"

"Crotch wore out," DeeJay said.

Doc let go a loud breath. "That's a little crude, isn't it?"

Her response was sharp, instant. "Don't scold me, Wallace! You do and I'll stomp your sailor hat and throw it in the creek. My Ah Fook fortune cookies tell me that Mattie Ellen Charlotte took off because she had a chance at a super-sweet shackup and she wasn't about to let it pass. You don't drag helpless babes from pillar to post and then dump them in the middle of Frontier Land with a couple Elmer Gantry types unless you are after *jollies.* I mean the big ones, the heavy breathers. The kind that make you swear you don't give a shit anymore about mundane things like hearth and home." Her voice softened somewhat. "But after almost a year of that she may have started to get her breath back. The honeymoon was over and there hadn't been any wedding bells. *That's* why she came back."

Doc leaned forward and grabbed DeeJay's hand where it

lay on the back of the seat and made a fervent show of kissing it. "Dear heart, I retract, I retract. I'll never scold you again. But promise you won't stomp my sailor hat. Even if I had one."

They laughed outright, all of them, and it wasn't just civility. They had touched the untouchable for the first time in their lives, had cornered the ghost of their childhood and faced it down without fear or pain. Now they were laughing and it was like a draft of victory wine. DeeJay lit a Pall Mall and Stewart unwrapped two Wrigleys while keeping one hand on the steering wheel, and passed one stick back to Tess and the other to Doc. Doc responded with, "You still want to get practical about those days, Stewart? If I asked you if you remembered those stringy beef roasts Aunt May used to serve on Sundays, would that be practical enough for you?"

Stew said he remembered eating tough beef but he wasn't sure it was Custer City. He didn't know where it was.

Doc elaborated for him. "That beef was stringier than pea pods. I'd chew it and chew it and it just wouldn't go down my throat. It was like the more I chewed the more it swelled. Probably the saliva, if I had any saliva left. Of course, Aunt May saw it as the child's rebellion against the adult, inspired by the devil, and wouldn't let me leave the table until I'd eaten every last bite on my plate. The guilt invoker she used was that there were poor, starving Crow Indian children who didn't have anything but ground corn and a few roots to eat, so I could rest assured I was going to finish my roast beef. Even if it took all day. She always added that part about all day. And it would have taken me that long except for the fact that Mattie helped me. Secretly, of course. She'd glide past my chair in that way she had of walking and manage to reach in and grab one of those pieces of beef off my plate. A few minutes later she'd float by again and sneak another piece. I don't know what she did with them, probably hid them in her hankie. She was always carrying a hankie."

"So where's the practical?" Stew asked, exaggerating it with hunched shoulders. "I thought you were going to give me practical."

Doc did a timing delay and then said, "After Mattie left I had to *eat* that beef. Is that practical enough for you?"

They giggled for a while then gradually grew quiet. After a few miles Stew noticed that the gas gauge was showing low and pulled off the Interstate at the first exit. The name of the service station was unknown to him and the posted price of $1.54 a gallon he thought outrageous, which he told the attendant. The attendant was an older man, dressed in a uniform of some sort, but hatless. His hands looked as if they had absorbed a lifetime of grease and his clothes smelled like a cold radiator. Stew didn't watch him fill the tank but studied the surrounding area. The land was flat and brown and brittle-looking, like pastry dough that has baked too long. His eyes sought the horizon and for some reason he remembered the time on Aurora Boulevard in Seattle when he glanced up and saw far to the southeast what looked like an unusual cloud formation. It proved to be Mount Rainier, darkish, snow-draped, a spectral pyramid adrift in the sky some seventy miles away. It was dramatic, even romantic, and he never forgot it. Here there was nothing. Flat, dull, empty space in every direction.

The attendant must have noticed the Buick's license plate, because he said to Stew, not looking at him, "Colorado, huh?"

"It's my brother's car. I'm actually from Wash—"

"In Denver once. During the war. Nice town. Quiet. Lots of factories there now, I guess."

"It's the first time we've been together in a lot of years," said Stew, nodding at the people inside the car. "We're on our way to see our father in Wisconsin. In La Crosse, on the river. The Mississippi. He's had a stroke."

The attendant withdrew the hose and replaced the gas cap. "Check that oil?" He still hadn't looked at Stew.

Stewart answered that he guessed it was probably a good idea and when the man had finished, Doc signed the credit slip and Stew headed back out onto the interstate. He was scheduled to drive until lunchtime, that was the plan. "I guess no one's hungry," he said to them. "I didn't hear any cries for food."

"Are you kidding? After *that* breakfast?"

"How about later? Anybody got any ideas?"

"We can look at something around Omaha," Doc suggested. "That's a couple of hours from here. Or maybe Council Bluffs. That's in Iowa. Across the Missouri."

"Sounds sinister," Tess remarked. "Across the Missouri."

DeeJay said it sounded like a John Wayne movie.

Doc said, "It means that once you cross the river it's goodbye *West*."

" 'Goodbye, proud world, I'm going home,' " Tess began quoting with a mock solemnity. " 'You're not my friend and I'm not thine; Long through thy weary crowds I've roamed, But now, proud world, I'm going home; A secret nook in a pleasant land, bosomed in yon green hills alone.' "

"God, that's sticky," DeeJay moaned. "Sticky, sticky, sticky!" and her eyes closed and she shook her head violently,

Stew could hardly avoid witnessing the performance, sitting next to her, but he chose to ignore it. It was hard to do. DeeJay's animation could be impressive in a small group, and of course language had always been her deadliest weapon. She could focus certain words as if they were lasers. *Shit*, for example. She could make the word *shit* actually smell. What she needed was to be bested *in kind*, but there were few who could do it. Perhaps none. The clearest recollection Stew had of Richard Kelley was that *he* had never been able to do it. In a fair fight, or a foul, DeeJay could shred Kell alive, could make him look like a gasping first-grader pretending he had to go to the bathroom so he would miss the hard part of the day's lesson. She was like a spirited horse, defiant, proud, and thinking now that he might head her before she charged again, he turned in his seat and said to Tess, "Do you still think of those hills as home? I mean, like in the poem?"

"Not home, not at all," Tess answered, and it was dismissive. "But I think of them as green, which is what the poem says. In fact, the color of Wisconsin hills is how I've often defined green." She stopped then to prepare her words, lining them up as she would pots of paint. "Vitriolic," she began, "that takes a decent first step toward saying what I mean. A deep, throbbing . . . *drenched* kind of green."

For DeeJay the words might as well have been a red flag, for she charged them instantly, her black eyes flashing. "Not today, kiddo!" she snapped. "Not in November. Even exiled natives like me know there's no green like that where we're going. Not now."

She was loose again, but before Stew could ready something, Doc stepped in. "Lord, you're no fun at all," he said to her, but the remark was so palliative, so full of allowances that Stew's first thought was, My God, he's afraid of her!

"Describing color is easy," DeeJay kept on, although a lot of the acid had drained from her words. "Try noncolor some time, like what's outside the car windows right now."

They all looked, it was as if a new game had been introduced and this was the beginning. "I see shit tones," Tess said, taking the first turn. "Old shit that's been in the sun for a day or two. Enough to acquire a little crust."

"I'm thinking more of dirty water," Doc put in. "The

(*168*)

stuff I threw in the yard on the ridge place when Mattie washed the clothes."

Stew kept it going. "I'm reminded of rainclouds. The kind that hang motionless over Seattle for ten days straight. This would be about the eighth day."

"All finished?" asked DeeJay. "If so, I will now describe to you what a noncolor is. It is the desert in southeastern Arizona on a June morning." Her voice had picked up some excitement. "A June morning in 1946 to be exact, seen from the window of a bus from Montana. I remember waking up when the light first came and looking out and seeing the greatest expanse of desert I'd ever seen. The only one, I might add. But it wasn't all sand, that surprised me. It was a million single islands of sagebrush surrounded by sand, plus some of those fancy trees with the traffic-cop arms standing around here and there. There was some creosote and some mesquite too, but all that stuff did was make the desert look flatter. God! And when the bus stopped at Benson, I think it was Benson, and I stepped out onto the ground—wham, I never knew heat like that existed! This was our new home? This was the much-anticipated Arizona?" She stopped to catch her breath. "For a long time after that I used to have this dream where I'd died and gone to hell and the devil was welcoming me. His tail would be dragging in the sand and he'd be wearing his red beanie and rubbing his hands together like some underworld Uriah Heep. 'Welcome, young lady,' he'd say, 'welcome to hell!' Then he'd walk over to this huge furnace and yank the door open. Cymbals would clash and trumpets would blare and this blast of heat would rush out. I'd peer at the flames and then at the devil and I'd say, 'Shit, devil, this is going to be a snap. I'm from *Tucson!*'"

No one could make a comeback like DeeJay. She could be tottering at the absolute cliff edge of disaster and suddenly turn everything around, march away from the abyss with her audience cheering instead of cocking their pistols for the *coup de grâce*. Her victories were inevitable, like George Blanda kicking field goals in the waning seconds of game after game. Stew remembered that as a young girl in the Tucson years she would do the same thing on Chrismas Eve, spitting out her contempt for present after present only to explode with gratitude over some insignif- icant, bottom-of-the-pile gift. Her devil-at-the-furnace reminded Stew of Mattie, how in those days she had taken the monotony of desert heat and given it a moment of sparkle. "Hey," he called to them, loudly, for they were still caught up in their enjoyment of DeeJay's story, "do you remember Mattie's summer thing in Tucson?"

That brought them back. "What summer thing?" DeeJay asked, resenting the intrusion and not totally able to keep it from her voice.

"About the heat." He was hurrying without intending it. "How she'd get up from the table in the mornings while we were eating breakfast and go to the window—"

"Oh God, yes!" DeeJay blurted, taking over again. "I remember! She'd go to the window with her huaraches slapping on the floor and pull the curtain aside and peer up at the sun and groan in this five-thousand-year-old voice, 'Another damned beautiful day in the Old Pueblo!' "

They laughed, remembering, and Doc kept it going. "That ancient voice," he said, "I'd forgotten she could do that. Actually, she could make her voice be anything she wanted, play it like an instrument . . . different keys . . . different moods. It was a real gift she had. I'd forgotten."

"She could do more than that with her voice," Tess exclaimed, going brighter now with a new memory. "We had this program one time when I was going to Tucson High. PTA maybe, possibly one of those Parents Go to Class things. Anyway, Mother was with me that night and this boy I knew—he was in several of my classes—came

(*170*)

up and introduced us to his father. I can remember looking at his father and thinking, *Oooh, good-looking man!* It embarrassed me a little because he had these real dreamy eyes and I wasn't used to that in men. Boys, yes, but not men. I glanced over at Mother, I suppose to lessen my embarrassment, you know how kids that age are, and I saw her whole face change when she looked at that man. Her eyes, her expression, her voice—"

"Voice?"

"She had on that black dress with the white diagonal stripe, I don't know if any of you remember it. Very tasteful, I can still see it. She had good taste in clothes, which was another thing I didn't realize at the time. She knew what went with things. Colors, patterns. If she'd had any money I'm sure she'd have been a real fashionplate. I imagine that black outfit with the stripe was the only dress she had then. I never thought of how many she had, you know how high school girls are."

"What about her voice? You said her voice changed."

"Yes. She said, 'Hello, Mr. So-and-So, I'm pleased to meet you. It seems our children are good friends. . . .' And her voice was so different, so soft and deep at the same time, so . . . aware. I remember looking at her and thinking, *What's happening? Why are you changing your voice?* She was suddenly another woman standing there. She was responding to this good-looking man as if she carried an antenna inside her. It shocked me. Her appearance changed too, it wasn't just her voice. You know how tall she was, well, she sort of eased her shoulders back and stood even taller. It was as if she were saying, *I'm not just anyone, I'm tall. Queens . . . the truly regal are tall.*"

"Talk about turning it on," DeeJay said, "how about those eyes of hers? When she moved her head a certain way and looked to the side and then looked back quickly—"

Stewart cut her off. "You want to talk eyes? I'll talk eyes with you. She used to turn them loose on those poor defenseless men in the TB cabins. She took me with her a lot in those days. She would stand at the foot of the patient's bed and study his chart and maybe write something on it, then she'd lift her head and fix her eyes on the guy and say in this voice I never heard her use anywhere else, 'Have you had your sponge bath, Mr. Goldberg? Would you like me to give you one? Give you a sponge bath?' " He laughed in remembered embarrassment. "Those poor helpless fools, they would just melt! They'd squirm under their sheets and look up at Mattie and their eyes would simply sag shut. Jesus!"

"She turned a lot of that power into the Gifts for Mattie Program, if I remember correctly," DeeJay said. "Things started showing up in our house. New things. Jars of creamed herring, chocolates, pieces of expensive crystal, doilies and napkin sets, furry slippers, slinky nightgowns, slinky robes."

Doc was next. "Tess said something a minute ago about Mother being *aware*. I suppose it wasn't what she was saying exactly, it was what she was thinking. Obviously, it always came out *bedroom*. That's why her lungers melted, she made them think of the same thing." DeeJay started to interrupt and Doc stopped her. "But I don't think she was interested in *them* so much, she wanted them to be interested in *her*. She wanted the . . . the power that represents."

Tess said, "We have waitresses at our restaurants who are like that. Dave has a special name for them. He calls them prick teasers."

No one spoke. Does she mean Mattie was one? Stew wondered. A semi truck passed them at high speed, shaking the car. It seemed a personal affront. When it was gone

(*172*)

he said, "Mattie was a lightning rod. She attracted, she drew in."

"You mean instead of putting out?"

"Funny, funny."

"I remember something," Doc began. It was preoccupied, as if the picture he was seeing hadn't caught up with his announcement of it. "I remember . . . she met someone . . . thought she'd get married. . . ." It was mostly question.

"Oh God, yes," DeeJay squealed, and the picture was obviously in focus for her. "That was . . . Mack Thomas . . . Thomas Mack. . . ." She let it go and turned to Tess in the backseat with something totally new. "Christ, that's the time you *slugged* her!"

A snort of surprise came from Doc. "You what?"

Tess said, "I didn't *slug* her. It wasn't like that," but the denial was oblique and Stew could see in the rearview that Tess was keeping her eyes averted. Ordinarily, DeeJay sprang at hesitation like a cat at a trapped bird, but not this time. "Well, maybe not slugged," DeeJay said, stressing the word yet not making it harsh, "but there was a definite laying on of hands." Her voice edged higher. "Don't forget, lady, I was there. I saw it."

"Well, you tell it then. You brought it up." It was snappish, unusual for Tess, but perhaps they were all being unusual. They were trying to free themselves from the awkwardness of being strangers and it was proving difficult. The years of separation were like a quicksand that kept pulling them back in. He wondered if four middle-aged people, despite sharing identical roots, could continue sticking their fingers down the throat of memory, hour after hour, without eventually spewing up some bile. Wouldn't they finally uncover some moment in the past when they hadn't all been on the same side of an event, not all Christians or all lions? Perhaps that same fear was touching each of them, because both Tess and DeeJay backed away from their sudden fracture. "You tell it," DeeJay said.

"No, you go ahead."

At last Tess took over and went on with the story. "Mother had brought this Mack guy over to the house on several occasions to play poker with Dave and me. Penny-ante stuff, quarter limit. Mother had an apartment out on North Stone. Doc, you were back East playing baseball and Stewart was in Wisconsin, I believe, and DeeJay, were you living with Mother or did you have your own—"

"I had my own apartment."

"Right. But you came to our place with Mattie that evening. It was the tail end of July, hotter than Billy Blue as Dave always says, and we'd made plans to take a cabin up in Flagstaff for the month of August. Just Dave and me and the kids, who were little then. In fact, I was packing their suitcases when you and Mattie got there."

"Your house smelled like a chili factory."

"You remember that? Hortense—that's our maid, she had just come with us—Hortense and her husband had gone across the line at Naco and picked up several bushels of chilies and brought them back. We were roasting them. You need a flame oven to roast chilies properly and Dave had installed one in the carport. If you do it right you can freeze an entire winter's supply. We've roasted a lot of chilies, Mirasol mostly, quite hot. Anyway, I went into the bedroom to do some packing for the trip and Mother came in and started telling me what a wonderful person this Mack was, how genuine and responsible, how they'd talked about getting married. She treated the word *married* as if it would frighten me. 'Mack's excited about it,' she said, 'but I told him I wanted Tess to be my bridesmaid, that it was the only way I would consent to the wedding. The four of us can drive over to Lordsburg for the ceremony—you don't

(*174*)

have to wait three days if you get married in New Mexico. I can get off from the san the first two weeks in August,' she went on, 'which is perfect because that's when Mack has his vacation scheduled.'

" 'Well, Mother,' I said, 'if you're excited about getting married then so am I. I don't know Mack but apparently you do and that's the only thing that matters. However, Dave and I are leaving in a couple days for the cabin. We'll be there the entire month of August and won't be able to stand up for you guys. But I'm sure Mack's got friends who can. You too. Surely there must be some nurses you can ask.'

" 'Oh Tess, no,' she said, and covered her mouth with her hands and gave me that little-girl look. Can't you just see it? I could almost hear the violins. Then she began telling me how *they* had to work for a living and couldn't take off just anytime they wanted, whereas *I* had the whole summer free of classes and of course *Dave* in his position could come and go as he pleased. He could easily take September instead of August.

" 'That may be true,' I said, 'but we're committed for the cabin in August, and that's that. You and Mack have scheduled your vacations in August, and that's that as well. I guess it's what planning is all about, isn't it, Mother? We go to Flag, you and Mack go to Lordsburg and get married.'

" 'Well, I won't get married!' she announced. 'If I can't have my Tessie for a bridesmaid then I won't have anyone. I won't do it!' Her bottom lip came out, something you don't see a lot in a grown woman. I actually expected her to stamp her foot, but all she accomplished was to make me mad. I could feel it coming and there was no way I could stop it. I said, 'Mother, this is silly. You have your life and we have ours!' But she kept pouting and when she realized I wasn't going to reconsider she threw her head

(*175*)

back and got this supercilious look on her face and said, 'Well, if you're not interested in my happiness and who I spend my life with . . .' And she just trailed it off like that, like she always has, wanting to make me feel guilty, acting as if I'd *betrayed* her. Something in me just snapped. I said, 'Why don't you just run off again, Mother? You did once. It should be easier this time, there'll be no little kids to leave behind!' "

"Which is when I walked into the room," DeeJay said, picking up the story. "Mattie's face was white as sugar and Tess's looked like a red pepper. I knew something heavy was going down but before I could make a move Tess walked over to Mattie and said in the coldest, deadliest voice I've ever heard, 'I owe you this. It's for Montana!' and slapped Mattie's face. Hard! So hard that Mother's whole body shook. She didn't go down but let me give you this qualifier in three-inch type—*I don't know why!*"

After a dead moment, Doc said, "I'd never heard that story. No one's ever mentioned it," and his voice sounded as if it were coming from the rear of the station wagon and not the backseat.

"What did Mattie say?" Stewart asked.

"Nothing," DeeJay answered. "Absolutely nothing. She just turned around and left the room."

A stillness dropped over them then that lasted for miles. The country turned hilly. Exits came closer together, an additional traffic lane abruptly widened their half of the interstate. There was a surge in the number of vehicles, especially delivery vans. "Must be getting close to Omaha," Stewart observed, as much to try his voice again as to declare the obvious. "Who's for chow? Anybody hungry?"

"It's third and long," Doc said to him. "Call the play that'll give you the first down."

DeeJay said, "I thought we'd decided on something across the river."

Stew answered that that was fine with him, whatever they wanted to do, he wasn't exactly suffering the bloat of starvation.

Doc said, "No truck stops, okay? I don't like them. Used to be, when I was on the road playing ball, that a bunch of semis parked outside a restaurant was a sure sign of good food."

"Actually," DeeJay said, "it was because the drivers were all inside gang-banging the waitress."

"Right," Stew answered. He unwrapped a fresh stick of gum and then massaged the back of his neck. The trip wasn't what he had expected it to be when he was riding to the airport with Bev. When was that, yesterday? Was that possible? It seemed more like a week. The time convolution was bad enough but he hadn't made allowances for the long hours in the car. The more appealing picture had been the one of him sweeping into the La Crosse hospital, doors opening magically before him, doctors seeking him out, medical personnel pressing back against the wall as he passed. *It's him, it's the engineer son from the Pacific Northwest.* Instead, he was sitting stiff-necked and headachy in a cube of dead air, a queasy movement in his stomach that might have been hunger, and might not.

The road became a bridge and he crossed the river, very narrow and cluttered, very unhistorical, then picked a restaurant on the Council Bluffs side. He felt satisfied with himself, there was a sense of goals established and met. He had made the river in safety and on time, delivering his charges to what looked like an excellent place to eat.

It was. The restaurant was medium-crowded, neat, there was no odor of hot grease and breading. The waitress came quickly to their table and left four menus and a pot of hot coffee. She returned with four glasses of ice water and with the pleasantest of smiles informed them she would be back in a few minutes to take their order.

"I'm impressed," DeeJay said.

Stewart said, looking at her, "You always were easy that way." She didn't respond. There was fatigue showing in her face but it was hard to say exactly where. She had a bruised, depleted look about her that the makeup didn't quite hide. He thought he'd noticed the same thing at the airport yesterday but there was a shock to seeing DeeJay for the first time that more or less took over. It was the height, the carriage, the great dark eyes. What was tired was inside, underneath, behind what you *saw*. It was as if somewhere in her life there had been a great many races to enter and she had entered the bulk of them, there'd been fads to follow that were exciting for a while before they fell off, candles to burn that had given a lovely light, and then gone out.

Tess broke in, suggesting facetiously that Stewart be elected Permanent Restaurant Selector, which motion being immediately seconded, was immediately carried. Scanning the dessert section of his menu, Doc muttered, "We gotta four kinds pie. We gotta mimce . . . we gotta stromberree . . ."

In unison the others lowered their menus and stared at Doc, but it was Tess who put it into words. "You know who used to say that, don't you?"

He looked at her. "Yes."

"You know something else? This is the first time Irv Donner has even come up. And he's the reason we made the trip."

T E N

IT WAS TWO-THIRTY when DeeJay drove away from the restaurant at Council Bluffs. Clouds still hid the sun and she could get no sense of direction, they seemed to be heading into a new world as well as a new state, a leached and gloomy place where the sun never shone. She felt an abrupt sense of loss. An image of blue-green deodar flashed through her mind, the orange of oleander flowers, a fountain splashing sun-blued water onto a red-tiled inner court.

The vision was short-lived, however, for a rank odor suddenly assailed her nostrils. Someone had broken wind, a fact that was unmistakable in a closed car. "All right," she said, speaking in an exaggerated protective nasal, "who cut the cheese?"

Stewart and Doc were sitting in the backseat. One of them coughed and the other fumbled for a window. So did Tess, who was riding in front, and with both windows open the smell quickly dissipated. "Confession booth is open," DeeJay announced. "Confidentiality guaranteed."

Stew said, "There is no disguising that smell, is there?" It sounded slightly disgusted.

Tess entered the conversation with an explanation of how her husband reacted to such things. " 'You know what?' he'll say. 'While we were in that restaurant eating, something crawled into this car and died!' "

They laughed. "Myself, I don't pussyfoot around," offered Doc. "I just say, 'All right, who shit?' "

"I've witnessed some masterful attempts at evasion in my time." This from Stewart. "I've seen people wave their arms and shake their head and go into all kinds of body movements in order to dissipate the smell. I saw a certain party one time breathing in through his nose and breathing out through his mouth, directing the exhaled air onto the offending gas by discreet movements of his head. All in complete silence, of course."

"What a price to pay," DeeJay said. "He must have suffered dreadfully on the inhale."

"Anyone we know?" asked Tess.

"Yes," answered Stew, "he happens to be in the car with us at this very moment."

"Confession box closed," DeeJay declared, flipping Doc the finger.

They laughed. Doc said, "At least we've kept it in the family."

"Speaking of breaking wind," said Tess, a new inflection in her voice, "the champion of all time had to be Irv Donner."

The name wasn't the conversational shock it had been in the restaurant because they had talked about him during lunch, questioning what had caused the stroke and expressing what they knew about thrombosis and *cardiovascular accident*, the term Stella had used on the phone. They wondered what Irv's condition was today, Wednesday, and decided that one of them would call the La Crosse hospital from wherever they stopped that night and ask for an update on his condition. Doc said they could possibly get as far as one of the towns north of Des Moines, perhaps Ames or Mason City, depending on whether everything went all right, no car trouble or bad weather.

"You didn't dare go into the front room with Irv after Mattie had fixed a big meal," Tess was saying.

"Front room, hell, *any* room."

DeeJay said, "Big meal, hell, any *meal*."

"Remember in the barn when he'd be milking the cows?" Doc asked. He didn't address the question to anyone in particular, he just threw it up to the group. Doc did that a lot, he liked to make things competitive.

"Yes," Tess said, "I remember the barn farts."

"Remember how he'd lift one cheek from the milk stool and rip one out? You knew there had to be damage, either to his overalls or to the stool."

Tess said, "I've actually seen the cows jump."

"Was Dad really crude about it?" asked Stewart, and the sincerity in his voice was almost painful. "I ask because I don't remember his farting. I wish I did."

"Not crude perhaps," Tess answered him, "just *devoted*." They all laughed at her emphasis. It was unexpected; the *bon mot* wasn't Tess's forte. She was totally disingenuous, she could laugh at her own humor, as now, but she was never wry, never droll. Not intentionally.

DeeJay said, "Stew's got a point. With the exception of the farting, Irv wasn't crude. I can't even remember him swearing, at least not around me."

"He didn't swear," Doc confirmed. "*Heck* would have been obscene in his mouth." Stewart started to interrupt, but Doc fended him off. "There were some other things Irv didn't do. To his everlasting credit he didn't shit in an

(*181*)

empty corn crib and wipe his ass on one of the cobs. Nor did he close one nostril off with his finger and blow a streamer of snot out the other. I've seen a lot of farmers do that. Usually they hit their shoe."

Stewart said, "Dad wasn't a farmer."

"He was at first. Before he got the sawmill going good he was a pure farmer. I remember his stories about his chickens, how one year they died faster than he could bury them. He loved to tell doom stories."

"What Irv Donner was," Tess said to them, and it was in her authoritative, oldest-child voice, "was a walking, talking, real-life contradiction. A paradox. He had an innate cruelty that was a wonder to behold, yet I never knew a man who could cry easier, or over so little. He was always spouting philosophy, yet none of it was his. It came straight out of *The Old Farmer's Almanack*."

"God, the almanacs!" DeeJay exclaimed. "I thought about them yesterday on the plane."

"Which means you haven't forgotten the pithies."

"Forget the pithies? Are you kidding? To forget the pithies would be to forget Irvin Donner. They defined the man as nothing else could have. He was Edgar A. Guest reincarnated. He was Mr. Hiram Overalls in that American Gothic painting by Grant Wood, except that he wasn't holding a pitchfork in his hand. It was a *Farmer's Almanack*."

The two men in the backseat laughed.

"In fact," she went on, heartened, "I want a contribution of pithies from each of you, something that will capture once and for all the essence of this man, this endless sayer of parochial sayings. I want your best effort and I want it now!"

"Oh Lord," Stewart groaned, "I haven't heard an Irv Donner pithy in so many years—"

"There will be no exceptions! We cannot possibly have forgotten that many adages and apothegms." There was an uncomfortable silence and she said, "I will ask for volunteers first, after that it's command performance."

Tess was first. *"Some minds are like concrete,"* came her contribution, *"thoroughly mixed and permanently set."*

DeeJay had expected Tess to be first. "Bully!" she cried. "Good start! Good example-setting!"

Life was the subject of Doc's entry. *"Life is not a matter of holding good cards, but of playing a poor hand well."*

"Page seventy-six, March 1943 issue, right?" DeeJay cried, and took her hands from the steering wheel long enough to applaud. "It is appropriate that I present my own offering at this time, which is as follows: *There is no smile so beautiful as the one that has struggled through tears.*" She waited. "How about it, panel? Is that sententious enough for you?"

Stew said tiredly, "Yes, but not very original."

"There *are* no original pithies, you dummy!" She searched for him in the rearview. "And quit stalling, okay? This is a communal project and full participation is expected. Otherwise, I start kicking ass and taking names."

Stewart groaned, and when he began to squirm in his seat, Doc leaned toward him and said, *"Itching for what you want won't do it, you've got to scratch for it."*

"Oh, top-grade, Wallace!" DeeJay cried, switching to him in the mirror. "But I was thinking more along the lines of *Talking is like flour, you must sift first.*" Then she switched back to Stewart. "Come on, little friend, we're waiting."

Tess took pity and turned to him. "Don't despair. Remember that *Everything comes to him who waits.*"

The shower of praise for these bonus efforts merely heightened the look of dismay on Stewart's face. "I'm supposed to *compete* with you guys?" he moaned. Then he laid his head back against the seat and rolled his eyes and muttered, "Shit."

"*Out of the mouths of babes*," Doc began, and DeeJay finished it for him, "*come words they shouldn't have used in the first place.*"

It did the trick. Stew sat forward in his seat, winked at Tess and said in a casual voice, "*Better to keep your mouth shut and be thought a fool, than to open it and remove all doubt.*"

A chorus of mixed boos and huzzahs closed out the contest and they returned to their individual silences. It was not unusual, their conversations had been tidal the entire trip, rising up to a central eminence, pooling, ebbing away.

DeeJay turned her attention to the Iowa countryside. It had been mostly jut and wallow when they first left the river but she could see that it had changed. The land was a vast sea that washed up here and there on tiny islands of farm buildings that were perfectly identical—huge red barns, immense blue silos, gray sheds, a windbreak of black leafless trees trying to hide a small white house. There were never any people visible. Livestock and an occasional dog, yes, but no people. Particularly no children, as if some sinister Pied Piper had passed through the land a few days before. Crouched behind the trees, the houses looked crushingly lonely. DeeJay knew that inside the houses the only sound would be a clock ticking in a room you couldn't see. There were no carpets, only a few throw rugs. There was wood everywhere, floors, cupboards, desks, tables, chairs, all polished and dust-free and yet, oddly, reflecting no light. On a mantel in the quietest room of all, twin lamps with floral shades framed a picture of a young man in a soldier's uniform. A benevolent visage of Jesus Christ looked down from one wall but on the others hung plaques and painted plates and, in the small room with the piano, a ponderous oval portrait of a stern old-fashioned couple, he seated, she standing beside and slightly behind. The faces were difficult to make out because an ancient oak tree outside the window had never let in much light. In the kitchen there were no dishes in the sink, no cloths or towels, nothing lying *out*, and on the stove a kettle sang . . . *How still this house, how still it is.*

Yet she remembered how busy farm kitchens could be in the fall, the men in a lot somewhere butchering and making sausage, the women canning fruit from the orchards and vegetables from the garden, "putting up" as they called it. For a moment she could actually smell the Wisconsin house again, the utterly rotten odor of sauerkraut that Mattie usually had "working" in the wooden half-barrels, the hot vinegar smell that permeated the house when she processed the last of the "eating corn" into pints of corn relish, the sweet-sour smell of rhubarb cooking down hour after hour into the thick pink sauce Irv loved. She could remember him hunched over his plate after the meal was finished and everyone else had left the table, a bowl of sauce in front of him, slabs of fresh-baked bread marbleized with cold butter, and it just came out of her mouth, shattering the stillness, "Lord, what a sweet tooth that man had."

"Dad?" It was Stewart's question.

"Sure Dad, who else? Mr. Irvin Donner, ex-paterfamilias. He could scarf up rhubarb like no one I've ever seen."

"Sherbet too. He loved sherbet." Doc this time. "Except he mispronounced the word. *Sherbert*, he called it."

Tess said, "He never went into town for any of that stuff, did he? I never saw him go into a restaurant. I never ate with him in a restaurant in my entire life."

"I think you're right," Stew added pensively. "That time he came to Seattle I don't remember us going out to eat. In fact, I know we didn't."

Tess offered the observation that Irv was not a monstrous

eater. "He was not a glutton. I never saw him attack his plate or stuff his mouth full of food, that sort of thing. Not like some men I've seen. Especially that kind of man."

Stewart said, "What do you mean, that kind?"

"Laborer, farmer, working man. The kind that wears overalls to the table."

"Nothing wrong with that."

"I'm not saying there is, Stew. I'm saying Irv Donner had his own special way of eating. And I'm saying that there was a curious sort of refinement in it. He wasn't up on his Emily Post, not like Mattie, but he had a form of manners nevertheless. He wasn't gross or uncouth."

"Except when he had gas."

There was a quick automatic laughter at the remark, but it didn't last. It wasn't what they wanted, not now.

"I'll tell you what he wouldn't do," said Doc, "he wouldn't change his mind about food. Once he decided he liked a particular thing, or disliked it, that was it."

"He wasn't fickle, that's for sure."

"If he liked carrots in a stew," Doc continued, "he wouldn't accept a substitution of turnips. He wanted horseradish with his beef, corn relish with his scrapple. He preferred his eggs over well, I remember that. Bacon crisp, almost burned. Fried potatoes well done, no onion."

Tess said, "I remember the time—"

"Yes, I know what you're thinking. You're thinking of the time Mattie bought those used appliances at the church —one of those fifty-cent sales they were always having— and served poached eggs and waffles for breakfast the next day. For a surprise." He gave a snort of a laugh. "Irv was surprised, all right. A little displeased, too, if you remember."

Tess said, "You bet I do," and it was harsh, there was none of the ease of fond recollection about it. "I remember that morning perfectly. One of you kids, I'm sure it was

DeeJay, got excited about the waffle iron and the poaching pan and asked if we couldn't have that kind of breakfast every morning. Irv immediately went into one of his eruption routines, nostrils flaring, lip trembling, the whole intimidating bit. Mattie backed off, as usual. Even DeeJay, as young and pushy as she was, knew that the price for a different kind of breakfast was too high to pay." Tess began to tap her knee, insistently, reprovingly, as if she were calling a student's attention to a faulty test paper, a term missing from an algebraic equation, the wrong declension of an irregular verb. "It was always that way for us then. We were trapped. And you know something else?" She didn't wait, she wasn't looking for answers. "Irv knew it. He knew we were trapped and he used it. He could indulge whatever mood he wanted to indulge and there was nothing we could do about it. That's cruelty. It may even be sadism." Under her breath she muttered an oath. It was inaudible, only the emotion came through. The emotion was disgust, a disgust so pervading and so ancient that in another person it would have been frightening.

They offered no agreement to it, nor any rebuttal. They sensed only that they needed to change the subject but they had no system of selecting a spokesman to do it. It turned out in the end to be Doc. "Childhood is a strange business," he said, and his voice was as edgeless as he could make it. "The time comes when we simply have to get out of it. All the way out. It's like that time Lil and I decided to drive to Wisconsin for a visit. Our kids were little then, we were at a baseball reunion here in Iowa, the eastern part, and Lil figured we'd never have a better shot. Irv had a house in Viroqua by that time and we went directly there. The first day was all right but then everything started to close in. The house was different, I'd never seen it before, but everything else was the same, the way things smelled, the way Dad lived, the regimen, the food. I felt like I was suffocating. I had to get out of the house, out of the town, out of my *childhood*. Do you see what I'm saying? There's a time to be young and vulnerable and that time was gone. I couldn't go back into it. And I didn't want to."

"I wonder," Tess began, and it was pleasant, even musing, "I wonder if that's true for all childhoods or just ours."

"You can't define childhood," Stewart put in, clearly glad to be involved and making a point. "They're all relative, there's no absolutes as to what a childhood *should* be. It's like the first time you stay overnight at a buddy's house. The people are weird, the house is scary, the way they live is lousy. Then a couple years later you stay over again and this time everything is real cool, much better than anything you've got at home. The buddy's family is brighter, sweeter. The kids have more freedom. They're never picked on. The family goes more places and does more things. Their car is better, their food, their furniture—"

"Hell," DeeJay broke in, "in our case it was true! Theirs *was* better," and she laughed exultantly, dragging the others in with her. They did so gladly, they wanted to laugh, it was time, the tide was back in. All except Stew. She could tell from the expression on his face in the rearview that he felt his contribution to the subject had been deprecated. Then his expression abruptly changed. "Your childhood is like your face," he said with a sudden confidence. "It's yours and yours alone. It's like the color of your eyes. It's like your name, you're stuck with it. If your name happens to be Donna Jean, you're really stuck!"

"Why don't you go piss in the fishtank, buster!" And she felt the heat rise in her face. "If you don't like my name don't soil your precious lips with it!"

"Hey, what's the matter, hotshot?" and his face was all archness now, all undisguised delight. "You can't be teased, is that it? Dish it out but can't take it, is that the rap on you, dear little Donna Jean?"

"Oh, we're getting brave now, aren't we? Actually, Stewart, courage is so new for you I worry about it. Really. I don't think you can handle the rush. You're too used to hiding in skirts and letting your brothers and sisters fight your battles for you. Which was never really fair because they didn't get the world handed to them on a fucking silver platter!"

"Time! Time!" Doc was suddenly hanging over the front seat making the hand signals that signified a request for a time out. "Let's cool it, huh? Let's take a breather and talk over our next play, all right?" His hands stayed in the T position and about the time she felt some of the heat drain from her face, he sat back again in his seat.

Tess stepped in then, soft-voiced, patronizing. " 'Be good, sweet maid,' " she said, " 'let those who will be clever.' "

"More poetry, Tess? Is poetry your solution to everything?"

Doc was immediately draped over the front seat again, this time ignoring DeeJay, addressing himself to Tess. "You see this, sister?" His voice flowed into the space between them like warm honey. "Do you realize that these two fallen angels in the car with us have allowed themselves to become angry?"

"As in *Every minute you are angry, you lose sixty seconds of happiness*? That kind of angry?"

"Precisely my meaning, madam. One wonders, for example, if they have considered that *People, like pins, are useless when they lose their heads*."

"Hopefully, they will. After all, *To speak kindly does not hurt the tongue*."

"And doesn't the parallel also apply? *Never throw mud, it will leave you with dirty hands*."

"My sediments exactly. And I remember what Father always said."

"I don't, unfortunately. What was it?"

"Go armed with a laugh, for what is a laugh but a smile that has burst?"

Stewart laughed suddenly, explosively, and so did Dee-Jay, despite herself. She turned in her seat and sought Doc out, winking at him lewdly. "You're so good to me, Smitty," she said, "and I'm so goddamned tired of it!"

The afternoon had hovered over them as thick and sullen as the morning but now, late, it turned hazy, blurring at all its edges. Then, at the last moment, the sun shot through the clouds. Everything brightened, shadows appeared, a consoling thing after all the sameness. The west windows of a passing farmhouse flared redly with the sun's reflection as if tiny fires were exploding inside. For some unaccountable reason, DeeJay remembered that Montana sunsets had looked like that. "Pretty," she said, watching in the car's mirrors, "in a mournful way."

The others had noticed and were turned in their seats looking back, making comments, all except Tess. She said nothing, and would not turn.

The display of life and color was short-lived. The clouds closed again and the light began to fail, the passing fields gave up their far ends to darkness. "I'd better start watching my gas gauge," DeeJay said, for the day dying behind them, and the night looming ahead, had put a sudden uncertainty on things. "Have we got a plan? What's the plan? Anybody?"

Doc told her she should pick up Interstate 35 at Des Moines and take it north. "Then we'll go until we get tired. Until you get tired, I should say, you've got the helm."

"But no charts, no compass. Thanks a lot, sailor."

"Tomorrow we cross into Minnesota and pick up Interstate 90 at Albert Lea, then it's a straight shot east to La Crosse."

A quiet fell and DeeJay could read the mind-flight of everyone in the car, navigating their thoughts to an invisible state line to the north, crossing it and then turning east into a morning sun, toward an unseen river, a hospital waiting in a city on the far bank, a parking lot, a lobby. . . .

"Sounds good to me," said Tess, who was beginning to stir now that the sunset was gone. "What's our estimated arrival at the hospital?"

"I'd say midafternoon. Depends on how far we get tonight and how early we can move out in the morning."

"I think I'll get gas now," DeeJay said, surprised at the blurt of it, at the sound of apprehension in her voice. She took the first exit that offered, and at the service station she instructed the attendant to fill the tank, check the oil, and wash the windshield. She popped the hood release and watched the man as he moved around the car, dipping, inserting, wiping, and when he had finished she said, from inside the car and its stillness, "Well done, thou good and faithful servant."

Stewart said, "I see you use a little poetry yourself once in a while."

"I try to stay open." She got out of the car and walked over to the attendant and handed him Doc's credit card. He took it with an obsequious gesture and said to her, "Kinda gloomy day."

"Kinda," DeeJay answered, and then the words came tumbling out of her mouth as though that single word had turned a key. "We're headed for Wisconsin. La Crosse. It's on the river. We haven't been to La Crosse since we were kids. We didn't live there, it was farther back in the state, in the hills. I mean, where we *lived*. Our father's in a hospital. In La Crosse, I mean. He's suffered a massive stroke. We were all notified last Sunday night. Telephoned. We live in totally different parts—"

"Nice town, La Crosse. River and all. Bluffs." The man

had looked at her that first time but now he wouldn't. "I was there once but on the Minnesota side. Winona, Minnesota. Had an aunt lived there. You been to Winona?"

She shook her head, strangely cut off now from her source of words.

"That'll be twenty-seven eighty-six," the attendant told her. "Your oil was okay."

When she got into the car and drove back onto the interstate she immediately told the others of the conversation. "The guy never once said, 'I'm sorry to hear about your father,' or 'Those things happen.' He just kept studying the credit card. Wouldn't make eye contact for some reason. He didn't—"

"He didn't want to get involved," Tess said.

Stewart said, "The same thing happened to me this morning in Nebraska. I told the guy about Dad and why we were going back and it's like he didn't hear me."

DeeJay said, "You'd think they could have at least been polite. Why didn't they say something?"

Tess said, "Why did you? What made you feel you had to tell someone about a stranger named Irvin Donner?"

They didn't answer, Stewart or DeeJay either one. No one said anything.

When DeeJay reached Interstate 35 she turned north. Downtown Des Moines loomed against the sky like the superstructure of an aircraft carrier that had anchored there and was just turning on its lights. Eventually they came to an exit which read State Fairgrounds. "Now appearing at the State Fair in an exclusive engagement," Dee Jay announced with an imitation trumpet flourish, "the USS *Goodship*. Accompanied by a full squadron of seaplanes. Takeoffs guaranteed, landings to be determined at a later date, depending on the amount of rainfall. An exciting, death-defying, once-in-a-lifetime show, don't miss it if you can!"

They could see the assorted buildings and show pens of the fairgrounds, deserted now. Tess said, "Remember the movie *State Fair* when William Holden and Kim Novak went to the fair?"

"The movie was *Picnic*," Stew corrected her, "and they went on a picnic. Holden sang to her, or she sang to him, whatever." He delayed a moment. "I don't remember the words but I know the melody. I can hum it for you." And he did, although he had to work through several bars of music before the melody could assert itself.

"Oh God," DeeJay moaned.

"I hope you don't call that a musical performance," Doc put in listlessly, whereupon Tess turned to him and said, "It's no worse than what you've been humming for the past half-hour."

"Humming? Me?"

" 'Sonny Boy.' You've been humming Al Jolson's 'Sonny Boy' ever since the sun went down."

Their talk ebbed. The lights of the city gradually disappeared behind them and the blackness became total. There was very little traffic, no one passed them and headlights approaching on the other side of the interstate became a sporadic event. There would be a single isolated light hanging in the darkness far ahead and then it would grow larger and split into a pair of lights, like the eyes of some mysterious creature who had been creeping toward them across the prairie and had finally reached their hiding place. There was no discernible shape to the creature, and no sound, just a faint whine as it passed. A semi truck was the exception; with its brightly colored running lights its approach was unmistakably festive. And it passed not with a whine, but a boom.

"Semi," one of them would announce anonymously, for

the interior of the car was dark and they were merely voices issuing from four separate quadrants of it. They too were creatures. They had journeyed from a visible world to an invisible and it had served not to unite them, but to isolate. They were reluctant to speak, the darkness was energy and they were feeding on it, alien-like, building private thoughts. When finally one of them spoke—it was Stewart—the isolation was thick in his voice. "I don't know . . . I think of him a lot of times . . . the way he used to be. I was awfully young when we lived on the ridge. I get impressions only, bits and pieces, nothing whole. He had a certain smell to him . . . sawdust I think. Maybe gear grease from the saws. I used to watch him shave, I remember, how his eyes would blink when he'd slap the after-shave on his face. The way he'd laugh without making a sound . . . just his shoulders moving. His arms were real big, I remember. And God, he had all that hair!"

"Odd," Doc mused after a bit, but it was a separate thing, unconnected to Stewart. "Odd that he never came to see us when Mattie moved to Viroqua. He never phoned. He was never waiting for us after school, never parked his truck by our house and waited for us to go by on the sidewalk. Regardless of what happened between him and Mattie, you'd think he'd at least want to see us. . . ."

DeeJay expected someone to keep the ruminations going when Doc trailed off, but there was nothing, there was only the engine noise and the wind at the window seams. Then a different sound began to intrude. It was constant, not rising or falling, and she realized finally that it was someone crying. It was the soft, caught sound that crying is when it's unstoppable and yet quiet, wanting no attention. She thought perhaps it was Tess but she wasn't going to look into Tess's individual space in the car to verify it, she didn't want to appear to be *listening*. She knew she wouldn't turn the dash lights back up and grow all alarmed and blurt out, *Who is it? What's the matter? Why are you crying?* They were adults, after all, they could use the darkness as they chose. What difference did it make? Darkness should be a private matter, like thought, like emotion. No one really had the right to ask someone about crying. . . .

It was just before she saw the *Ames Next Exit* sign flash at her from out of the endless monotony that she suspected her body had somehow doubled its weight and was in the process of sinking through the seat. Some of that heaviness was pulling at her eyelids as well, and when she shook her head to throw it off, her neck felt like a breakable glass rod. "That does it," she declared, sitting abruptly erect, and in the next moment she saw the sign that read *Ames Exit*. "I have conferred secretly with my old friend Turkey Lurkey and he has convinced me that the sky may indeed be falling. He suggests that I refrain from further highway driving and seek shelter immediately, for the sky, he insists, is really quite unsafe in this part of Iowa." She reached down and located the rheostat and restored light to the dashboard. "And guess what else, gang? Turkey suggests that I take the whole lot of you with me."

The exit produced the expected arterial stop with a white arrow on a green background pointing left, but it didn't produce the town of Ames. After driving what seemed an excessive distance, she was moved to say, "Well, the town's here somewhere. The Iowa Highway Department gave it a name and an exit number off the interstate system and that's usually a reliable indication. It's not their problem, it's mine. I can't find the damned thing."

The others began to stir in their seats, partly coming back to life and partly deciding to help her look. There was a long curving stretch of road with periodic light poles ahead of them, but apparently nothing at its far end, nothing she could see. "Looks to me like the city of Ames didn't pay its utility bill," Stewart offered, his voice hoarse from disuse, "and the state has cut off its lights."

Several minutes passed and still nothing clustered and electric loomed up to define what a town at night should look like. Tess said, "Should we begin to worry?"

"Should we begin to pray?" asked an equally hoarse Doc.

"I recommend song," DeeJay said. "That's what they do in the lifeboats, the downed aircraft. Song will keep our spirits up and enable us to present a united front, whatever that is. Will you join me, therefore, in singing that beloved Methodist hymn from the Montana frontier, 'O Where Shall Rest Be Found?'" She hummed a suggested key and they cleared their throats and mouthed a few uncoordinated belches of lyric, more like an orchestra tuning up than a quartet of human voices. And it was at that precise moment, as they rounded another blind curve in their mysterious road, that the town of Ames appeared. It burst on the night like a suddenly illuminated gift tree at a surprise party. Their singing voices strengthened accordingly and they entered the blazing oasis of streets singing in surprising harmony—" 'What to do when darkness falls . . . where to flee when sin enthralls . . . where to hide when Satan calls . . . O where shall rest be found?' "

Rest, it turned out, was infinitely easier to find in Ames than the city had been, and to celebrate the luxury of so large a choice of motels, or perhaps to prove that Ames was really more than just a white mirage in a black desert, they traveled the full length of the main street, turned around, then drove leisurely back to their point of entry at the south end, where they took adjoining rooms at the Colonial for fifty-two dollars, plus tax.

Carrying luggage in from the car, DeeJay was surprised

to discover that a wind had come up and blown all the clouds from the sky. It was active in the motel parking lot as well, alternately gusting and swirling as if on a hunt, as if searching for something hidden in the darkness beyond the lights.

Needing the exercise, they walked two long blocks to a restaurant that seemed as though it would be a warmly reclusive place, given its soft lighting and dim interior. Once inside, however, there was a lot of noise and the lights were too bright.

DeeJay noticed that Tess's eyes were swollen. She seemed preoccupied and spoke very little during the meal.

Doc looked tired. His temples seemed grayer than before and the downward lines at the corners of his mouth were clearly visible. And he was nervous, chewing his lip, tapping one hand constantly into the palm of the other as if expecting a hard ground ball to come his way. He ordered a deluxe hamburger with a side of onion rings, plus a piece of pie with milk, and ate quickly. When he finished he sat back in his seat, his neck stalky and his shoulders lightly sloping, and shot imaginary baskets with crumpled napkins, arching the wadded paper balls through the air with a deft motion, whispering, "Two points . . ." then another shot, ". . . two . . ."

Stewart appeared more interested in events beyond their booth. He concentrated on watching the waitresses, the busboys, the customers, the cooks in the serving window that he could see perfectly from his side. He sat erect with his elbows on the table and made comments on everyone who passed with a disjointed mumbling sarcasm, a restless-cherub look on his face.

Back at the motel, DeeJay stood outside and smoked a final cigarette while the others went in and threw themselves into bed. The night, like ice, seemed to harden around her. The wind was still prowling, there was a sound of dead leaves running away through the darkness. Overhead, the sky looked shallow and transparent. There seemed to be a light *behind* it, skittering rapidly back and forth, reluctant to stop and show itself. Like the day to come, she thought. Like tomorrow.

ELEVEN

IT WAS THE DAYLIGHT that woke Doc. Weak as it was it had no difficulty filtering through what he suspected was the thinnest window drape in the state of Iowa. It didn't do much to keep the morning cold out either, and he pulled the covers up to his chin and lay perfectly still in the bed. At one point he suspected that Stew might be lying awake beside him (there is often a noticeable difference in the sound of the breathing, the shallow patterns of being awake versus the deeper rhythms of sleep), but Stew didn't turn on his side and pull his knees up into a fetal position as he had when he was a boy. The truth was, Doc didn't know how Stewart slept anymore. He'd assumed that sleep habits stayed the same throughout life but perhaps that wasn't so. Smiles certainly did. Look at Stew's, it was exactly the same, still roguish, still trying to spill over into an outright laugh. The way people walked ordinarily stayed with them, as well as certain mannerisms such as how they showed surprise or the way they held their head when they were concentrating. The trait that absolutely never changed was the voice. He remembered the time at Christmas when the phone rang and he'd picked it up and the voice said, "Hello, Doc, how you doing?" He knew it was Stew, even though they hadn't talked to each other for over ten years. Fifteen, twenty, thirty years, no matter, he'd still have known the voice. The problem was that he didn't know *Stew* anymore. At age forty-one, what was Stewart James Donner like inside? Did he stand for something? Did he have his own set of likes and dislikes and not just society's? What were his values? He'd changed, but what was it that caused people to change? Marriage, children, jobs? Or just time?

How about DeeJay? Her body was still as slim and brisk as a young girl's, that was easy to see, and she had that same impressive mismatch of skin coloring and eyes that invariably drew the second and even third look from strangers. And that *La Dame aux Camélias* flair, Mattie's old trademark, she'd kept that intact—the head lifting at precisely the right moment, the eyelids sagging daintily and the hand going to her face in that grandly fatal gesture. Mercurial too, still pouty one minute and exuberant the next, seeming at times to veer out of control but not quite, something always saved her, the fuse sputtering out an inch from the powder charge, the tree branch jutting from the cliff face to break the fall, the valid will found and read at five minutes to midnight. He sensed that DeeJay should have had a great cause in life, should have been a Madame Defarge hurtling toward the barricades, waving and shouting, so she could have burned off some of that energy. So fiercely aggressive, this younger sister. But what about in private? Did DeeJay Kelley ever break down and cry? Did she ever just give up and dissolve into tears? One of the girls had cried last night in the car. He couldn't see who it was, he could only hear, and it was difficult because the crying was so soft, so nearly hidden.

It was probably Tess. Tess could cry easily. Bruise easily too, he remembered. Sensitive, perhaps even timid, she'd always been slow to defend herself. Yet she endured, she went the distance, forgoing the flash and excitement of the short dash for the plodding, often unwitnessed grind of the longer run. You could depend on Tess to be there at the tape, unspectacular, wanting no praise and diverting any that came, seeking neither press nor camera, never playing the stands but content to slip quietly into the back row and praise those who had finished the race before her, to cheer for those still on the course. For a moment he saw his older sister as he had seen her in Denver two days before, unmistakably the matron and yet making no attempt to disguise it with hair dye or a gauche splashing at the mouth and eyes. One had only to stand back and watch Tess to realize that elegance required no spotlights or banners. *I will still be here when all the trumpet blasts have died away*, her presence seemed to proclaim. Physically, one couldn't fail to notice the large head or the wider-than-normal face that flashed smiles seemingly too soft and fragile for it. And the eyes, who could escape them? Not black and volatile like DeeJay's, but sad. Ineffably sad, even when the rest of her appeared jolly. Eyes, as yesterday afternoon in the car, that turned away from sunsets. . . .

At this point, except for realizing the weakness of it, Doc nearly allowed himself to sink back into sleep. But an abrupt sitting up and a sharp "Stewart, we overslept!" got them both out of bed and into the bathroom, one showering while the other shaved, and then the reverse. After they had rapped on the wall and gotten a response from the girls, and had dressed and packed and finally left the room, they discovered it was cold enough outside to see their breath. The sky was clear but the sunlight was so thin it only added to the coldness. When Doc got into the Buick and warmed up the engine, the exhaust bloomed in the air like a bizarre, blue-white flower.

The first words spoken when they got underway were from Tess, announcing in her guileless way that she remained constipated, that this—what was it, Thursday?— would mark her third consecutive day without a bowel movement and could they please skip breakfast entirely? "I have no place left to put the food."

"Displacement," countered DeeJay in her best Nurse Nancy voice. "Displacement is the solution to your problem. If your intestines are packed with what we in the trade call *shit*, then the intake into the system of any amount of new food will displace a like amount of old."

With that hopeful beginning, Doc stopped at a Country Kitchen that sat miraculously on the same stretch of frontage road that the night before had proved so deserted. They consumed their orders of toast or pastry and coffee or juice but when they returned to the car and Doc drove out onto the interstate and headed north, there was no resurgence of the earlier levity. Tess said, "I still can't go. I drank my coffee very hot and very fast but it didn't help." Nothing came of the remark and they settled into a kind of preordained lethargy. Doc tried on several occasions to initiate a conversation around which some interest might form, but he failed. There was only awkwardness, the returned awkwardness of the first afternoon. They'd had some fun that night in Ogallala but laughs were the first and easiest part of any reunion. Their repeated attempts to go back across the years to isolate an experience they had shared, perhaps even enjoyed, had served in the end only to stress the changes that had befallen them. They were strangers, strangers whose voices alone had remained the same.

He shook his disappointment off as best he could and

(*202*)

concentrated on the Iowa farmland, so drear and lifeless that he was tempted more than once to expound on it. Frail as it was, the midmorning sun had leached the color from everything in sight. It was as though a painter had begun a rural landscape and then given up, his paints proving too weak. The only difference from the previous afternoon was that the fields appeared to have gotten larger, the buildings fewer and more huddled, the houses rimmed not by trees now but by frost-blackened gardens and the limp, sagging poles of hollyhock. An old shed stood at the edge of one field they passed, peering at them over the fence like a worn gray horse. The famous golden spears of Iowa corn were gone, only a stark grid of stubble remained.

At one point, Tess remarked from the backseat, "We must be heading straight toward Minnesota." Her voice picked up on the last word as though she meant to elaborate, but there was nothing.

"Yes," Doc said, and then later he added, "We're going straight north." The words hung in the car, isolated and ridiculous.

Some time later, Stew asked at what place in Minnesota they would turn and head east, adding that he had forgotten Doc's explanation of the morning before, or was it the afternoon? Doc explained that the name of the city was Albert Lea, that Interstate 35 would intersect at that point with Interstate 90, which was an east-west highway. All the even-numbered highways were east-west, all the north-south were numbered odd, had any of them noticed that?

"That's heavy," DeeJay mumbled.

"How far from Albert Lea to the Mississippi?" Tess asked.

"I'm guessing a hundred miles. Maybe one-twenty."

Again that almost malignant silence crept in behind their words.

Then suddenly, off to the right, a billboard materialized, standing in the middle of an empty field like a misplaced blackboard, its red-and-blue brilliance as jarring as a stadium cheer. The borders of the sign were festooned with gaudy orange streamers and it read: GO HAWKEYES, BEAT THE GOPHERS!

"Looks like frat-house work to me," Stewart remarked. "Bunch of troops hyping the Big Game." His observation was curiously dull, measured against the vivacity of the sign.

Tess said, "Maybe the *I* Club did it, if they've got an *I* club in the state. Or maybe the guy who owns the field is a rich alumnus and he put the sign up."

DeeJay said, "What difference does it make who put it up? Corn is corn, rah is rah."

Stewart turned in his seat and watched the sign shrink into insignificance behind them. "Big Ten schools," he said. "The Gophers are Minnesota and the Hawkeyes are Iowa. They used to play us. Wisconsin was in the Big Ten too. Wisconsin Badgers." The sign was gone and he turned back. "Dad was always trying to get down to Madison and go to one of the games with me. It was about an hour-and-a-half trip from Viroqua in those days, two at the outside. Good highway, once you got out of the hills. He had a Nash sedan then, I think it was. Old, but in good shape, you know how Dad was, he wouldn't replace anything until it fell apart. Good tires, not a lot of miles, he really didn't travel much. The Badgers had great teams those years. Everytime we'd have a home game I'd sweep up the apartment, dust a little, wash out the sinks, trash the beer cans. The empty ones." He started a laugh and then cut it off. "I didn't live in the dorms, I had my own apartment. I'd go to the deli over on State Street and pick up some fresh sauerkraut and franks, then I'd stew up a bunch of prunes and have a box of Quaker Oats handy for Sunday breakfast, plus a big loaf of bread and lots of strawberry jam, you know how Dad liked that sweet stuff. We were talking about it yesterday." He coughed. "But he never made it down. Got sidetracked, I imagine. He was always busy with something or other, especially at the lumberyard. Hard worker, that man."

From the backseat, DeeJay said, "You were at the university four years, right?"

"Right."

"And how many home games were there in a season? Six?"

"Probably six, yes."

"Four times six is twenty-four. Twenty-four times Irv couldn't make it down to Madison, is that what you're telling us?"

Stew didn't turn and look at her. "Well, don't forget, you're looking at some potentially bad weather in a Big Ten football season. Those last couple Saturdays in November can get real nasty sometimes."

DeeJay raised her hand over her head and snapped her fingers. "All right now, I want pithies from each of you to cover this. The subject is *Broken Promises*. Remember your *Farmer's Almanack* pages and give me your very best effort."

No one responded. Finally Doc said, not looking at Stew, "You're lucky. At least Dad talked to you about a game, even if he never showed up."

Stew didn't answer immediately but when he did his voice was peevish and frayed. "What do you mean, I'm *lucky?*"

"You just are, that's all. Irv Donner acknowledging that an athletic contest even exists is an accomplishment. Maybe even a miracle." He looked at Stew for the first time. "How long did we live with Irv? How long did I? Twelve years? Thirteen? You know how many times that man played catch with me during that time? Caught a ball from me or threw one back? Threw an apple or a potato or an acorn squash instead of a ball because he didn't have one? The answer is never. And the difference between the athletic contests you're talking about and the ones I'm talking about is that I *played* in mine. *I was on the team!* Church team, school team, Junior Legion team, you name it, I was on it. I even played for Viroqua Co-op, for God's sake, where Dad did business. I bought the lettering for my uniform shirt myself, with mole-trap money. And you know how many of those games Irv Donner went to? You want to take a guess?" He swept the rearview, craning his neck to catch them all. "I'll give you a clue on this, gang. What is zip times zero divided by aught subtracted from nothing? That's your correct answer. And I was more than just a good ballplayer. I was the best Vernon County ever produced and on my way to being one of the best in the state. I knew that, the players knew, the coaches knew. Then I'd come home after a game and stand there in the yard or in the living room where the radio was, wherever *he* was, with my baseball cap on my head and my glove on my hand and wearing my Co-op shirt and the spikes Mattie bought for me out of cream-and-egg money, just praying for him to ask how it went. If we won or lost. If I got any hits, knocked in any runs. Got beaned. Broke an ankle." He lifted his shoulders and then let them drop. "I said it right, Stewball. You were the lucky one."

The Buick's tires reeled up the miles. If they talked at all there was no buoyancy in it, the topics were emotionless, without people in them, such as the reputed richness of the Iowa farmland ("Loess soils are what they're called," Stew explained. "That's the geologic name. I hadn't thought about that until now. Perhaps all those laboratory field trips pay off in time"); estimates on the cost of the green-and-yellow farm machinery sitting everywhere ("How many eggs equal the price of a twelve-row seeder?" DeeJay wanted to know. "How many bushels of corn will pay the note on a hay baler?"); the weather as it related to farm planning ("Do they have radios in tractors like they do in cars?" Tess wondered. "Can they get weather stations?"). The patter simply bought time, filled in the hours until a highway sign appeared to give them something to concentrate on. When the sign *Albert Lea 12* appeared they hailed it with weak applause, then fell silent again.

The country began to change. It grew hillier, there were more trees. The farms were smaller and less prosperous and the sky seemed to have become a stretched blue plastic that anything tall might have pierced. But there was nothing tall in sight.

At one point a nameless village appeared to the right of the highway and from the ring of timber that hid it a trickle of smoke lifted into the air. Doc wondered if someone was burning leaves, if children were there watching the fire in that wistful detached way they had of studying destructive things. Unexpectedly, an image came to him of the waiflike rag doll Tess had had on the ridge farm, a wistful creature in its own right, not resplendent enough to be a bedroom doll but consigned mainly to a table on the porch where she sat propped against a wall, looking out. Their dog Mick usually lay with her on the table, obviously convinced she was a member of the family. Tess forgot the doll when Mattie moved to the apartment in town and Doc wondered how long the doll had remained on the porch, her hair knotting and her dress fading, the snow covering her in winter and the sun coming in spring to melt it away, all the while watching for the little mutt dog to jump up beside her, waiting for the little girl to come and fold her in her arms and take her home. . . .

(*207*)

"My God," DeeJay broke in, jolting Doc from his reverie, "we're in Minnesota!"

"How can you tell?"

"We just passed a sign that read '*I-90 two miles*.'"

She was right. They reached the intersection in a matter of minutes and it was definitely I-90. Doc slowed and then turned to the east, yet so mundane was the junction after all their anticipation, so totally without civilization of any kind to welcome them, that they felt cheated. "Hey, where's Albert Lea?" one of them asked. They looked out the side windows and out the back but there was nothing visible except a distant steeple sticking up out of yet another clump of leafless trees. "What a dumb place," one of them said, and it was sullen and disgruntled.

So they faced east and rode on. After a few minutes Tess said tonelessly, "Next town we stop and eat, okay?"

"What town?" Doc said. "Minnesota doesn't have towns, just steeples and signs."

But a town showed up nevertheless, for all their distrust. Austin. Surprisingly, it was neat, tidy, Scandinavian-looking. A Hobo Jo's restaurant sat on the frontage road and they stopped there, hitting the rest rooms en masse and ordering a pot of coffee when the waitress brought menus to their table. "I'm not terribly hungry," DeeJay sniffed, and had a garden salad. Doc wondered aloud if there was anything in the world that grew tiresome quicker than restaurant food, then polished off a cheeseburger and a bowl of chili, his hunger growing as he fed it. Stewart settled for his customary grilled cheese sandwich and didn't finish it, spending most of his time complaining about the waitress. "Coarse," he whispered. "Talks like a Bohunk. Accentuates the wrong words and bites the end off the others. Very coarse." Tess drank a single cup of coffee and sided with Stewart, but sarcastically. "Bohunks love this country. Paul Bunyan gave it to them years ago as a gift."

"It may get better when we get to the Mississippi River bluffs," Doc offered. "Remember how pretty the bluffs used to be?" But no one said anything.

Back in the car, heading east in the thin, wasted sunlight of midday, DeeJay stared out her window and finally she said, not raising her voice, "What the hell are we doing here, anyway?"

Stewart turned to her as if to ask for a repeat but at the last moment he did not. "I can't believe this," she went on, not looking at Stew, not looking at any of them. "When I realize we are actually here on this superhighway in this less than super state, I begin to have trouble with the reasons *why*."

"Be patient," Stew advised. "Doc said it would get better as we got closer to the river."

"I'm not talking about the country. Minnesota's not any uglier than Iowa or Nebraska, even Colorado. I'm talking about why we made the trip."

Stewart's eyebrows arched in disbelief. "To see Dad, for God's sake."

DeeJay came right back. "But *why*? He didn't ask to see us. The only name he mentioned was Mattie's and that's got to be the joke of the century. It makes about as much sense as the Pope asking to see Martin Luther."

"When a parent becomes ill," Stewart began solemnly, looking slightly past DeeJay, "and the children are called—"

"That's what I mean. Somebody says *your father is dying* and we drop everything and come running. My God, we're as conditioned as Pavlov's dogs. That's bull-shit!"

Stewart's eyes flared with a genuine surprise, but it gave

(*209*)

way quickly to a resolve not to be intimidated by her. " 'Honor thy father and thy mother,' " he began, and it was so instantly wrong that Doc winced in spite of himself. DeeJay was going to rip Stew to pieces on this one. " '. . . so that it may be well with thee,' " Stewart was saying, " 'and thou mayest live long upon the earth.' That's a commandment."

DeeJay pounced. "That's a canard! You honor your father and mother because they *deserve* it, not because some catechism tells you to. That's just almanac pap in another form, made up to keep children from making judgments on their elders. A man ejaculating into a place where a woman's eggs are waiting doesn't automatically qualify him for honor and respect." She wasn't spitting the words as she usually did, there was no venom in them, merely intensity. It was disarming. "Irv Donner honoring and respecting his children is what I'd like to see. And wanting to be with them more than once in a quarter of a century would be a real good start. Cardiovascular accidents have nothing to do with that."

Stew must have sensed the new restraint in her too. "You want to remember," he said evenly, not the least hint of argument in his voice, "that Dad did come to see us."

"You!" she said, and the word ripped out of her, her eyes flaming blackly. Here was the familiar DeeJay Kelley. "He came to see you, Little Beaver! The one frigging trip our master took out of his kingdom was to your house in Seattle."

"You think I planned his trip?" Stew demanded, the outrage of being trapped thinning his voice.

"Who was next on Irv's itinerary that time? It was me, wasn't it?"

"Yes, but you can't hold me responsible—"

"You know what I did for that visit, Stewart? I fought forest fires for three days and cleaned my house for two. I trained one side of my body to sleep while the other worked. I scrubbed walls, shoveled mud, washed grime out of everything I owned, including my children. I got them shined up and slicked down and ready to meet their grandpa "from the old country," we called it. They'd never seen him and they were thrilled to death, which also includes Kell. I even held a three-hour seminar on table and various other manners just to make sure Dad would be proud of them. And guess what? *He didn't show!*" The words foamed in her, building pressure. "I sat there in that smoked-up house and waited for that man like a little girl waiting for her first look at Santa Claus. And he didn't come. The father I'm rushing across half this goddamned country to be with didn't care enough to come and see me." Her breath suddenly gave out and she began to pound the back of the front seat with her fists. "*He . . . didn't . . . care!*"

Doc pulled onto the shoulder and stopped the car. He got out, opened the back door, reached in and took Dee-Jay's arm, and pulled her gently from the car. He stood close, his hand touching her lightly and his arms forming a possible nest for her to come to if she wanted, a place at his shoulder for her head, for the tears that could break her anger as a chill will many times break a fever. But no tears came. She did not speak or lift her head to show him what her pain was or whether it would go away by his holding her, and eventually she walked around and got back in the car and stared straight ahead down the highway.

Doc drove back onto the interstate and no one spoke. They didn't look at one another. Perhaps five miles later a sign announced a rest area and someone in the backseat said, "I need to stop," but the voice was so emotionless he couldn't tell who it was.

He pulled into the rest area and stopped. It was a neat

uncrowded place with a mansard roof on the central building as well as on the smaller individual pavilions spaced around it. A sidewalk traversed the entire length of the grounds and when he and Stew came out of the men's room they could see that at its far end the walkway curled up onto the knoll and stopped at an overlook railing. He said to Stew, "You want to walk down to the end with me?"

"No, I think I'll stay here."

"It wasn't you DeeJay was mad at, Stew."

He nodded.

"What came out is a hurt that's been there for a long time. I didn't know."

"I didn't either. It doesn't matter."

"Yes, it does. Whatever hurts, matters. I think maybe we forgot that."

Stew reached out and rapped him lightly on the shoulder. "Take your walk, Doctor, then come back, you've got the car keys."

Doc walked all the way to the end and as he went he could feel autumn around him. It was dun-colored, rustling, a thing of sticks and straws. What had the poem said? *Naked woods . . . meadows brown and sere.* The air had the sweet-sour smell of an apple picked some time ago and only now bitten into. It made him think of orchards with fruit rotting on the ground, of cider presses and a phalanx of waiting mason jars. Minnesota, Wisconsin, the whole upper Midwest was apple country, but what were the names? Jonathan? Winesap? McIntosh? What else? He gave up, it was too long ago, he had forgotten. Yet he remembered in that moment that Irv could peel an apple with the small blade of his pocket knife and produce a single unbroken curl that hung nearly to the ground.

He stopped when he reached the overlook railing. He saw an empty pasture on his left and on his right a long field of corn stubble leading down to a creek bottom hidden in thicket. He suddenly wanted to be in the middle of that field—gun, dog, shells in the pocket, the cap pulled down and the red cartridge vest on. He wanted his son William walking the stubble with him, stalking the thicket with the dog out front. He was seized with an overwhelming need to be with all his children, to show them the availability of their father. He fiercely, deeply, wanted that.

He turned and walked back to the car.

After several miles the interstate began to curve to the left and the sun, lower in the sky now, swung around to shine directly into the car through the back window. The country had changed since lunch, becoming a broken land of small fields and scrub-clotted hills, giving a sense of rawness like new stumps. Here and there a slough appeared, an occasional old shed crouched at its edge like a hungry dog waiting for a hurt duck to land.

Apparently Tess was also watching the country slide past, for when she spoke the struggle to come back from distant thoughts was plainly audible in her voice. "Hill country," she said, "ridge and hollow, hollow and ridge. Bony on top, misty and cramped at the bottom, like something out of an Hieronymus Bosch landscape. But at one time I thought of this country as a fairyland. A paradise."

Stew said quickly, "Well, don't forget, this is November."

"But it isn't a fairyland," Tess went on, her voice stronger now as though Stew's attempted reproof had emboldened her, "and it isn't a paradise. I was wrong. It's a land of ghosts." She stopped at that point and Doc knew she was searching for something imbedded in memory. " 'I have wandered home but newly . . . to this ultimate dim Thulee . . . By a route obscure and lonely, haunted by ill angels only. . . .' "

"That's Poe," Doc said, then wished he hadn't said it.

"Well, if there are ghosts and ill angels around, we're them," said Stew, "because we were born in this country." It was less of an admonishment than the previous statement and easier for Tess to ignore.

"It's the same country as up ahead, across the river," she went on, and it was obvious that the memories were flooding out of her now. "It's where I lost a father, if I ever had one. It's where the beatings started. I haven't forgotten them. I remember being afraid to go up to bed at night because that's where they happened, and when I finally got into bed I would pretend I was so well hidden under the covers that Irv couldn't find me. I began to pretend all the time. Sometimes I would pretend I was sleeping so sound that nothing could wake me until morning and that way I couldn't feel the beatings. And if I couldn't feel the beatings it meant there hadn't been any. Some mornings I would wake up and realize that my thighs weren't cut and my rump wasn't swollen and there wasn't any blood on the sheets. I'd be so happy I'd throw off the covers and jump out of bed and dance around the room, not knowing if it was the pretending that saved me or if Irv hadn't come upstairs the night before. I never asked which was true. I didn't really want to know. All I wanted was for the beatings to stop."

"Tess, don't," DeeJay said, and it was so softly spoken they almost didn't hear her.

"But I never knew why they'd started so how could I judge when they'd stop? I didn't know what I'd done. I know it's silly but I used to go around asking myself things like, Did I snore in my sleep one night and keep

Irv awake? Did I get snippy without realizing it? Did I embarrass him in some way in front of company or at church? Was he ashamed of me? Was I too tall, too slow to move?" She stopped and Doc could feel her voice seek him out. "Was I, Doc? You'd remember. Was I that . . . unlovable?"

DeeJay said, "Please, Tess."

"I can remember hearing the stairway door open when I was lying in bed trying to get to sleep, or else doing my pretend things, and then I'd hear his footsteps on the stairs. He was such a big man and he had those heavy work shoes. When he'd reach the top of the stairs I always knew which way he'd turn. He never went to any room but mine."

A stillness prevailed in the car.

"And that belt, my God, how it stung! Sometimes when you slam your shinbone against something or bump your head on a sharp corner there's a second or two before the pain starts. But not with a belt. It's instant. And the edges are the worst. They cut. More than anything, I used to pray that the belt wouldn't turn in midair and the edge come down and cut into me. The sound is even different when it's the edge that hits you."

Now Doc spoke. "Stop, Tess."

"Why a belt? Why would a grown man use a belt on a child instead of his hand? I know the answer finally, I've thought enough about it. It's because he wants to hurt the child more than he wants to reprimand it. Hurt it and break its spirit and still be somehow removed from the physical act because it wasn't flesh against flesh, not his against the child's. I couldn't fight Irv, I was too small. All I could do was beg him to stop. I'd even practiced this helpless little voice that I hoped might get through to him, 'Please, Dad, don't hit me anymore.' "

"Tess—"

(*215*)

"Then the beatings stopped." Doc could feel her voice isolating him again. "Do you remember why, Doc? It was because of you, you did it. I was in bed one night listening to Irv climb the stairs and all of a sudden I heard this voice say, *Stop! I want you to stop! If you don't stop beating Tess we're all going to run away and never come back!* You sounded so frightened, Doc. I never heard a more frightened voice in my life. I can still hear it. Over the years, whenever I'd think of you, I'd hear that voice."

There was no sound in the car except for the weeping. It wasn't Tess, it was DeeJay. She was crying, softly, steadily. It was the first time in his life Doc had ever heard her cry and he wanted to turn and look at her, to *see* it, but he did not. He drove and watched the white highway and the dead brown hills and tried to concentrate on the assorted car sounds, the tires and the engine and the wind. He heard them distinctly, but they only intensified the weeping.

Then Stewart said, without turning in his seat, "You've forgiven Dad for that, haven't you, Tess?"

She wasn't quick to answer, yet no one stepped in to answer for her. "You can forgive a parent anything," she said finally, "but only if they love you."

"You cried for him last night in Iowa. I heard you."

"I cried for what was lost, Stewart. You were reciting what you remembered about him, his smell, his arms, the way he laughed. It's what grown children should do with their father, remember the dear things about him. They're dear for you but they're not for me, I have only the lost things. That's why I cried."

"That was a long time ago," Stew said. "Dad's probably changed. In fact, I know he has. When I was up here going to school in Madison he never laid a hand on me. I never even got a hard word."

In a voice so cold and biting it was barely recognizable, DeeJay said, "When I think of a sensitive, understanding human being," and here she took a deep breath and released it noisily, "I will think of you, little brother."

Stewart turned to her, ready to do battle, but Doc deterred him with a hand on his arm. "Tess is right. DeeJay is right. Irv didn't love us. I think it's time we accepted the truth."

Stew said, "Are you sure you're not substituting personal opinion for truth?"

Doc restored his hand to the steering wheel. "No, but you are. You're hung up on some romantic idea of childhood, parents doting on children, children worshipping parents, all laughing together, all living happily. I'm sure we loved Irv at one time. I think all children start out loving their father. And they make no demands that he be a special man. What he does for a living, his success in life, the mark he makes on society, children don't care about that. Irv made a success of his sawmill business but I'd have gladly traded that for a hug at bedtime, maybe a pat on the shoulder for laying down a squeeze bunt in the last of the ninth to win the game. My God, think of what the words *I love you* would have meant, coming from him." He swallowed and went on. "But he never said them, Stew. It's because he didn't feel them. And I don't buy that crap about certain people being unable to express themselves, that's just an excuse. It says that a kiss or a touch requires some sort of educated language. It doesn't." He lifted one hand from the steering wheel and let it drop. "I don't say we're any the less for not getting love from Irv. I don't think we're impaired. But we missed something it would have been nice to have. It seems such a waste. Such a damned waste."

Tess spoke again, her words soft, nearly obscure. "Com-

(217)

ing all this way to see a dying father isn't easy," she said, "but the hardest part is going back into childhood. Maybe," she added, "they're the same thing."

Doc waited and then said, "When was it, yesterday . . . the day before? . . . we were wondering why Irv never made an attempt to come see us after Mattie left and moved into town—"

"That must have hurt him deeply, her leaving like that."

"Oh, Christ, Stew," Doc said. "Can't you be honest just once in your life? Are you ever going to come up with a response that's genuine instead of one you think is expected? We're talking about why Dad didn't want to see us, not whether it hurt when Mattie left. I'm sure it did, but if Bev walked out on you tomorrow wouldn't you still want to see your kids? Wouldn't you want to know how they were doing, whether they were happy? Whether they were crying for you at night?" His glance at Stew was not returned. "Let's not kid each other, buddy. Irv didn't come to see us because he didn't want to. He didn't care. The truth is, we only had one parent who did."

At that moment, faintly, as from a distance, Tess said, "'. . . how bright and true they were, even for country folk, and yet they were betrayed by their kinspeople and had their hearts broken by those they loved. . . .'"

Stew didn't turn to the backseat this time, but he reacted. "What have we got now, more poetry?"

"It's from the story Mattie used to read to me. A long time ago. About Tess of the d'Urbervilles and her family. The way it turned out," she added, "it could have been us."

A silence fell over them and no one made any attempt to breach it.

Under the changeless song of the tires the miles swept by. A square of late-afternoon sun lay on top of the dash like a present they had bought earlier in the day and were rushing home to give someone before it got dark. Steeper hills began to block their way and the highway chose to climb directly into them, winding, curving, bridging creekbeds that lay in the mouths of the cramped hollows like discarded snake skins. Then the road burst abruptly onto a crest of bluffs and the land fell sharply away before them. "Look!" Stew cried, pointing. "There's the river!"

The Mississippi lay at their feet, twisting skeletally through the trees, the city of La Crosse huddled on its far bank. Beyond, across the valley, loomed a similar rampart of winter-dark bluffs.

DeeJay said quietly, "I'm not going."

Tess said, "Nor me. I won't cross the river."

There was a deserted turnout on the left side of the highway, obviously a summer viewing area for the spectacular river scenery, and Doc drove into it and stopped the car.

Stewart's face had gone white, and he stared at each of them. "You mean we're just going to turn around and go *back*?"

"Yes," they answered, not in any confederacy but in a sort of accidental unison, much like what had happened in the cocktail lounge in Ogallala, which seemed now as they sat atop the bluffs and watched the silent river, a long time ago.

·

TWELVE

Agitated, pale, the grin gone from his mouth, Stewart said, "We need to talk. We need to understand what we're doing," and before any of them could reply he reached across and shut off the ignition. The stillness was immediate, eerie, isolating.

Then Tess spoke, starting the flow once more. She had always been the one to start things, creating the word games when they were kids, finding the old discarded books in which to "do the vowels," forging the library cards and initiating the home reading contests where the monthly winner could paste a homemade gold star on the bedroom door, or on the dresser mirror. She'd always drawn substance into herself in order to make new substance out of it. Doc remembered the sign she had made and hung on the wall in one of their innumerable houses in Tucson. *TAKE, HAVE, KEEP, Are Lovely Words*, the sign had read. The quote was from Thomas Hardy but like so many literary things Tess had gotten it wrong, she'd inverted, misquoted, made another solecism out of what she had hoped would be deathless words. For her, such proclamations were a form of celebration, little victories that helped make up for those times when she had stood on strange winter lawns or in wind-hounded bedrooms, defeated and alone, locked in yet another rejection. Now she was on a bluff overlooking a winter-threatened river, telling them that it was finally over. "Whatever relationship we were destined to have with Irv Donner," she said, "we've already had. There's nothing left, for him or for us. We're . . . committed now."

Doc studied the bluffs across the valley, the way the city seemed to huddle against them for protection. A *V* of geese flew over, following the river south, and with the windows rolled up he couldn't hear them. It was just as well, theirs could be a lonely sound, the call of something lost, destined never to find its way. He said, "On the phone Sunday night, Stella kept saying *if you kids want to see your father*. She repeated it several times. It was never *he wants to see you*. He had a chance to ask for us if he'd wanted to. Stella told me he was conscious for the first thirty minutes in the ambulance. *If you want to see your father*, she kept saying. Well," he said, swallowing hard, "we don't."

"Wait a minute," Stew said, his eyes sweeping them. "What are we saying here? That we were better children than our parents were parents? Can we say that?"

DeeJay replied, "Of course we can." Her voice was calm. "We don't need one of your Sir Walter Scott rules for this, Stewart."

"But *were* we better children?" His words were jamming in upon themselves. "Those two people . . . whatever happened since . . . at some point at one time in our lives . . .

after children have had their noses wiped and their butts cleaned a thousand times, after they've been protected, fed, crooned to and prayed over . . . can they honestly say they're better than their parents?"

"You're quoting from the Granny Samplers again, Stewart." It was DeeJay. "They look nice hanging on the wall or covering the sofa pillows, but they seldom apply."

Stew turned away and looked down into the city. "What about Stella? We told Stella we'd be here. She'll be expecting us."

"We didn't come for Stella." This was Tess. "We didn't come for Irv. We came for ourselves."

Stew flipped his head to one side and snorted in an exasperated way as if to say, *What do you mean we came for ourselves? What kind of a remark is that?* But it was apparent from his eyes that he didn't want to go on arguing. He sputtered again but it was more desperation than anger, a searching for words that hadn't been spoken yet, words that came rushing and tumbling around them, struggling to find a voice.

Tess said, "A thousand miles and almost half a century to find out about our parents, that's why we came. I'm not saying that it's our right to complain about them, maybe we don't get that. Maybe what we get now is a chance to understand." She too was studying the river valley. "We can sit here and tell each other that we won't allow our parents to reach out and put their mark on us, but it's too late. They already have. And I don't mean physical things like Mattie's eyes and Irv's hands, I mean the other. I mean longing for something you can't identify. Feeling a sadness that never goes away. My God, I'm almost fifty years old and I still can't watch the sun go down."

No one added anything, not right away.

Doc said, "I remember when I was a kid how I'd lie in the hay and stare into that square of blue sky that the mow door made. I wondered where I'd go when I grew up. Would I leave the county, maybe even the *state*? I'd think about who I might marry and what my kids would look like, what their names would be as if the names came with the babies. I tried to imagine what would become of the four of us . . . we were so united then. Would we survive, would we make it through?"

From the backseat DeeJay said, "I have the answer for you, sailor. It's yes."

"We inherited some stubbornness from one of them, the need to stay with a thing. Look at our marriages, we're still living with our original mates. We became real stickers, you ever think of that?"

"It's because our parents weren't," DeeJay said.

"One was," said Tess, her voice gaining strength. "In a roundabout, second-chance way, it turned out to be Mattie. Oh, I know she blew it in Montana. Really bad. She committed what is probably the closest thing there is in a woman's life to the unforgivable sin. She deserted young children. But she came back. She put out the fires, whatever they were, and came back and stood in the stocks until we were grown and gone. And with no help from us, I might add. In fact, we were probably her biggest tormentors. She was a woman and by God she was going to be the perfect mother!" Tess paused. "Of course she wasn't. She couldn't be. She married bad and when she finally got out of that she was too alone, too full of failure. And frightened, God, how frightened she must have been. Couldn't drive a car, never held a job before. I remember how I'd catch her crying some nights, in the dark." She paused. "But as the current slang would have it, she hung in there. Whatever she was, Nurse Nightingale or *La Dame aux Camélias* or the real Tess of the d'Urbervilles, it doesn't matter. For all her flaws she was the one parent who stuck with us, which makes her the only one we ever had."

"And as a reward," said Doc, rapping the steering wheel, "we actually considered putting her in a nursing home."

"Ooooh," DeeJay moaned, sinking into her seat. "Some-one take a memo, please. A memo that states, unequivo-cally, that we will . . . *not* . . . *do* . . . *that*! A memo that offers her a lifetime extension to our current contract, the popular Four-Year Rotation Plan." She leaned forward and lit a cigarette, blowing the smoke out in a long relieved streamer. "And we must hope that she signs it."

"Yes, we've got to keep her," Tess said, "even though she's exactly the same as she always was. Still peeping out from under her hat at all the men in the neighborhood. Still off center, out of sync, always at right angles to every-one and everything. But still trying to make it all work, still trying to put together," and here she laughed softly, "her cactus garden."

"It's really us, you know," Doc said. "The four of us, we've been Mattie's cactus garden."

He reached down, turned the key in the ignition, and started the car. "We can probably make it back to Austin by dark," he said to the others. "Maybe even Albert Lea."

"This is wrong," Stewart said.

DeeJay said, "I'm not sure there is an Albert Lea."

Tess said, "I hope my Arizona car is still in that parking lot in southeast Denver."

"Better hope the wheels are still on it," said Doc.

"If we really were our mother's cactus garden," Stewart said, "it's because she handled us wrong, gave up too soon and then ran away. If we run away from our father now, like this, won't *we* be making the cactus garden?"

Dr. Larimer stood in the window of the hospital cafeteria and looked down onto the hospital grounds and the river valley beyond. He was tired, his legs ached, his low back grew tighter by the minute. Long hours in surgery did that. It wasn't that he was in poor physical condition, or that he was old—the Olympic pool and the racquetball courts and the oval track at the athletic club put the lie to that—but he had inherited a lumbar weakness from one of his parents, probably his mother. Mothers bequeathed to their children more of the gene-chromosome matrix than did fathers. He thought of women as embryonic, swirled and knotted with internal patterns and forms, like a child's marble.

The young woman in OR today had been such a marble, except that at the very core of her splendor, dormant and undetected for all her twenty-five years, had existed a flaw, a flaw that had finally erupted. After six hours of surgery they had saved her, though at the cost of a kidney so prematurely strangled by stones that it had to be removed. They had positioned her on the table on her side, knees up and head down as in ancient burial rites, and cut through half her body at the middle as you would cut into a ripe melon to get at useless seeds. She would convalesce and survive, an equally young husband at her side to assist and to abide and to give the love that was in the end the premier therapy.

The doctor took a sip of his coffee. In this single hospital day he had witnessed salvaged life in OR, new life in Maternity, impaired life in Intensive Care. The old man, the CVA from the little hill town in Vernon County, was slowly emerging from his coma but not to the hope of full recovery. Something vital inside him had been irrevocably damaged. He could linger for several weeks, even months, but the end was ordained. His wife, the small, stout, handsome woman with the Slavic face, would be at his side throughout. She too would provide the therapy of love.

The doctor's eyes caught movement in the parking lot and he glanced down and saw four people approaching the hospital, two men and two women, obviously middle-aged and looking somewhat vague in the shapeless rumpled clothes that people for some reason elect to wear when traveling by car. One of the men, indicted by size and a certain impishness of face to be the youngest, led the group by several steps, but just before reaching the edge of the lot he stopped and turned back to the others, whether on his own initiative or by reason of being summoned, the doctor couldn't tell at that distance. When the four merged into a single group they conversed briefly and then sort of knotted up and hugged each other and continued on, arms locked now, across the parking lot. He wondered who they were.

When the foursome reached the front walk and disappeared into the hospital, the doctor's attention turned elsewhere. Beyond the grounds and the city proper he could see the river winding through the trees. It wasn't silver now as it often was in the afternoon. The sun wasn't right, it was too late, a rather sad time of day all in all. A sad time of year, actually, with the trees stripped and the vitality gone from everything and the barren gods of November determined to surrender the land to winter. One day soon he would come to this window and find the river trapped in snow and ice, seemingly frozen to the earth forever.

But nothing locked itself in place forever. There was a time for ice and a time for fire, a time for silver and for green. In the world beyond, as in this hospital on this very day, some would enter life and some would leave it, some would find new meaning. And months hence the river would free itself in a great grinding agony, and spring would come. Spring always came, it was the instrument of man's hope. It sang in his memory, even at the coldest darkest hour, with the poignancy of remembered music.

WILLIAM DIETER was raised and educated in the West. He is the author of three previous novels, *The White Land*, *Hunter's Orange*, and *Beyond the Mountain*. He lives in Denver.